CORRUPTED BY SIN

Copyright © 2022 B.J. WARBURTON. All Rights Reserved.

This book is a work of fiction. Names, characters, organizations, places, events, businesses, and incidents within this book are fictional and the product of the authors imagination. Any resemblance to actual persons or events is unintentional.

No part of this publication may be reproduced, distributed, or transmitted in any form or by any means, including photocopying, recording or other electronic or mechanical methods, without the prior written permission of the publisher, except in the case of brief quotations embodied in reviews and certain other non-commercial uses permitted by copyright law.

ISBN: 9798792793637

COVER DESIGN BY JOELEE CREATIVE

I WISH I COULD BE PAID TO READ…

OH, NOW I CAN.. AND SO CAN YOU…

CHECK OUT BOOKSHIB @BOOKSHIB

DEDICATIONS

Firstly, I'd like to thank you... yes you... reading this now. Without you, it wouldn't be possible. I can only hope you enjoy reading this book as much as I enjoyed writing it. I ask that you leave a review. I will read all feedback. Also, if you want to stay updated, follow me on social media platforms @AuthorBJWarb. Feel free to use the hashtag, #CorruptedBySin.

Secondly, I'd like to dedicate this to BookShib and the team for their partnership and sponsor. Reading is fun. Why not earn whilst doing it? Check them out at @BookShib

Thirdly, I'd like to thank any local law enforcement located anywhere in the world, in advance, in the event that a situation arises involving anything to do with cheesecake. Let's hope that doesn't occur...

CORRUPTED BY SIN

A NOVEL

BY B.J. WARBURTON

ARABELLA HARPER

"Roses are blue, violets are red—"

"Shut up and pay attention," says Dakota and shakes her head, as her mysterious companion contains his smirk in his first-class plane seat next to her. "When we land, we're going to Devil's nightclub and then the hot—"

"Roses are blue, violets are red, I'm a seducer..." and smoothly leans left over the arm rest, casting his deadly green gaze at her divine brunette beauty, "...so get in my bed," he seductively whispers. The cabin fills with a loud slap.

"Say that again and I'll start calling you by your real name."

Shaking off the red imprint, he chuckles and stands from the vanilla leather. Stretching his muscly arms amidst the turbulence, he walks right and takes grip of the royal blue curtain entrance into business class. Looking over his right shoulder, he watches Dakota elegantly sip from her champagne glass. "Continue then. What's the plan?" He peeks through the curtain and glimpses at the rows of passengers tightly packed together, noticing a couple kissing, as she places her glass down.

She turns to face him. "As I was saying, we need to—"

He turns to her. "I think we should join the mile-high club." Leaning against the wall, he tilts his head and observes her glare. "I see that naughty twinkle in your eyes."

Shaking her head, she looks down at the floor and resurfaces with a shifty smile on her scarlet red lips, locking her grey eyes into his tall, dark, and handsome complexion. "I think you're right." She stands and approaches him in her red ruby dress, and black heels. "Why didn't you just say," she sweetly says, as she looks up and flutters her long lashes at his towering beauty.

He widens his eyes. "Seriously?"

She bites down on her bottom lip and nods. "Mmhhmmmm."

"Well, well, well. It only took you a law degree and a holiday to Italy.

She runs her dainty fingers down his crisp white shirt; enjoying his hardened abs. "Wait twenty seconds and then come join me."

He widens his eyes again, watching as she exits through the curtain. He can't believe it; it's really happening. It's only taken four years. Reaching into his black suit trousers, he pulls out his peppermint spray and freshens his breath.

Rubbing his veiny hands, he exits through the curtain with a smirk; his bad boy image projecting across the plane, as all eyes turn to him. With an ego to fill a mirror, he proudly walks down the aisle, catching the back of her red dress entering the restroom behind the brunette hostess smiling at him. Shimmying past her, he leans into her ear. "You should be a model," he seductively whispers, and moves on, too busy thinking with his dick to notice Dakota laughing at the idiot, as she struts down the other lane and back to her seat. Reaching the bathroom, he grips the black handle. Cracking his neck, he opens it and looks at her brunette hair, as the occupier applies makeup in the mirror. He turns around, and steps inside backwards; his eyes peeking through the closing gap for any hostesses. "You're in for a treat. There's a reason they called me the chopper in university."

Staring at the back of his shirt through the reflection, she applies the final stroke of her lip gloss. "Why would that be?" Closing her lipstick, she chucks it back into her makeup bag and turns to face him, as he locks the door.

He raises his eyebrow at her angelic voice. "Look, I know we're doing this whole New York thing now, but at least keep the British accent." He spins around in the tiny space and towers over her, brushing his hands down her devil red playsuit and gripping the back of her thick thighs; her arms and legs wrapping around him, as he lifts her up. Hit with her coconut shampoo, as their cherry, and ice breath collide, he closes his eyes and captures the moment in silence. "Ahem… it must have been a long and strenuous battle, having to stare at me in all those lectures but let's put that behind us. I'm here. You're here. That's all that matters."

She breaks into a giggle. "Are you sure you have the right girl?"

He leans back and inspects her. "Green eyes. You aren't Dakota."

She shakes her head sideways. "Nope."

"Did you know green is my favourite colour? Must be fate."

She blushes. "Fate?"

"Do you believe in fate?"

She glances over his stunning composure; drawn by his strong jawline and wild black hair, as his woody cologne and majestic green eyes attack. "Perhaps. Perhaps not," she says, and combs her petite fingers through the back of his thick hair. "I'm Arabella Harper by the way."

Hit with turbulence, as if it were fate, the gap between them closes as their foreheads press together. "And what would a beautiful woman like you Arabella Harper, be doing on a plane from Heathrow?"

She deeply exhales through her nose, struggling to stay composed as his dominant gaze and fine beauty screams alpha. "Umm... I'm visiting—"

Hit with yet another round of turbulence, they grip each other tight as it throws him against the door; the gentleman in him catching her parted lips. Regaining his step, he breaks their locked lips. "That's the sweetest thing I've tasted all day. Candy floss?"

She grazes her pink glossy lips against his. "Kiss me," she passionately whispers, as her chest drowns in a whirlwind of pleasure.

Using his fingertips, he stimulates her smooth thighs, feeling her cherry warmth steam against his upper lip. He looks her up and down. "How old are you?"

"Twenty-three."

He smirks. "Welcome to the mile-high club." He spins her around and slams her against the door, leaning into her, as she parts her cupid lips. Slipping, and sliding between the mounting moisture, he keeps her pinned with his muscly chest, as he removes his hands and begins journeying up her playsuit.

Gripping his hair tight, as his rough hands continue upwards, she breaks the moment and gasps the bathroom air. Pressing her forehead against his, she gazes into his dominance. "What's your name?" She widens her eyes and nervously giggles; her back vibrating as someone knocks aggressively against the door.

He spins her around and gently lowers her. "It's probably just a hostess checking in." He turns around and unlocks the door. Giving her a boost of confidence, he looks back at her. "I've got this," he says, and faces front, smiling his pink stained lips as he opens it. He starts to chuckle, met by his sly companion Dakota, as she looks his lips over. "Well, well, well… if it isn't my—"

She grabs his white collar and drags him out. "I haven't planned an operation for an entire year, only for you and your fuckboy ways to mess this up. Got it!" She looks Arabella up and down feistily and looks back to him.

He chuckles and raises his hands. "I got confused. I thought it was you."

She rolls her eyes. "That's why I will never sleep with you." She looks her up and down again and fake smiles, slamming the door on her and escorting him back to his first-class seat.

Exiting through airport security, Arabella waits at the crowded, rotating carousel for her suitcase in Terminal Seven. Glancing to her right, she looks through the gap of the other passengers in search for her mystery man. No luck. She gulps amongst the surrounding chatter and looks down at the shiny square tile; her reflection looking back at her, as she twists her cupid lips. *If it's meant to be, it's meant to be.* She feels the brush of a black suit jacket against her smooth skin, and looks up, staring at the back of a tall, dark, and handsome man, as he goes to grab his luggage; her heart racing, as he slowly turns around.

"Help me hon," he says, and smiles as his wife brushes past her. She sighs and watches the couple vacate, spotting her hot pink suitcase. *Well at least that's not lost.* She grips the handle and lifts it from the conveyer belt. Turning around, she places it on its wheels. Gripping the handle, she makes her way through the large crowd and heads for the exit.

Waiting for her best friend, Clarissa Campbell, she stands on the sidewalk in the pickup zone, swapping the musty airport smell for the New York exhaust fumes amidst the evening summer breeze, as it carries her brunette locks around her pale, and rosy face. *It's good to be back.* She takes out her smartphone and scrolls through her social media; her attention broken as a loud clap occurs.

"My man," says the deep voice. She peeks to her right, watching as her mystery man exchanges handshakes with an older Italian gentleman; unable to do anything as the brunette hovers around him. *Why does she have to be there?* She hears a car pull up to her left and looks, smiling her pearly whites at Clarissa in her black Range Rover. Rolling her suitcase along the path, she approaches and opens the back passenger side door, sliding the suitcase across the creamy white leather. She closes it and opens the front passenger side door; met with a cheeky scarlet red smile, from her elegantly stunning, blonde bestie.

"How was your first trip to England?" asks Clarissa.

She looks through the gap of the open door, observing the three enter a Rolls Royce Phantom. "It was good," she unenthusiastically says.

Clarissa follows her eyes and looks at the phantom. "Are you going to get in?"

She snaps out of it and looks to her. "Oh sorry." Hit with the pine air freshener, she shuts the door and fastens her seatbelt. Pulling away from the curb, she watches as they drive past them, continuing to observe from the wing mirror. Smaller, and smaller, they fade; her stomach sinking as the odds of ever seeing him again may as well be zero.

Clarissa taps her thumbs against the steering wheel amongst the silence. "How was it then?"

Entering onto Interstate 678, she leans against the window and observes the speeding cars. "Yeah, it was ok." She looks up at the orange sky and sighs. She turns to her. "Actually, no it wasn't ok."

Clarissa keeps her eyes on the road, looking in the reverse mirror as she switches lanes and gulps. She had a feeling this was coming. "It happens. Look at my parents."

Arabella leans forwards and places her flushed cheeks in her dainty palms, staring down at her feet. "Your mom didn't cheat on your dad though." Thinking about her dad and his new wife, she can't help but feel anger; it's like both her parents have forgotten about her, whilst they go onto create their own lives. "Maybe, I'm just overreacting."

Clarissa nods and hits the play button, adjusting the volume to low as she bops her head to the catchy club remix. "Exactly," she says, and risks their lives as she casts her naughty look at her. "Did you lose your virginity to any British guys then?"

She rolls her eyes. *What is it with her and sex all the time?* "Noooo."

Clarissa raises her eyebrow at her unconvincing tone. "Arabella Harper!"

"What? I actually didn't." She raises her dainty hand over her cupid lips and looks to her. "I did kiss a guy though."

Clarissa drops her jaw, looking into the reverse mirror as she attempts to switch lanes again. "And you've only just told me?"

"It only just happened." She reaches into her cross-shoulder bag and retrieves her blush pink lip gloss, pulling down the sun protector mirror.

"What! Where?"

"On the plane," she switches to her bottom lip, "in the bathroom."

"Where has the innocent Arabella gone," and looks to her, "who waits for her soulmate?"

"So I go in to do my makeup and I forgot to lock the door. He walks in and I thought he was just going to notice me and be like oops. Instead he saw me and closes the door. Then he picks me up—"

Clarissa raises her eyebrow. "What! Are you ok?"

Oh my god. Shut up and let me finish. "You didn't let me finish. He's not a predator. He was with a girl who looked like me, so he thought I was her." She puckers her lips and closes the gloss, as Clarissa sits in silence processing this absurdity. "Oh… as for the kiss, he slammed me against the door."

Clarissa widens her eyes. "You absolute animal, Miss Harper!" Arabella breaks into a giggle and slaps her arm. "I think your nickname should be changed from A to mile-high club, or MHC."

She yawns. "Funny. I'm going to catch a quick nap." She reclines the leather seat back. "I think the jetlag has already set in."

Pulling up outside Arabella's apartment block on Cypress Avenue, located on the corner of East 137th, Mott Haven, Clarissa shuts off the engine and looks to the sleeping beauty. "We're here now." No answer. "We're here now!" and watches her bloodshot eyes slowly open.

"That was… quick," she yawningly says and sits up. "Thanks for picking me up. Any plans for tonight?"

Clarissa looks in the reverse mirror and fixes her hair. "I'm off to the opening of Devils nightclub with Beatrice, then off to Miami for two weeks in the morning to see Father."

She unfastens her seatbelt and looks to her. "Wait, are you missing B's wedding?" She grips the door handle. "Also, what's going on with the shop?"

"Apparently she wanted a small wedding. So I'll be back on the day and I'll pick you up for the reception in the evening… and don't worry about the shop. I've hired cover so the wedding flowers are being taken care of. You just relax and I'll see you when I'm back."

"Sounds good," she says, and opens the door. Stepping out onto the sidewalk, she opens the back door and retrieves her suitcase. She slams the door and leans back in for a hug. "Thanks for the lift. Have fun tonight and I'll see you in two weeks." She releases her and exits. "Don't be a slut and make sure to text me."

Clarissa looks back to her with a naughty look. "I still can't believe you kissed someone. Who even are you anymore?"

She giggles. "I'm still an innocent angel," she says, as she flutters her eyelashes. She slams the door and waves through the tinted window. "Byeeee."

Listening to Clarissa fade into the nightlife, Arabella looks at the church in front, sniffing the sewage air. *London smelt better.* She turns around and lugs her suitcase up the graphite grey, seven step staircase, reaching into her tanned brown cross-shoulder bag at the top and retrieving her keys to unlock the rusted, black community gate. She ascends the outside staircase of the redbrick apartment block, and turns right, listening to the filthy pleasure from her neighbours open window. Walking through the communal door, she steps onto the burgundy carpet and looks at her creamy white apartment door, number one; first on the right. Sliding her key into the lock, she peeks left at her chattering neighbours under the staircase.

"Looking sexy tonight, Miss Harper," says her neighbour.

She opens the door and enters her modern white wall, L shaped apartment, hitting the light switch and wheeling her suitcase along the light brown carpet. She lifts it onto the cream white couch to the right of the entrance and throws her bag on top of it. *Hmmm... maybe I should. Fuck it!* Retracing her steps, she pops her head out the door, her heart racing as her lips tremor. "Y-Y-You... look like shit tonight, Jerry!" She slams the door and bursts into a giggling fit, kicking off her caramel sandals and walking her bare feet onto the shaggy cream rug in the center; the fluffy fur caressing between her toes, as she gazes into the standing mirror next to the couch. Dropping her playsuit beneath her, she slides her hands down her hourglass figure. *Not bad.* Turning around, she looks back into the reflection, bouncing her cheeks up and down. *Must work on that more.* Raising her left hand, she releases the hairclip; shaking her head as her brunette locks unleash their thickness around her beauty bones. Walking back over to the couch, she grabs her smartphone from her bag and hits the light switch, using the torch on her phone as she walks straight ahead to her queen size bed, facing the kitchen. *Ahhh comfort. Time to text Beatrice.* "Just got back, have fun tonight with C. Wish I could have come but super tired. I will see you in two weeks at the wedding reception xx." She leans over to the oak side table to her left and places her smartphone on charge before laying back with the duvet smothered over her. Sinking into the fluffy pink pillow, she shuts her eyes. *Welcome to the Mile High Club... why did she have to be there! Those eyes were so beautiful. Please, please, please god, if you're out there or whoever, let me meet him again. It's all I ask.*

Five hours later, the dark apartment shines from the backlight of her smartphone; the light sleeper in her catching the vibrations. Opening her eyes, she reaches for her phone and holds it away from her face, as she hits the unlock button. Adjusting her eyes, she opens the text from Clarissa.

"OMG. Just kissed this 11/10 guy at the nightclub. So hot!!!"

HOTEL L'AMOUR

Gazing over herself in her apartment, Arabella slides her dainty hands down her tightly fitted white dress; the tight wrap showing off her perfect hourglass. Fixing her wavy brunette hair, she hears Clarissa beep her horn and panics. *Make up? Check! Hair? Check! Dress? Check! Shoes? Check! Bag? Where the hell is it?* She looks over to the couch, spotting the brown strap hiding under the fluffy pillow. *There you are.* She puts it on and assumes her position. "Make up? Check! Hair? Check! Dress? Check! Shoes? Check! Bag? Check!" She exhales a sigh of relief. The horn beeps again; this time never ending as Clarissa holds it down. *Wtf is wrong with her!* Rushing out the door, she descends the outside staircase into the summer's evening warmth.

"Can you tell your friend to shut the hell up!" shouts the neighbour, from their window.

She gulps. Reaching the car, she opens the door and looks at C. "Will you stop that!"

Clarissa starts the engine. "Took your sweet time…"

With her cheeks rosy, red, she climbs in and fastens her seatbelt. "Just drive." Hitting the gas, they reverse straight into the parked car behind; the back of their heads feeling the force, as their hearts race. "Oh my god! What is wrong with you today?"

Clarissa rolls her eyes and switches into drive, pushing down on the gas and leaving the wreckage behind as they veer right, onto East 137th. "I doubt they even noticed, probably just a scratch." Arabella exhales her frustration; the last thing she needs is a neighbour slipping a repair bill under her door. It would be the death of her bank account. "The wedding gifts in the back in case you were wondering," says Clarissa.

She looks behind at a large, hot pink, ribboned box. *Thank god for that.* "Well I'm glad you remembered because I've been so busy with work." *Shit! Why did I say that?*

Clarissa raises her eyebrow, keeping her eyes on the road whilst looking back and forth at her. "Wait! You didn't take the two-week break?"

She gulps. "I was bored, after a day of binge-watching crap, I didn't know what else to do! So, I just sort of just went to work."

20

"You seriously need to lose your virginity already. Like what are you waiting for?"

Oh piss off. "Soon! I'm going to close my eyes for a moment, it's been a hectic morning."

Reclined back in the comfy leather, she imagines a figment outline of the tall, dark, and handsome man from the plane. He raises his right hand. "Come closer," he seductively whispers, and signals to come here with his index finger. She can't resist, step, by step, she moves closer, as he stands in his white unbuttoned shirt. She takes his veiny hands and curls her dainty fingers between his, pressing her body against his hardened abs, as he towers over her. "It's just you and me," he says, as he presses his forehead against hers. She flutters her eyelashes, her chest drowning in chaos as she deeply exhales, creating a sauna of steam between them, as their green eyes burn their eternal flames. Grazing their noses, she parts her lips, as he starts to—

"Wake up you horny bitch!" shouts Clarissa.

Opening her eyes wide, she looks at the blonde queen. "What the hell?"

Clarissa gives her the look. "You are soooo filthy. Did you know you sleep talk?"

"No I didn't," she says, as she looks out at the marble lions. *This isn't the wedding?* She looks to her. "Why have we stopped outside the Public Library?"

"Umm... I thought it was here. I tried to text her but no response."

She pulls out her smartphone. "Ohhhh. I forgot. B text whilst you were away. Since they met in the library, the ceremony had to take place there. Not sure why the sudden change." She opens her messages from Beatrice. "The ball room at Hotel L'Amour?" She types the address into the satnav. "It's behind us. Take a left on East 41st and then left onto Madison."

Driving down Madison Avenue, Arabella looks Clarissa up and down. "Love the white dress by the way."

"Thanks. It's a silk slit maxi dress. Only cost $1200."

She looks away and rolls her eyes. *Only... god she is so spoilt.* Unlocking her smartphone, she scrolls through her messages with Clarissa; the last two weeks have been non-stop going on about that guy from the club. "You haven't mentioned that eleven out of ten yet?"

"Don't get me going again..." Trying to remain focused on the road, she struggles to concentrate as her club experience intrudes. "Fine! He was just so hot. Not just hot... next level hot... like godly hot."

She looks at the satnav, as they pass East 61st street. "You've missed the turning?"

Clarissa shakes her head. "That's your fault." Continuing along, they turn left onto East 66th, and onto 5th Avenue. Enjoying the gift of darkness as it sweeps the evening sky, they soak up the vibrant colors as Manhattan's city lights create that warm, magical feeling. Reaching the towering hotel, they swing left into the porte-cochere and join the other guests, slowly rolling along the neon white lit, red cobbled brick lane, as they reach the center. She looks out her passenger side window, as two red coated valets approach. "This reminds me of Vegas," says Clarissa, as she gazes out her window at the extravagantly large, stone fountain.

"I've never been," she says, as the redcoat open her door and holds out his sparkling white glove. She takes his hand and climbs out; her rose gold heels touching the crowded, grey sidewalk as he escorts her to safety. "Thank you," she says, and smiles her pearly whites at him. Joined by the blonde princess, they turn around and stare goodbye as the valet sets off to park the Range Rover in the underground carpark. *I wonder how long it'll take her to realize she's left the gift in the backseat.*

"Clarissa?" shouts the groomsman, from the top of the hotel entrance.

Looking at the blonde queen, Arabella peeks over her shoulder, and widens her green eyes, as he descends the staircase. "Why is B's brother calling you?" *Let me guess. They slept together. That's disgusting.*

Clarissa sighs and turns around, with a fake smile. "Bret. Fancy seeing you here," she says, and signals her blue eyes left at him.

"You didn't return my—" He catches on and looks to Arabella, then back to her. "Hey Arabella. Didn't see you there."

This is so awkward. "Hey." She looks to Clarrisa. "I'll leave you two alone, so I'll meet you in there," she says, and gives her a look of disgust.

Making her way through the congregating guests, she walks along the Lyon red carpet and stops to look up through the glass overhead roof, appreciating the grand architecture as she scales the hotels mirrored exterior design and extravagant size. Holding onto the gold railing, she ascends the four, fresh white steps, elegantly smiling her beauty at the redcoat doormen; their white gloves each holding a golden handle, either side, of the expensive gold framed doors.

"Welcome to Hotel L'Amour," they say, and pull it open.

"Thank you," she says, and steps inside. *Holy shit.* Hit with warmth, she moves inside the modern, fresh cream spacious white lobby, and looks right, widening her eyes at the exquisite and fine art hanging in gold frames along the right wall; enough to open a local gallery. *Why is it all Italian Renaissance though?* Gazing left as she moves through the bubbly, chatting guests towards the center, she stares over the stunning blonde receptionist behind the walnut mahogany desk. Avoiding eye contact, as the receptionist catches her, she looks up; her chest sinking in awe as her favourite past time twinkles before her through the sky-high glass ceiling. *That's gorgeous.*

"Champagne?" asks the white coat waiter.

"Don't mind if I do," says Clarissa, as she rejoins her side and takes a glass.

She grabs a glass. "Why thank you," she says, and parts her pink glossy lips, swishing the dry fruity flavor around her mouth. She turns to Clarissa with a frown. "What the hell was that?"

"Not now," she whispers, as the glamourous Tiffany, owner of Brides and Grooms across the street, and her husband Benedict approach.

"This is amazing girls. I couldn't believe it when we walked in. The mahogany brown skirting, with the modern cream combination is what I've been telling him I want in the house for years," says Tiffany.

Clarissa takes another sip and scales the room. "This sure is some fancy décor. This must have cost a fortune."

Arabella nods in agreement with her blonde bestie, as the ballroom double doors open straight ahead of them.

Benedict, not one for being last, looks at all the guests moving. "Yes, well Tiff, ladies, it's quite something. On that note, let's find our seats, shall we?" He links arms with Tiffany and smiles at them. "Enjoy the night girls." He turns around with his wife and heads for the ballroom.

Nearing the ballroom, with a hallway either side, Arabella looks to the right side and raises her eyebrow, silently sipping away as she observes a man dressed in a black suit, guarding a control panel like a Doberman on a stool, next to a set of steel doors. *Hmmm… rather suspicious.* She looks left, as they reach the ballroom entrance, looking at the blood red carpeted hallway. *I wonder where that leads.*

"Please find your allocated seats. Your names will be written on the cards. Enjoy your evening," says the doorman.

She smiles and passes through the double, gold framed doors, following behind Clarissa as they walk along the walnut glossed floor, hit with a sprinkle of nostalgia as the fond memory of her prom rushes back. Deeper into the room, that nostalgia fades drastically. *Who in their right mind would design this?* Walking amongst the crystal glass rounded tables, she looks to her left and raises her eyebrow. *Why is the room lit a winter blue with summer mural walls? This is dreadful.* She lavishes up the pastel pink and blue hydrangea smell, scattered across the summer mural walls with banquets of extravagant flowers from every part of the globe; compliments of her and the Campbell empire. Arriving at table five, she looks up at the icy, tiered pendant, chandelier, hanging from the maple ceiling, and takes her seat, positioned to the left of her bestie. "Why is it winter themed with a summer mural?"

"They met in winter obviously," says Clarissa, as she swoons over the magical room. "This is so dreamy. B has really outdone herself this time. God I'm going to have to do bigger and better on my day."

The white coat waiter reappears. "Champagne?" They can't possibly resist, as they both take two and sip away.

Giggling away on the copious amounts of flowing champagne, the room falls silent as the newly wedded couple, Beatrice and Tristram Levington, make their way onto the stage in front, from the side entrance, and take their seats in the middle of the long table, overlooking the floor. Beatrice waves to them both wearing a white drop-waisted wedding dress to die for; its delicate lace bodice, and appliques beautifully crafted throughout the skirt, with a halo-style headpiece to compliment her brunette wavy curls.

Tristram, in his traditional black tuxedo, picks up his glass and taps it with his fork twice, creating a ringing noise. "Thank you all for coming. Today marks a significant moment in the Levington history, for not only did my darling wife and I meet six years ago, on this very day, but that my parents also married on this day."

Arabella lowers her glass from her lips and leans into Clarissa. "They didn't meet in the winter?" she whispers.

"I'm such an idiot. Blame the champagne."

She leans back and looks around the spinning room, squinting her eyes at the ballroom entrance. She sits confused and curious as a well-dressed man with his arms crossed leans against the entrance and watches the speech. *Who is that?* She refocuses on the speech.

"— you all enjoy the night, drink as much as you can, and we thank you from the bottom of our hearts for all the gifts."

Clarissa widens her eyes and leans into her. "I forgot the gift. I'm terrible," she whispers.

She spits out her champagne into the glass. "Ha-ha, I'm sorry," and places the glass down, "let's go get it." She stands and follows the clutz to the entrance. *Where's he gone?*

Waiting on the ranch brown, leather couch, in the lobbies waiting area, artwork side, Arabella leans forwards and places her flushed cheeks in her dainty hands. The alcohol starts to kick in. *Christ… I need air.* Peeking to her right, she looks at the guard again. He hasn't moved a muscle. With her overheated, raspberry colored face dripping, she looks across to the left side of the ballroom and reads the

28

small hanging sign. *Garden this way. Yes please.* She stands and follows the carpet to the end and turns right, looking down the long, glossed white hallway. *This is long.* Managing to not stumble, she reaches a silver door. Gripping the crystal handle, she twists and opens it. She gasps. *Oh my god. Oh my god.* Stepping out onto the oak wood decking, as the evening breeze cools against her sweaty skin, she approaches the panoramic glass railing and leans over. *It's so beautiful.* Silently gazing out at the highly exquisite and well-lit garden, enriched with rare flowers and vibrant colors, she hears the flick of a zippo lighter. Glancing left, she observes a deep, blue flame amongst the shadows; the cherry embers of the cigar burning a deep fiery red, as the thick white smoke rises around their face. *Well that's not creepy at all.* With her guard up, she faces front and peeks over, watching and listening as his penny loafers tap along the hard oak floor.

He leans over the glass railing on the other side, in his tightly fitted custom, black suit and looks out into the garden. "If only this garden looked half as good as you," he seductively says. She discreetly scans the area for others, as he stubs his Cuban cigar out in the ashtray on the glass table and steps along the decking. Approaching her, he takes a sharp left and descends the two steps into the garden; her heart racing as she stares at the back of his black hair and observes him strolling deeper along the path. Stopping halfway, he points to a neatly arranged flower bed. "What's this one called?"

Let's just answer then go back inside. "Umm... a Juliet Rose."

"Juliet?" He crouches down and delicately brushes its beauty. "I guess that would make me Romeo wouldn't you say?"

She places her dainty hand over her lips and giggles. *Control yourself.* "I mean... it's an extremely rare flower though."

"Extremely rare you say. What if I'm rarer?" he charmingly asks and stands up.

She bursts into laughter. "I'm so sorry, but where did you—"

The garden fills with a loud gasp, as he spins around with his hands in his pockets and smirks. Locking his devilish gaze into her, he slowly trails back up the path, as she stands frozen. Ascending the steps, he turns left, as she turns to him. "The next time you want to selfishly gasp in a garden Dakota, spare a thought for those poor insects and their families you disturbed this time of evening." He spins around and walks towards the glass table, holding in his chuckle with his tongue pressed against his cheek, as she stands there in shock. Looking down at the ashtray, he's surprised by her silence – usually it's insults. Turning to face her, he approaches. Towering over her, she looks up and flutters her lashes; their eyes reigniting their green flames as they lock. "You're not Dakota?"

She shakes her brunette locks. "Arabella—"

"Harper." He leans into her ear. "Must be fate," he whispers. She struggles to contain her tingling sensation, drowning in a whirlwind of pleasure as his woody spiced cologne leaks from his exposed, veiny neck. Exhaling against his clean shave, she grabs his left wrist and guides his hand to her champagne lips. He presses his forehead against hers; their eyes connecting as she softly bites down on his thumb and soaks her moist lips around it. She breathes heavily; her chest exploding in waves of sensational flutters as his stifling complexion teases. He brushes her glowing cheek with his right thumb and curls his fingers; the stimulating touch of his fingertips shooting through her, as he sweeps her brunette waves behind her ear. Removing his thumb from her succulent lips, he brushes along her other cheek; the smell of her sweet perfume hitting him, as she moves her wet lips closer.

"Kiss me," she passionately whispers.

Grazing against her cupid lips, he whispers, "Whilst I would love too, you're drunk."

"What's your—" They both look to the garden door. He steps back, as the handle turns.

Clarissa bursts through the door and looks to her. "There you are. You've been ages." Arabella smiles at her blonde friend and hints with her eyes in his direction. "What are you…" Turning her head left, she widens her crystal blue eyes, as her heart starts racing.

With a sexy smirk, he slowly steps towards her, closer, and closer, brushing his suit jacket against her smooth skin, leaving her in a tease as his fragrance hits. Opening the door, he turns around and uses his muscles as a doorstop. With all eyes on him, he looks down at his white shirt. "What do you prefer? One or two buttons undone?" He looks up; his godly complexion locking on to Arabella, as Clarissa blushes.

"I—"

"Enjoy the evening ladies." He winks to her and turns around; disturbing the gardens nature as he lets the door slam behind him.

Clarissa turns to her. "Why was he here?"

She raises her arms. "Do you know him?"

"That's the man from the club," she says, and takes a seat on the glass bench, left of the door. Arabella gulps. *Should I tell her?* She swears an oath of silence and takes a seat next to her, gazing out into the garden through the glass panel, as the champagne flows through them. "Did he like say anything to you, about me?" asks C.

"Why would he? We've just met," she says and stares up at the twinkling display. *Why does she always have to ruin everything!*

"Did he tell you his name? I need to find his socials."

No. You ruined my chance! "He didn't say."

Listening to the garden's nature chirp and buzz, as the champagne effect hits, they close their tipsy eyes and rest; each enjoying their own version of the mysterious man.

THE ORDER

Squinting her bloodshot eyes as her alarm rings, Arabella rolls over in her dawn lit apartment bed and reaches over to the oak side table; desperate to turn it off as her head pounds from last night. Restoring the crisp silence, she returns to her sleeping position. Her phone vibrates. She sighs and rolls over again, unhooking it from its charger and unlocking the screen; the bright light blinding her, as she opens the message.

"Hope you got home safe," texts Clarissa.

How did I get home? She sits up and drops the phone on the duvet; panicking as she inspects her body. *Everything seems ok.* She looks around the bright, muggy room. *Everything seems fine to me.* She wipes the sweat from her forehead, and leans forwards, resting her puffy face in her petite hands. *I feel like shit. How much did I drink?*

Finding the energy to stand, she stretches and yawns. Moving to the kitchen, she opens the refrigerator and grabs a green juice. *I was on the bench and then?* Quenching her dry throat, she places the empty bottle on the granite, kitchen counter and retrieves her smartphone. "How did I get home exactly?" she texts Clarissa. She looks at the time, 08:30. *Maybe I should call in sick... better not actually.* She opens the local cab app. *9:30 is a good time.* Attempting to pay, an alternative option to use crypto currency appears. Intrigued, she clicks and waits. *What the... A reading dog. I can pay with a dog.* Finding humor amongst the confusion, she converts her dollars to BookShib and is redirected to the payment screen. She taps the book cab option. *I can't believe I've just paid with a dog lol.* Chucking it on the bed, she enters the bathroom and leans into the shower, hitting the power button. She heads back to the mirror and undresses. *You look awful.* She turns around and re-enters; the room heated like a sauna, as she steps onto the dark white shower tray and slides the steamed glass door shut. She spins around and stands under the hot pressure. *Mmhhmmmm.* With the steam building around her tight skin, she bends over and reaches for the shower gel; her peachy ass leaving an imprint on the panel as she stands. *I can't believe it was him.* Closing her eyes, she lets her imagination run wild - his drop-dead gorgeous complexion, the smell of his cologne, and his words, all overwhelming her. Flicking open the cap, she hovers it over her soft, rounded breasts and lets it rain. Dropping the bottle, she cups them; creating a silky foam as she caresses them. Catching her rosy nipples between her spread fingers, she bites down on her sultry bottom lip; the desire to moan building as her body stimulates to her sensational twisting. The apartment door knocks. She stops and sighs. *Who is that now?*

Only half dry, she races to her wardrobe. Slipping on a white tee shirt and hot pink G-string, she opens the door and raises her eyebrow at her dissatisfied, mature neighbour, Barbara.

"Sorry, I was in the shower," she says, and looks over her curly light brown hair and tacky leopard print dress.

"I can see that dear."

Following her eyes, she looks down; her eyes and mouth widening, as her hardened nipples show through the soaked fabric. She gulps. "I am so embarrassed!"

Barbara flicks her hand. "It's fine dear. The reason to have disturbed you so early is because someone has crashed into my car. I know it can't be you of course sweetie, as you don't drive, but I was just wondering, since your apartment is looking out onto the street, whether you happened to of noticed anything?"

The whiplash moment of Clarissa crashing pops into her mind. "No, I didn't see anything. How bad is it. I hope it's just a scratch?"

Barbara shakes her head. "I'm afraid it's a little bit more than a scratch dear. Sorry for bothering you anyway. If you hear anything let me know. I'm just above."

Slamming the door on the old woman, she races to her bed and grabs her smartphone. *She is unbelievable.* She hits dial on Clarissa. Listening to it ring, she answers. "You are unbelievable! Do you know that?"

"Hey, I'm sort of busy. Did you get my text?"

She looks in the mirror. "Nooo? I was too busy dealing with a neighbour!" she furiously says.

"Get down the shop already. Father decided he liked the idea so much that he has already updated the company website and found a supplier for the eternity roses. They are being delivered soon. Sooo, get your ass down there, ASAP!"

Panicking, she rummages around the room for clothes. "Are you not already there?"

"No, that's a long story. I think the car valet last night must have reversed into something, I have a right mind to sue, but anyway, getting that fixed so won't be in today!" The line cuts off.

Is she serious? She throws her smartphone on the bed and shakes her head in disbelief. Facing the mirror, she peels the soaked top from her moist skin; her breasts bouncing as the tight fabric catches her rosy tips. *They've got bigger.*

Clipping her thick, brunette hair up, as the cab waits outside, she does one last mirror check, looking summery in her pastel pinky white playsuit, and tanned brown gladiator sandals. She grabs her cross-shoulder bag from the couch and exits her apartment. Descending onto the sidewalk, as the summer breeze sweeps her rosy, glowing skin, she walks towards the yellow cab and climbs in the back.

"What happened to that?" asks the driver, as he stares at the wreckage. She shakes her head in silence, feeling nothing but shame for poor Barbara.

Driving along 5th Avenue, she stares out at Central Park, wondering about the mysterious man. *What's his name? Why was he in the garden? He wasn't a guest at the wedding. He wasn't dressed as staff.* Pulling up along East 90th Street, she smiles to the driver and exits the cab. She's already paid on the app. Reaching into her bag, she retrieves her keys and looks through the large window into the empty lounge of the meadowy green exterior shop front. Walking to the door; right side of the window, she listens to the morning traffic pass behind her as she unlocks the door. Entering the Campbell enterprise, she flicks both switches to her left – the lights to the shop, and the bright gold sign reading 'Campbell and Co' on the exterior front. Moving inwards along the grey carpet, she places her keys on the glass counter straight ahead and turns left into the open lounge, throwing her bag over the glass coffee table and onto the chocolate brown, leather couch.

Sitting behind the glass counter, she opens a business email. *Oh my god!* The shop fills with clapping as her excitement takes over. Grabbing her smartphone with a wide smile, she messages Clarissa. "We have our first order!!!" She places it back on the glass and looks straight ahead, smiling as an older, grey haired, suave gentleman enters the shop. Using his back as a door stop, he stands with a box in his hand, allowing two exceedingly attractive blonde women squeeze past him with their hands also full of extravagance.

Letting the door swing behind him, he approaches the counter. "Hello. I have spoken to your father, I'm the supplier for the Eternity Rose. Where would you have us put these beauties?"

"They really are beautiful," she says, and points to the archway door between her and the lounge. "Just in the back if you don't mind." The two girls descend the creaky wooden steps into the workshop and carefully place them on the large wooden table. Making their way back onto the shopfloor, they smile to Arabella and wave goodbye, leaving the older gentleman alone with her.

He scales the room with his hands clasped. "A mighty fine establishment, Mr. Campbell has here. You must be Clarissa."

She shakes her head sideways. "I'm afraid not. I'm her best friend and colleague. We went to floristry school together."

He nods his head. "I am impressed. I hope you enjoy the exquisite, and truly immaculate, Eternity Rose. I will be delivering them every fortnight. My name is Peter Hoffman, and yours if I may ask?"

She pleasantly smiles. "Arabella Harper."

"Arabella, what a sophisticated name. Nice to meet you." He turns around and grips the silver door handle. "I will see you soon, Miss Harper."

"Bye," she says, and waits for him to exit. Racing down into the workshop, she hovers over the beauties, and deeply inhales their divine floral scent. *This is heaven.* With no time to waste, she prepares the first order. Delicately removing the twenty-four-karat gold dipped roses from their resting spot, she places a dozen onto the special clear bouquet wrap, encrusted with a white gold trim to enhance the luxurious feel. Turning around on the stone floor, she opens the wooden draw and retrieves a gold florist ribbon. Creating a perfect floral bow around the bouquet, she smiles and returns to the laptop for the delivery address - located on the west side of Hudson Yards - Manhattan's gated community of wealth. Worried the delivery driver will mess up, she takes zero chances and books a cab with her BookShib on the local app.

Wrapped and ready to go, she locks up the shop and proceeds to the back of the taxi, holding her babies in her hands tight. Opening the back door, she delicately positions the flowers on the middle seat and carefully slides in.

The driver looks over the seat and sniffs. "They are incredibly strong."

She smiles and looks down at them. "Yes. Words can't describe these," she excitedly says, as the driver pulls away from the curb.

Looking back in the reverse mirror, the driver says, "My wife would love them. I'll pop into your shop next valentines' day."

Staring out the window from the backseat, she looks up at the tall, skyscrapers; the summer rays reflecting its godly shine off the world's elite. The cab pulls up. "Could you wait here? I need a lift back to the shop after this."

"Yes, that's fine."

She opens the door and steps out smelling of roses. Turning around, she leans back inside and lifts the bouquet from its resting place, as the summer breeze sweeps the back of her glowing legs. She closes the door and approaches the black community gate. She presses the buzzer. No one answers. She rings again. No answer! She peeks through the thick black bars that hides the elite in their luxury. *Please answer.* She tries one last time and patiently waits, as her nerves simmer. *No. No. This can't be happening. Not on the first order.* Unable to leave them, she whips out her smartphone and opens the order, examining the confirmation email. She widens her eyes at the billing address and rushes back to the car. "Change of plan. Do you mind if we go to another location please?" she asks, as she places them in the middle seat and slides in.

He takes a sip of his ice-cold water. "What's the address?"

She shuts the door and looks at her phone. "Hotel L'Amour on Fifth Avenue." The cab sets off again.

"Just to make you aware, I'm clocking off after so you will have to arrange another lift back to the shop."

"No problem." She reinspects the address, gulping as her anxiety kicks in. It doesn't mention a room number. *Seriously. Why is it always me?*

Pulling up in the cobble lane, the driver leans over his seat and takes a final whiff. "Gorgeous. It says you've paid for the first trip already. Consider this one a freebie. I'm feeling generous today."

She smiles, as the red coat valet approaches. "Wow. Thank you so much." The door opens. She takes his white glove and climbs out. Standing on the sidewalk, she waits as the valet retrieves her flowers and hands them to her with a smile. "Thank you." She turns around and ascends the steps, listening to the fountains soothing flow bounce off the glass roof. She smiles to the doormen, as they open the grand entrance to match her pace. Holding the roses tightly, she steps onto the freshly waxed, white marble floor and approaches the reception to her left. Placing the bouquet on the mahogany desk, she smiles to the blonde receptionist.

"Welcome to Hotel L'Amour. What is the nature of your visit today?"

She looks at her nametag. *What's with the high pitch voice Chloe.* "I work in a florists called Campbell, and Co, and we received an order. No one was at the delivery address. The billing address is registered to here. There isn't a room number though so I wondered if you could help?"

Chloe smiles. "One moment please." She picks up the reception phone and places her hand over her mouth, nodding away. She hangs up and smiles. "Please enjoy your visit," she says and turns around.

She raises her eyebrow. *What? She didn't even say anything.* Hearing footsteps approach her, she turns around. It's the guard from last night.

"Please follow me, Miss." She grabs the roses and follows the black haired, muscly guard towards the steel doors. *He sounds Italian.* He presses the control panel and retakes his seat. The steel doors reveal their secret, as they slowly open. It's an elevator. "Please step in!"

"Umm… where is this taking me?" He says nothing. *It can't be that bad. It's a hotel.* She enters and turns around, watching the lobby light fade in the reflection, as the steel doors shut. *Jesus!* She flinches, almost dropping the flowers as the lift floods with devil red lighting. Feeling the force beneath her feet, her ascent begins. Looking left, then right, she turns around. *What the hell?* She's in grandiose heaven, as three mirror walls capture every feature of her; only the devil himself would be this vain.

"Welcome to floor one-hundred. The Penthouse," says the recorded, seductively, deep and sexy sounding woman. The doors begin to open. Blinded by an intense burst of sunshine through the opening gap, she rapidly blinks, adjusting her eyes as the black and white interior reveals itself; a cooling touch to keep out the heat. She steps onto the black, and white, large tiles, and scales the right side, a veneer white wall with even more Italian Renaissance art, as a strong mixture of cologne hits her. Directly ahead, a glass door attached to the back wall. Unable to see more, she walks inwards and reaches the corner wall, scaling it right to left. *This is… wow, classy.* Continuing straight ahead, she approaches the sliding glass door. Her jaw drops. Widening her almond eyes, she observes through the glass at the starry black, glossed terrace overlooking Central Park, fit with a swimming pool in the center.

She breaks out of her drooling state and looks left, met with one long Tuscany cream leather couch positioned along the glass wall – a shorter version either side of it, all facing inwards towards a glass coffee table standing on a cream white, Persian rug in the center. She turns around and walks along the back of the short couch, and turns right, and right again, along the Persian rug, placing the bouquet on the glass table before sitting on the long couch; the need for a sunbed unnecessary, as the sunshine reflects from behind. She leans back and spreads her arms across the top. Relaxing in comfort, she looks straight ahead at the red brick wall fireplace and a long-stretched mirror above it, enjoying her own reflection, as she patiently waits for the owner.

THE PENTHOUSE

Returning to the main couch, Arabella spreads her arms along the top and leans her head back, enjoying the summer shine, as the smell of sex and cologne linger. Having had the opportunity to inspect the penthouse for the last 20 minutes, she's convinced the occupier must be a woman; the luxury lingerie strewn all over the floor gives it away. She perks up to the sound of a door opening around the right side and stands. *Remember they are a customer so act professional.* Hearing footsteps, she moves left to the short couch and faces the right-hand side, masking her nerves with a professional smile. She widens her eyes. *Keep calm.* Watching as the side of a golden god - tall, dark, and handsome appears, she plays with her hands as he turns his back on her, wearing nothing but a white towel wrapped around his toned waist. *Do I interrupt him?* Sliding the wall, he reveals a secret wardrobe, full of expense and high-quality fashion. He reaches for the top shelf, flexing his power as he retrieves a pair of penny loafers. *You can pick me up anytime.* He drops them on the tiles, creating a loud bang. She bites down on her left index finger, as he reaches back inside for his white boxers. *What are you?* He drops the white towel. *Oh gosh. Please turn around you sexy thing.* She flutters inside; ignoring the pain of her strengthening bite as his perfect ass sends her into a drooling paradise. He bends down and slides the tight fabric along his smooth and muscly calf's, snapping the elastic waist against his V line as he finishes and opens the next wardrobe to find his suit trousers. He stops, as the pinging message of a smartphone comes from behind him.

  She releases her bite marked finger and widens her eyes, gulping as her heart races. *He's going to think I'm a pervert now.* "Ahem... hey, sorry to—" With his trousers on, he turns around. She gasps. *It's you.* He starts to approach. Locking his smirking gaze into her, she breathes heavily; her body hit by a tsunami of waves as a cluster of uncontrollable emotions shoot through her. He throws the white shirt around him; the sleeves wrapping around his tight muscles, as he nears. Enjoying the V.I.P view of his glowing pecks inches away, she lavishes the smell of his woody cologne leaking from his exposed neck, as he crouches down and reaches behind her with both arms. Taking hold of his luxury belt from both ends, he stands up and smiles; the fine leather caressing the back of her neck, as he pulls her in closer with it. She looks up and flutters her lashes, exhaling against his icy breath in his towering trap of tease.

"Must be fate," he charmingly says.

"It's starting to appear that way," she breathlessly says and presses her dainty hands against his hardened pecks, biting down on her bottom lip as she glides down his rippled abs.

"I'm afraid our third time wasn't so lucky," he whispers, and releases her from his tease; turning around and perching on the couches armrest opposite.

"Who are you?"

"They call me Mr. P," he says, as he slips his black socks on.

She places her hand over her lips. "Mr. Penis?"

He stands and steps along the Persian rug; their eyes locking again as he presses his forehead against hers. "Could you do me a favor?" he seductively asks. Fluttering her lashes, she nods. Sweeping his curled fingers behind her ear, he leans in, as her body tingles to his stimulating touch. "Would you never join a comedy club for me?" He turns around and walks towards his wardrobe, containing his laughter with his tongue pressed against his cheek.

She rolls her eyes. *So immature.* "You seem very different to other guys."

He slides into his penny loafers and looks down at his watch. Spinning around, he perches back on the armrest and looks to her. "Have you ever done speed dating?"

She shakes her head sideways. "No."

He chuckles. "No neither have I. Anyway you have two minutes before I need to go. Tell me about yourself."

What do I say? "Umm... My parents are divorced. Dad is British, Mom is American. That's why I was on the plane."

He starts to button up his shirt. "Have you ever heard of Canterbury?" He looks up to her nodding. "Have you ever been?"

"No. It was my first time, and I was in London. Are you British?"

He stands and grabs his custom-tailored black suit jacket from his wardrobe. "Did the accent give it away?" he asks, as he throws it around his torso.

"Yes it—" The elevator opens. She breaks eye contact and turns around, listening to the tapping of shoes approach and turn the corner. She smiles at an older, Italian gentleman, dressed in a black suit.

He smiles back and looks to Mr. P. "Ready boss?"

Mr. P looks at her. "Change of plan. Take Arabella home. I will delay by thirty minutes." He grabs the flowers and hands them to her. "They're yours now." He kisses her on her rosy cheek and turns around.

I forgot about those. "Will I see you again?"

He stops and sighs. Shaking the back of his head to her in frustration, he knows he can't. "That's for fate to decide," he says and walks into the bedroom around the right-hand corner.

"Hello, my name is Gino."

Ooo, I love that accent. She turns to face him with her hands smelling of roses. "Hello, I'm Arabella."

He nods. "I know. I took you home the other night. Please grab all your personal belongings and follow me."

She widens her eyes. "Took me home?" she nervously asks, as she grabs everything and trails behind him towards the elevator.

He hits the call button and looks to her, as the doors open. "Yes. You were passed out alone on the garden bench. No cab would take you, so I stepped up," he says, as he lays out his hand. "Ladies first."

She smiles and enters. *Oh god, I hope he didn't come into the apartment. It was rather messy.* Following behind her, he stands next to her and watches as the doors close. The elevator turns red. *What is with that stupid lighting.* Choking on the strong floral scent in silence, he stares at her half-parted lips tremoring as if they want to ask a question.

50

She can't hold back. "Mr. P. Hmmm. Phillip? Preston? Pierre? Peter?" He stands in silence with his hands clasped in front, listening to her guessing game as they descend.

Reaching the lobby, he exits the lift first; apparently leaving his manners behind! She follows behind, stepping along the white marble floor with the bouquet in her hands. He takes off his right, black leather glove and shakes the doorman's hand. Descending the white stairs, he smiles to the red coat Pippo who stands at the ready with his car keys.

"Your car is always the best car I drive," says Pippo, as he throws the keys to him.

"One day Pippo, you will have your own Phantom," he chucklingly says.

Pippo opens the passenger side door for her. "I hope you have enjoyed your visit, please enjoy your journey in my dream car." She smiles her pearly whites and leans inside, delicately placing the roses on the middle, creamy leather seat and sliding in.

Exiting the lane and turning left on 5th Avenue, Gino looks back at her through his reverse mirror. "Are you comfortable in the back?"

She looks up at the sparkling gold lights of the interior roof. *So pretty.* "Yes, thank you." Staring out at Central Park, she says, "Tell me about Mr. P."

"I've known him for a little while now. British man. Love brunettes."

He sounds like a player. Maybe his name is Mr. Player. "Charming."

He chuckles. "I think you have got me confused with Mr. P."

She looks down at the flowers and smells them. *Gorgeous.* "Can you tell me what Mr. P stands for? It isn't Mr. Player is it?" *God, I hope not.*

He taps his thumbs on the steering wheel, trying to conjure up a suitable response, without revealing his client's mystery. "It is a name, but not a name. It is his name, but not his name."

Is this guy stupid! "So, you could have just said nickname?"

"It's not a nickname as you or I would call it. Think of it as symbolic."

Turning onto Cyprus Avenue, the onlookers stare as the Phantom parks in front of the wreckage. "Thanks for the lift," says Arabella.

"That is one messed up car," he says, and climbs out. Sitting in silence, she rolls her eyes and unfastens her seatbelt. Grabbing the bouquet, she steps out onto the sidewalk and smiles.

"Thank you."

He shuts the backdoor and looks to her. "On behalf of Mr. P, he wishes you a fulfilling and prosperous future, and every success in your flower business."

She smiles and watches as he re-enters the driver's seat and shuts the door. *That didn't sound good.* The engine starts. *Shit. What if I never see him again?* Breathing heavily with fear, she acts spontaneous and opens the back door. "Sorry, I can't accept these flowers. Tell him to give them to one of his other brunettes!" She places them on the middle seat and slams the door. Turning around, she reaches into her bag and retrieves her keys.

Gino pulls away from the curb, tapping his thumbs on the steering wheel, as he watches her enter the gate through the reverse mirror. "I see what he meant now," he says and chuckles.

THE LETTER

Scratching her claws down his oily chest, Arabella bites down on her plump bottom lip; the sexual tension becoming unbearable, as she turns around and looks up at him in his strong arms. "How can I trust you, Mr. P?"

"Take a leap of faith," he whispers, and gently nibbles down her neck, listening to her parted lips release their gasp, as his feathering touch explores her curvy temple.

She closes her eyes and breathes heavily; her body drowning in sensation, as his pleasuring graze trails up her smooth skin. "I'm ready," she breathlessly whispers.

He releases her neck and turns her around. Reaching behind her, he grips her thick thighs and swoops her off her feet; her legs and arms wrapping tightly around him, as their warm passion steams between them. "Trust is—" An unexpected knock at the door occurs.

"Why is there a knock at the door?" He throws her onto the bed. "You don't deserve me," he wickedly says, and turns around, fading into darkness, as the door knocks again.

"Don't leave…" Dripping in sweat, she gasps the apartment air and opens her eyes, her heart racing as she wipes her flushed face. *It was just a dream…* Restoring her breathing, she lowers her hand under the sheets and glides along her toasty skin. *Yuck!* She wipes her wet hand on the duvet. The door knocks for a third time. "Coming!" Throwing the covers off her, the cold air swarms her rosy, warm body, as she scurries to get dressed. She checks the time on her smartphone. It's 07:00. *What the hell?* She opens the door.

"Good morning. Are you Arabella Harper?" asks the delivery driver.

"Yes? I didn't order anything," and peeks out into the half-lit hallway, "and why are you so early?"

He hands her an electronic signature device. "Please sign here, Miss."

She signs it and swaps it for a white gold, encrusted envelope. Closing the door behind her, she returns to her stained bed and inspects it; running her fingers across the rough bumps, as she reads her name 'Arabella Harper' perfectly centered on the front in fancy black italics. Preserving the envelopes beauty, she delicately opens and removes the fancy letter. *Dear Arabella, I have never received flowers before. It brought a tear to my eye when it set off my allergies.* She giggles. *Nevertheless, my driver will pick you up at 7pm this evening. Don't worry about an outfit, my assistant has picked one out for you. Make sure to wear your hair down. ~ Mr. P.* She throws the letter to one side and pulls the duvet over her. She shuts her eyes and rewrites her penthouse experience, as her hands move downwards.

"Must be fate," he says, as he sits on the couch.

She walks right, around the coffee table and along the Persian rug. Pushing his golden chest, she stops him doing up his shirt and towers over him; her knees resting either side of his muscly thighs. Tightly gripping the back of his wild black hair, she raises his neck and looks down, exhaling her delight against his lips as her eyes lock their seductive sparkle. "I've been a very naughty girl."

"Yes, you have," he says, and takes hold of her curvy waist; his strength lifting and pinning her on the couch. Towering over her, he presses his forehead against hers and exchanges his fierce alpha glare. "I'm the dominant one."

She bites down on her bottom lip. "Explore me…" Her penthouse imagination fades, as her legs spasm. Checking the mail in silence, a look of distraught sweeps Barbara's face, as her intense orgasm spreads into the communal hallway.

Laying in her own cold, and wet mess, she looks at the time. It's 10:00. She heads for the shower. Waiting for the water to steam, a cast of doubt shadows over her. Stepping in, she looks up at the shower head, hit with a stream of soothing pleasure as Clarissa clouds her mind - she can't help but worry about breaking girl code. *If she found out, she will never forgive me.* She reaches for the pink shower gel and rains it from above. *Maybe I shouldn't go.* Caressing the foamy mix into her tight skin, she sighs. *But then if it's meant to be?* Catching her nipples between her fingers, she gently twists; letting Mr. P enter her foggy cloud. *Mmhhmmmm. That mysterious hair, and those beautiful green eyes. Pin me down with those godly arms.* She lets him take over her temple; breathing heavily as the steam rises around her. *I surrender.* Rinsing the foam under the stream, her chauffeured journey home interrupts. *Gino said he had a thing for brunettes. What if I'm just another brunette?*

With her vision no longer distracted by lust, she steps out the shower; the cold air hitting her warm tight skin, as she reaches for a warm towel. *He must be a player, right?* Drying herself down, she exits the bathroom and walks over to the bed. She looks down at the letter. *I'm sorry Mr. P but you come with way too many red flags for me.* She reaches for her smartphone and checks the time, it's 10:32. With 28 minutes to get to work, she texts Clarissa. "Might be slightly late C, I was busy with a guy x." Throwing her smartphone on the bed, she drops the towel and moves to the wardrobe. *Not another playsuit. I think... ooo that's cute.* Switching it up with a cute white top and dark blue denim jeans, she moves towards the mirror and brushes down her curves. Turning around, she looks back. *Such a fire ass.* Opening the apartment door, she walks out onto the landing and checks the mailbox. It's empty. She hears a set of high heels descending the staircase to her right.

"Did you have a good time sweetie?" asks Barbara.

She looks at her; raising her eyebrow as she observes her in a leopard print dress, red heels, and one heavy casing of makeup. *What is she talking about?* "Good time?"

"Say no more," says Barbara, and reaches the bottom of the stairs. "You girls make me feel alive. I sure need it at my age."

She smiles. "Where are you off to?"

Approaching Arabella, she pats her on the shoulder. "I have a date with someone uptown now. I can have fun myself you know at this age."

That's disgusting. "Well then... you have fun. Tell me all about it another time," she says, as Barbara slowly steps along the burgundy carpet and exits the apartment building. Turning around, she remembers she didn't book a taxi. *Shit!* She descends the outside stairs and looks left at her opening the community gate. "Barbara, can I come with you? I need to be at work soon if you don't mind?" she shouts.

The glammed-up cougar turns around. "Yes Dear!"

Gesturing one moment, she rushes back into her apartment and fetches the remainder of her outfit. Performing one last mirror check, she slams the door behind her and races to the car. She enters the cab and smiles.

Sitting behind the driver, Barbara leans forwards. "Can you please take this young lady to the Campbell flower shop please on route." He nods. "Thank you, driver," she says, and leans back.

Cruising along 5th Avenue, Arabella stares out at Central Park to avoid unnecessary eye contact with the wild woman. Listening to Barbara complain about her old cell phone, she looks to her. "Everything alright?"

"May I use your phone sweetie? I need to tell my date that I am on my way and my phone isn't working," she says. Passing the smartphone to her, she looks back out to Central Park as Barbara constructs her text. A text message appears on the screen. She accidentally opens it and reads.

"Arabella Harper!! You slut! How big was he?" asks Clarissa.

59

She widens her eyes and glances over to Arabella for a split second. Sending her message, she pretends she didn't see it and hands her back her smartphone. "Thank you for that."

Smiling back at her and the awkwardness broken, Arabella becomes curious. "So, tell me about this mystery date?"

Barbara dreamily sighs. "He sure knows how to take care of an older woman."

She raises her eyebrow. *Older?* "How old is he?"

"He's thirty-three years younger so that would make him twenty-three. His name is George. He's American Italian. How about you? Any dates for a young, and gorgeous girl?"

"As a matter of fact, I do. Tonight at seven, his name is Mr. P." She shakes her head. *Why did I just say that?*

"Well that's lovely sweetie. How old is he?"

She grimaces her lips. "That's what I'm wondering myself," she mutters. Barbara plays with her hearing aid; unable to catch that, as the cab pulls up outside the flower shop. "Oh look, we're here. Thanks for the ride, enjoy the date," she says, and rapidly exits. Slamming the door behind her, she steps onto the sidewalk and approaches the front of Campbell, and Co.

Surrounded by flower trimmings, she snips away in the backroom alone, contemplating her dilemma. *Should I go? What about*

Clarissa? She sighs - torn between her curious nature to explore his mystery with her heart screaming he's the one; whilst her mind yells it's a façade and the aftermath if C ever found out.

Clarissa enters the shop and races down into the workshop, interrupting her intense decision. "Why didn't you reply to my text? How big was he?"

She looks to her. "What text?" She looks down at the wooden table and grabs her smartphone. *Oh my god.* Widening her eyes in disbelief, she gulps. *Barbara would have seen that!* She looks to the blonde queen with a flushed face. "I got your text. Only I didn't see it. A cougar did instead."

Clarissa gives her a look of disgust as she walks around the other side of the table. "A cougar? As in an older woman cougar?"

She raises her hands. "I was in a cab with her."

Clarissa can't believe what she's hearing; the innocent angel in front of her appears to have turned into an uncontrollable sex addict overnight. She puts her bags down and props herself on the seat opposite her. Playing with the trimmings in silence, she imagines her with an older woman and another man in this threesome. She can't contain herself. "You lost your virginity… in a threesome… oh my god!"

She rolls her green eyes as she continues to trim away. "Obviously!"

Clarissa bites down on her finger. "Well, whilst you were exploring your fetish, I saw mine last night."

She looks up at her. "Your fetish?"

"That guy. He gave me some business card with his name on it." Clarissa reaches into her designer bag and retrieves the plain white card. "It's completely blank but has his name in the bottom right corner in black ink. He's called Mr. P. He's just so mysterious."

Hit with a wild storm of jealousy exploding inside, she gulps; her heart racing as her face turns strawberry red. She puts the scissors down. "Did you have sex with him?" she nervously asks, as her stomach sinks.

"Sex with him? I wish ha-ha. God, you are so dirty these days, Miss Harper."

She looks at her smartphone. It's 15:00. She books a cab on the app and pays with her BookShib. "I've got to go C."

Clarissa checks the time, it's 15:01. "Where are you going now? I've only just got here."

She scrapes the metal chair legs along the cement floor and stands, leaning over the workshop table as her breathing heavies. "Just something I have to do. I won't be in tomorrow."

"Is everything alright?"

She nods and looks down at her vibrating smartphone; the notification for her cabs arrival has come through. Rushing into the open lounge, she grabs her belongings and exits the shop without saying goodbye.

Exiting the yellow cab, she unlocks the black gate and rushes up the stairs in a disoriented state. With her hands shaking, she struggles to insert the key into her apartment door. Holding her breath, she focuses and unlocks it. She enters. Slamming the door behind her, she leans against it and gasps the apartment air, blocking out the world as her breathing becomes erratic. Throwing her bag on the couch, she moves to her bed and lays back. Closing her eyes, she parts her lips; taking deep breaths to establish a sense of rhythm. *Calm down. Calm down. She didn't sleep with him.*

Returning to normal, she spreads her arms out and brushes her fingers against the envelope. *What have I become?* Grazing over the white gold envelope, she opens her eyes and sits up to re-read the letter. *Oh screw it.* She drops the paper and positions herself in front of the mirror, staring deeply into her torn image; the mirror unable to reflect her overwhelming nerves as she accepts the risk. Smiling her cupid lips, she swaps her doubt for confidence and turns around, gazing back at her peachy bottom and lioness beauty.

SEVEN PM

Sitting on the edge of the bed with her smartphone in her hands, Arabella stims her legs against the floor. She hears a car door slam. She looks down at the time. It's 18:59. This is her last chance to back out. She stands and glances over her reflection, smiling her pink glossy lips at her flawless glow. *I hope he likes it.* She looks down at her clutch bag on the couch and grabs it. The door knocks. *What the hell?* She breaks out into a giggle; her date starting on a good note as Gino's attempt at opera of an unknown old Italian song belts under the door.

Switching into her lioness state, she opens the door. "You sound wonderful," she says, sassily.

Gino smiles. "Did you get the letter?"

"Yes, but that doesn't mean I'm coming?"

He raises his hands above his head and plays with his hair.

She raises her eyebrow. "What are you doing?"

"On our last encounter, your hair was up. The letter told you to wear it down. Is yours not down?" Well that went well! She rolls her eyes and locks up. Exiting the building, she follows her Italian escort to his Phantom. He holds the passenger side door open for her and waits as she climbs in. Shutting the door and entering the driver's seat, he looks back at her. "Seat belt please."

She locks herself in. "There you go, Grandpa!" He lets out a chuckle.

"Thank you." Pulling off from the sidewalk, he turns the corner of East 137th and picks up the speed; the luxury ride drawing attention from the nightlife crowds. Looking back at her through the reverse mirror, he watches as she plays with her hands. The father role in him takes over. "Are you ok in the back there, Arabella?"

She looks to him. "Yes, why wouldn't I be?"

"You remind me of my daughter. She used to do that thing with her hand when she was nervous." She looks out the window in silence, watching as the onlookers pile into the nightclubs and restaurants. *Every one of them must have their own romance.*

Driving down 5th Avenue, she gazes up at the starry interior lights. "Gino, do you believe in soulmates?"

He grimaces his lips. "I don't know. Even if there was such a thing, the odds of finding them is beyond my math's," he says, and turns right onto West 57th. Cruising in silence, they reach their destination. Pulling along the sidewalk, he cuts the engine and leans over the chair to face her; filled with fatherly advice. "Emotions are both beautiful and ugly. What one might feel for someone, that someone might not feel for them. What one person might consider morally wrong, the other will consider as morally right. This is the world we live in." He points to the shop in front. "Your dress is in there. Be quick. We're on a tight schedule." Stepping out into the evening breeze, she scales the street left to right. She widens her eyes in awe, absorbing the luxury cars parked amongst the tall skyscrapers as the bypassing crowds drip in their high-end designer. She takes out her smartphone and loads up the location, her jaw dropping as her brunette locks blow around her face. *This is billionaires row.* A sense of not belonging kicks in as her stomach sinks to the fear of being judged upon entering. Gino taps on the car window. She looks to him pointing at his watch.

Tapping away at the steering wheel for 20 minutes, Gino gets out and enters Billionaire's Boutique. Stepping inside the fresh white tiled room, he leans on the glass counter as he gazes the high-end fashion from afar.

Turning the dressing room corner, Chantelle, the tailor, makes her way behind the counter and claps with joy. "The girls are just in the back. It's my best one yet."

Gino chuckles. "Better than mine?"

She pats him on the arm. "Now, now, Gino."

He reaches into his jacket pocket. "Whilst I'm here, I best give you Mr. P's order." He pulls out a piece of paper and hands it to her.

"He sure does keep me busy," says Chantelle, as Arabella makes her way into the center of the floor. All eyes are on her. Chantelle walks over to see her creation. "Absolutely stunning! This is a one-of-a-kind, black, silk satin, draped with a front slit dress. It complements your figure so well hon. How are the breasts feeling? It has the built-in shelf bra."

Arabella twirls around in front of the mirror. "I love it, it's gorgeous." She feels her cups. "Oh yeah, it sits perfectly... just wow. Thank you is all I can say."

"Time to go," says Gino, as he looks at his watch.

Chantelle smiles. "It's been my pleasure." The assistant comes from the dressing room and hands Arabella a small bag with her original clothes.

Climbing back into the Phantom dressed like a princess, she can't stop smiling. He checks the time. It's 20:07. Shaking his head with 23 minutes to go, he pulls off. "Do you like heights?" asks Gino.

I thought this was going to be a meal. "What do you mean heights?"

"Heights? You know, up in the sky, 30,000 feet."

She raises her eyebrow. "What are you saying? Wait! Where are you taking me? Where is this date actually?"

He chuckles. "Teterboro Airport." *Whatttt!* She cracks the window open and attempts to stick her head out. Luckily Gino has a control panel and stops that. "You'll ruin your hair!"

She parts her lips trying to hide her smile. "Slight problem. I don't have my passport? Commercial airlines aren't going to let me on."

He looks at the time and puts his foot down on the gas, testing the Phantoms limits as they approach the strip. "Commercial? Ha! Mr. P does it in style. Private."

Staring out the front window, she observes the bright floodlights lighting up the clear starry nights sky from afar. *This isn't real.* They stop. *This is for me?* Staring at the security with their hands clasped in black suits, either side of the jets staircase, she still can't come to terms with this.

"Have a safe trip, I will be here when you return," says Gino. Still in shock, she smiles to him, as a security guard approaches. She looks left, as the passenger side door opens.

"This way please, Miss," says the security guard.

She gets out. Hit with the whirring noise of jets taking off, she watches as the Phantom U-turns and exits. Following behind the guard, they approach the expense of the one percent. Closer, and closer, the powerful machine gets bigger. *This is so fancy.* She flutters inside, as the jets fresh white veneer exterior sparkles. She looks near the tail. *Oh! Of course he would have his name imprinted on it.* The captain looks down from his cockpit, smiling and waving, as she approaches the red-carpet staircase. She smiles her pearly whites back. *I can't believe this is all for me.* Climbing the stairs, she steps onto the jet and turns right. *Holy shit!* The flawless interior resonates a vintage appearance; furnished with vanilla leather seats, a black marble bar, built-in lighting projecting a star lit clear night sky and a cream carpet to finish off the cozy feel. Walking along the carpet, she takes a seat at the front, right side. The overhead radio comes on.

"Welcome aboard, Miss Harper. This is your captain speaking. Would you like to take a guess where we are heading?"

She giggles and raises her hands. "Spain?"

"One more guess."

"Monte Carlo?" She hears an electronic noise and casts her eyes left, watching as the door traps her inside. This is it! The engines start to whir.

"I like those guesses. Mr. P loves Monte Carlo, but not today Arabella. Please fasten your seatbelt and enjoy the flight. We're heading for the Bahamas." She fastens her seatbelt, as the jet turns left on the strip. Gripping the armrests, the g force builds against her body as the intense whirring pierces through the windows. Zooming down the runway, the interior wobbles like an earthquake, faster, and faster, as the G force works against her. She leans her head right and gazes out the window, as the jet starts its ascent to 30,000 feet; her stomach sinking as they climb the nights sky. The cabin changes pressure. She shakes her head as her ears pop.

Floating vertically at 30,000 feet, she massages her earlobes. The radio comes back on.

"I hope that wasn't too bad, Miss Harper."

"Just my ears ringing."

"Move your jaw up and down."

She bites up and down. "Ah there we go."

"Works like a charm. We're scheduled for arrival in approximately an hour. Please check under your seat, Mr. P has left a gift for you."

Unfastening her seatbelt, she leans forwards and reaches under the seat. Brushing against the gift bag, she finds the handle and pulls it out from underneath her. *Wow.* Lifting, and placing the large bag onto the seat next to her, she removes its contents. *It's shoes. Must be heels.* She reads the white signature writing and widens her eyes. *Oh my god.* Opening it, the signature red heeled black stiletto in a size 8 stares back at her. Gushing in awe, she throws her old heels to the side and tries them on; the extra three inch of heel making her steps more difficult. Using the aisle like a catwalk, she struts up and down. "These are –" Hit with sudden turbulence, she's thrown into the middle seats. *Oww.* She regains herself and flicks her hair.

"Sorry for that," says the captain.

She laughs. "I'm ok," she says and returns to her seat. Placing the box on the floor, she scoots over to the window and looks down on Manhattan's nightlife glowing; a sensational image of a city that never sleeps. *So pretty.*

Caught up in her own star gazing world, the radio interrupts.

"I hope you enjoyed your view, Miss Harper. Unfortunately, it's time we descend. May I ask you fasten your seatbelt as we prepare for landing. Enjoy your date." Fastening her seatbelt, she says goodbye with her eyes to her favourite stars, as the jet slices through the clouds. Descending rapidly, the cabin wobbles as the air pressure adjusts.

Gripping onto the arm rests, she hears an electric doors opening amidst the rattling. "Please sit tight, this is the fun part," announces the overly, excited captain, as he releases the wheels. Touching down on the tarmac, she jolts forward. *Please know what you're doing. This is so fast.* The engines roars as they zoom down the strip with extreme speed. In a split few seconds, they come to a rapid halt. The radio comes on again. "Well that was quite the adrenaline rush wouldn't you say?"

She fixes her wild hair. "Yep!"

Descending the staircase onto the tarmac, she looks at the white limo in front, distracted as the Bahama's breeze sweeps across her glowing face. She inhales the fresh non polluted air, rolling her eyes up as her nostrils devour every moment. *Why can't we have this in New York?* Smiling at the Italian Chauffer holding the door open with his black leather glove ahead, she approaches. He tips his hat to her, as she enters the poshly lit interior. *Very fancy.* Taking a seat on the cream leather, she spots the complimentary, local made champagne from the table. *Don't mind if I do.* She takes a sip as the limo sets off. *Mmhhmmmm.* Leaning back in comfort, she reclines the window; sipping away on the delicacy as she absorbs the islands stunning sunset.

Tapping her acrylics against the glass, she listens to the ringing noise as her breathing heavies. *This is happening. What if he doesn't like me.* Sitting up straight, she looks down into the glass; her champagne reflection swishing around from the limos motion. Parting her lips, she practices her smile. The limo stops. She gulps and sits back; her heart racing as the driver's door slams. She throws back the champagne and places the glass on the table. The door opens.

"Enjoy the date," says the chauffer, as he holds out his hand.

Oh god, Oh god. Filled with nerves, she takes it and steps out onto the white spotlight path. "Thank you," she says, as the oceans breeze hits her. Staring at the greyish brick walls and neon red light exterior of the cliff tops only premise in front, she proceeds down the pathway entrance and reaches the luxury black double doors with gold handles. She reads the glowing electric red sign on the right, 'Clubhouse 47'.

"Wrong way!" shouts the driver. She turns around, as he points to his right. She retraces her steps and turns left, announcing her arrival with her heels tapping away against the white patio floor as they follow the path around. Slowing her pace, she turns the bend as her body spikes with nerves.

CLUBHOUSE 47

Arabella exhales. *Here we go.* Stepping under the romantic arches, she enters the pebbled plant courtyard. *Oh wow.* She looks left at the contemporary outdoor fireplace, captivated by the beauty of its burning flames. Stepping further along the white stone slabs, she faces front and peeks around the water feature. *There he is.*

Sipping on fruity champagne in his tight fitted black suit, Mr. P rests against the stone balcony, listening to the tapping of her stilettos steal the soothing crash of waves as he watches the jet skis race across the moon lit ocean. Placing the crystal glass on the ledge, he stands up straight and plays with his right cuff link, as she stands by the fountain.

With a smile across his face, he turns around. "Wow," he says, and approaches.

She blushes and scales up his towering beauty, deeply exhaling her nerves away as their sparkling green flames lock. "Hello," she softly whispers.

"Arabella. How do I look?"

She presses her tongue against her bottom lip. *Surely, he's joking.* "You look—"

He chuckles. "I'm joking. You look absolutely stunning."

She shakes her head; struggling to conceal her protruding smile. "You look... ok," she says, as her eyes and nose devour everything about him. *Please kiss me.*

He fake wipes his right eye. "That's the nicest thing anyone's ever said to me."

Bursting into a giggle, she hovers her dainty hand over her mouth; fluttering her lashes at him as her cheeks turn bright pink. "You are very unique."

He lowers her hand and leans in, pressing his forehead against hers. "As are you," he says romantically. Steaming his fruity breath against hers, as their lips, and noses graze, he watches as she closes her eyes. "This was only meant to be a three-course meal," he murmurs, and lifts her up; her arms and legs wrapping around him.

"I don't—"

Caught between his lips, she grips the back of his hair and exhales her pleasure through her nose, exploding inside with a fiery warmth as her excited lips share their gloss. Opening his right eye, he carries her towards the clubhouse backdoor entrance. Bouncing up and down in his strong arms, she tries to stay afloat on her slippery voyage. Making their way under the doorframe, she breaks their sensation and looks behind her, smiling her smudged lips at the private venue - the layout screaming a 1930's Italian red and white vintage look with a hint of goodfellas. Moving inwards, he carries her along the crimson red patterned carpet and reaches a candlelit, white clothed round table positioned underneath a gold chandelier. Lowering her down onto the seat, he turns around and snaps his fingers as he takes his seat opposite.

Casting his eyes right, he watches the Italian waiter emerge from the kitchen.

"Good evening, Mr. P and Arabella, welcome to Clubhouse 47, the finest dining in Nassau. May I start with drinks?"

"Hold that thought for one moment my good man," he says, and looks to her. "So, any guesses to my name?"

"Mr. Pervert."

"Absolutely." He turns to the waiter. "This pervert will have a Caribou Lou and for the queen, a bottle of your finest champagne for the finest lady please."

She smiles her cupid lips at the waiter and waits for them to vacate. She looks to him. "It's not actually that is it?"

He shakes his head and leans back in his chair. "How did you know I would come biting?"

"I guess I'm not like the others, Mr. P," she says, and bites down on her index finger.

He leans forwards and rest his elbows on the table. "Exactly why you're here. You have this unknown aura about you that I can't quite place."

She taps her pink and white polka dot acrylics along the white cloth. "Do you know what they call more than two coincidences?" He shakes his head. "Synchronicity. We have met on three unplanned and separate occasions now," she says, as the waiter approaches.

"A Caribou Lou for the gentleman," says the waiter and places it in front of him before turning to her, "and a glass of Dom Perignon for the lovely lady. The mains will be served soon."

Watching the waiter place the bread down and vacate, she takes her first sip of perfection; weightlessly swishing the fruity extravagance around her mouth. *Why is he drinking that?* "Why are you drinking a girly drink?" she asks.

He swallows and lowers his glass. "You are like this drink. I don't know why I am, but I just can't get enough of it."

He is so smooth. She lowers her glass. "How are you this charming?"

He brings his glass down again. "How are you this beautiful?"

She lowers her glass again and swallows the expense. "Let's be serious. I'm not."

He places the glass on the table and leans forwards. "I see my date is humble. Another exceedingly attractive attribute."

She starts to giggle. "Oh for fuck sake."

He starts to laugh. "And a girl that swears. Even more attractive. Shows intelligence."

She rests the glass on the table and leans against the cloth, placing her warm, blushing face in her petite hands; the champagne starting to take effect.

"Tell me the basics then. Name. Age. Birthplace. Job."

"Twenty-eight, Sagittarius, England, and a bit of luck investing. Now I have created my own paradise." He winks to her through, as she peeks through the gap of her hands.

"You missed one?"

He reaches for his glass and sips on his fruity delight, releasing a refreshing sigh as he places it back down. "I know it's killing you inside to find out what my name is," he mysteriously says.

She rests her chin in her palms, gazing over his mesmerizing features. *He is perfect.* "Your voice is very deep. Did you know that?"

"Mysterious. Seductive. A bit like you."

She closes her eyes. *Just kiss him.* Sliding the chair out from under her, she stands and approaches. She climbs on top and throws her arms around his neck. Trickling her right fingers down his clean shaved face, she soul searches into his luminescent green eyes, as their fragrances tease. "I see a man that's hiding something," she whispers.

He brushes his veiny hands up and down her curvy hourglass. "We all have our secrets, what's yours?"

She leans into his left ear. "I sometimes dream about you," she says and giggles, as she presses her forehead against his.

"You are truly mesmerizing, and you're right. You're not like others," he says and swoops her brunette waves behind her right ear, "because I've never met anyone like—"

Kiss him already! She closes her eyes and catches his lips; seeping her gloss in deep as their champagne and pineapple breath creates a passion cocktail. Clawing her nails against the back of his head, she grips his thick hair; her body exploding in sensational tingles, as his fingertips lightly tease along the sides of her smooth thighs. She breaks their intensity and gasps. Brushing noses, she combs through his hair, looking deep in his green flames as her steamy warmth mists his upper lip. "I've never met anyone like you either," she breathlessly whispers.

He gulps; his chest tightening as a cluster of emotions he hasn't ever felt brew inside. "Let's eat," he says, and taps her leg.

Exiting the kitchen with a large black tray, the waiter approaches the table. "For the finest lady of tonight's service, homemade Tagliani pasta, topped with a pound of lobster, caught fresh this morning, infused with black truffle. This dish was inspired by Manhattan's finest itself."

"Thank you," she says, with a smile.

The waiter looks to him. "For the finest club owner, your favorite dish, a medium rare, sliced porterhouse steak, accompanied by grilled asparagus and dauphinois potatoes, finished off with a touch of lavish white truffle shavings. Please enjoy the meal."

Picking up the silverware, Arabella raises her eyebrow. "Club owner?"

He picks up his cutlery. "One of many."

"That explains how you can afford to live in a penthouse."

Cutting into his tender steak, he takes his first bite; the white truffle adding a rich decadence, as it melts in his mouth. He swallows. "My hotel you mean."

Twirling the pasta around the silver fork, she catches the lobster in silence and raises it to her mouth. She chews on the exotic flavors; her lack of fine dining confusing her plain palette as they explode in her mouth. *Yuck.* The waiter arrives with another round of drinks.

Mr. P nods to the waiter and takes his drink; washing down the buttery taste as he observes her playing with the food. "How's the meal?"

She slowly rests the fork on the bowl and looks to him. "To be honest, it's not for me… none of this is for me."

"Why would that be?"

She grabs the champagne glass and sighs, twirling her right index finger around the rim as she stares into her champagne reflection. "We're from two different worlds. I'm this 23-year-old florist who comes from a middle-class family at best. I live in Mott Haven and I don't like truffles."

He wipes his mouth with the napkin. "What world am I from exactly?"

She rolls her eyes and looks at him. "I don't know how to explain it. I can't understand you. This. Any of this." He prompts her to continue with his hands. "Ok, let's start with a few things. The name?"

He rolls his eyes. "The nickname was adopted in university, it's not a name, but a meaning to represent who I am. Next?"

She raises her hands. "Why all the secrecy?"

He bites his tongue. "I can't tell you at this time."

What is wrong with him? "How do you expect us to progress if I can't know your basic information?"

"When the time is right, I will tell you everything."

I give up. She rolls her eyes and sighs. "Tell me why you give out cards to people?"

"How did you know that?" he laughingly asks.

She slides the chair from under her and stands. "You gave my friend one."

He slides his chair from under him and stands.

"You're quite the detective," he laughingly says.

"Don't patronize me!"

He stands in awe at her fiery glare and aggressive tone. "You just get more attractive by the second," he smirkingly says. "Tell me about your friend. Blonde I assume?"

She leans on the white cloth and snarls. "She doesn't shut the hell up about you!"

He laughs and mimics her movements; their faces inches away as they fiercely showdown. "Well there you go. A gift. A little reminder of me that lives rent free in the minds of many."

Wow! She widens her mouth and presses her tongue against her cheek; astounded by his god complex. "Wow! Wow! Wow! Wow!"

He chuckles. "What I meant was... I have a particular taste. Those I don't, I just give them a card. Saves me having stalkers."

She lavishes the smell of his powerful woody cologne. "What taste is that then?"

"Oh, I think you already know." He watches her smirk. "You don't fool me you know."

"Fool you with what?" she innocently asks and flutters her eyelashes, as their foreheads meet again.

He glares his smoldering inferno deep inside her. "Your manipulative personality."

She cunningly smiles. "Maybe I am. What are you going to do about it?" she asks and attempts to bite his lip. Dodging her, he snaps his fingers and ends the meal before holding out his hand. She looks him up and down; his allure giving nothing away.

Walking hand in hand, he leads her through the club house and into the courtyard. Reaching the fountain, he lets go of her hand

and returns to the stone balcony; the crystal glass still standing strong against the oceans breeze. Leaning over, he listens to the crashing waves, as she looks up at the clear nights sky, both silently gazing at the full moon as it outshines the twinkling stars in all its glory. He observes a beach party from afar; looking at the orange lit flame burning from the firepit.

Tapping his hands against the ledge, he sighs and stands, adjusting his cufflink as he continues to watch the party. "What do you truthfully see when you look at me?" he asks.

She breaks her dreamy gaze and looks at the back of him; her thick brunette hair flying around her face as the wind sweeps across her champagne sweat body.

"I don't know."

He rolls his eyes. "Close your eyes. Be confident. Tell me everything you see and feel."

Following his wishes, she inhales the islands air and taps into her emotional catharsis. "I see a man, a muscly man, with green eternal flames staring at me. I can't help but be drawn in."

He turns around and leans against the stone with his arms crossed, as he absorbs her beauty. "More," he loudly says.

She smiles and giggles. "He's not like anyone else; he has his own rule book. How can someone be so confident and charming naturally?"

He lavishes up her angelic voice. "More," he loudly whispers.

"I don't care about his wealth. I can't explain this feeling, I don't even know him. I wonder what he truly thinks of me. What does he see in me when he can get—" Caught in his towering surprise, her soft lips melt away as her chest overloads in a whirlwind of explosive passion. Racing inside to the brush of his hands down her dress, she stands on her tiptoes and throws her arms around his neck; keeping her eyes closed as he lifts her up. In his strong arms, she combs through the back of his hair, creating a passion cocktail between them.

He taps out first and gasps for air. "That was—"

Not finished yet, she pulls him back in and bites down on his lip. *Dominate me.* Fluttering her lashes at her alpha, he gets the message and tears his lip from her trap. He walks her across the courtyard. *Please put me up against—* Slammed against the wall, she widens her mouth and looks up; releasing a sensational moan, as he bites down on her neck. She rolls her eyes back – digging her acrylics into him, as he sucks harder. Clawing away, she loses herself in the euphoric sensation shooting through her. "Keep going," she pantingly whispers. The courtyard drowns in orgasmic moans, as he switches sides. Breathing erratically to his trailing fingertips under her smooth thighs, she doesn't stop him as the stimulating pleasure spikes through her. Feeling his feather touch move closer, she flutters inside as his fingertips brush the outside of her warm, and wet lace. *I think I'm ready.* "Do you have anywhere we can go," she breathlessly whispers.

He releases her from his love bite and pulls his hand out; firmly taking grip of her thick thighs, as she rewraps herself around his muscles. "I might own a condo nearby," he seductively says, and pulls her away from the wall.

Entering the beach view condo, he carries her through the white door and swipes it closed. Dimming the lights in passing, he walks along the white tiles and lays the sober queen on his fit for a king-sized bed before turning to face the mirror. Listening to her take off her stilettos behind him, as he kicks off his penny loafers, he reaches into the magnolia mirrored dresser and whips out an exquisite bottle of 1942 tequila. "You're going to like this," he says and cracks the aged bottle open.

Oh who cares about drink. With her endorphins skyrocketing, she slips off the bed and sneaks up behind him. Bringing her hand around the side of him, she places it over the top and stops him, their hands gently lowering it together. Taking a step back, as he turns around, she locks onto the green storm brewing in his eyes. "Now be gentle, Mr. P," she says, and bites down on the remainder of her pink gloss.

"Oh, I'll try." Towering his dominance over her, as she wraps her arms around his neck, he grips her thighs and lifts her up. Swiftly spinning her around, he slides her onto the dressing table, too entangled in their burning kiss to be distracted by the loud bang.

She breaks their passion. "I thought you said you would be gentle," she giggles.

"You haven't seen it rough yet," he seductively says and lifts her up; her head near missing the ceiling as he wraps her thighs around his neck.

Maybe I should tell him? That would probably be wise Arabella! *I mean it's the same as a sex toy I'm sure.* A sex toy doesn't come with emot—

She squeezes his hair. "How do I taste?" she taunts. Or don't?

He palms her cheeks and squeezes. "I'll let you know soon," he says, and nibbles along her inner thigh.

Mixed with excitement and nerves, and stupidly not telling him, she lowers her right hand between the gap and brushes the outside of her wet laced front, pressing her dainty fingers inside. She widens her mouth and looks up, exhaling her building pleasure as his caressing lips move closer. *I guess this is it. I'm ready.* Brushing her knuckles against his nose, she slides the fabric to the side, as he helps from the back. Taking grip of his hair, she feels his warmth approach. Closing her eyes, she waits. Hit with the first stroke, she pulls his hair; drowning in waves of flutters as her legs begin to tremor. Thrusting her hips to the speed of his licks, the condo fills with sultry moans as her body spirals into sin. Panting away, she tightens her wrap around him, breathing heavily as her champagne sweat slides down her steamy hot skin. She lets go of his hair and pulls her dress up; her body shaking to the sensational lust spiking through her, as the dress hits the floor.

Licking away, he scratches up her back and reaches for her red laced bra strap; his sleight of hand blindly unhooking it with one attempt. Retracing her smooth back with his nails, he holds her by the strength of his burning neck and removes his jacket. Nearing the point of suffocation, he unbuttons his shirt; the arousing scent pumping him with adrenaline. Lowering her down onto the bed, he gasps the condo air, as her legs unwrap.

Teased by his rippled abs, she glides her red laced bra along her arm, as he slides her matching thong along her smooth legs; her rounded breasts and soaked pussy breathing the Bahamas as the lace hits the floor. "You look like you can't handle me!"

He chuckles and moves onto the bed. "You've never had my kind," he says and wraps his godly arms around her curvaceous thighs, listening to her gasp as he buries his tongue deep inside her.

Parting her lips, wider and wider, she loudly moans as her fingers twist his wild hair. With his tongue licking goodbye, she pulls him up her temple; her stomach rapidly moving up and down to the intense flutters consuming her, as he leaves a wet trail along her soft skin. *Mmhhmmmm.* Drowning in an overdose of sensation, she tugs his hair; almost ripping it out as his fingertips deliver their stimulating tease either side of her hourglass in a race to the top. Biting down on her plump bottom lip, she swaps his hair for the sheets, digging her claws into them as tight as she can as her body melts into chaos. "God this is something else," she pants.

"We've only just started," he mumbles and journeys his carnage onto her rosy tip, whirling around her areola as he feels her nipple hardening.

With her pleasure mounting, she reaches underneath him and undoes his belt; her sexual desire becoming unbearable. Whipping it from his waist, she holds it by both ends and slides the leather along his back. Wrapping it firmly around the back of his muscly neck, she pulls his come soaked lips towards her and sinks her cupid lips into him.

Sliding their moisture as the room heats with intense passion, he lets her have at him and removes his trousers, gripping the gold waist band of his boxers along with it as they slide down his muscly calves. Trapped in her web of romance, he kicks them to the floor and brings his hands up to her flushed face, caressing his fingers along her rosy cheeks before sweeping them through her thick brunette locks. Listening to the belt hit the floor, he grips her hair and breaks their blazing kiss. Raising her neck, he attempts to bite down again, failing as she slaps him; unleashing the beast in him as he pins her wrists above her head. Seeping his dominance into her green flames, he raises her legs with his thighs.

Staring into his inferno, she bites down on her lip and rests her heels on his lower back. *I hope you don't hurt.* Feeling the tip brush her tight entrance, as her heart races, she pushes down. She loudly gasps. *Owww.* Painfully moaning away to his gentle strokes getting deeper as her lube soaks around it, she closes her eyes and tilts her head. She feels the tightening squeeze on her wrists suddenly release, with his warmth leaving as he vacates the bed. "Everything ok?" She watches as he slides his trousers back on in silence and reaches into his suit jacket pocket for his smartphone before moving to the glass door and opening it. *What is he doing?* She watches as he leans over the balcony ledge overlooking the sands. *I hope I didn't do anything wrong.* Filling with worry; the door knocks. She stands and races over to her dress. Throwing it over her head, she proceeds towards the door and opens it.

"I'm here to collect you, it's time to go home now," says the smiling chauffer.

"But…" She looks back at him, gulping as her stomach sinks. Turning around with tears sliding down her sweaty face, she grabs her stilettos and sits on the edge of the bed. *What did I do?* Slowly putting them on as she stares at the back of him, she wonders how emotionless this guy must be. *This is a new kind of asshole.* She stands up and wipes her teary eyes in the mirror, looking back at him one last time as she shakes her head in utter disbelief.

CRUEL LOVE

Drawing circles on the glass counter of Campbell and Co, Arabella sits alone, staring aimlessly at the Autumn leaves piling up outside the shops entrance. It's been six, long and overly depressing weeks since Mr. P pulled his stunt; leaving her to get on with her life. Unable to get him off her mind, she sits trapped in a deep, and dark void, bearing this pain alone as she can't tell Clarissa; the betrayal would be catastrophic. *What did I do?* She looks down at the countertop, losing herself again in the reflection as her flashbacks return; the tingling touch of his fingers sweeping behind her ear in the garden; the heavenly belt lock at the penthouse; and the moment she gave herself to him, hammering away at her. *Just why?* Clouded with sadness and watery eyes, a single tear escapes and hits the glass. A grey suit jacket arm swoops in and wipes it up.

She looks up, met with a smile. *Oh wow.* Trailing her teary eyes up and down the customers grey suit trousers and crisp white shirt, she wipes her flushed wet face and stands. "I'm so sorry," she says, as she looks over his light ash brown hair and locks onto his warm brown eyes.

"Oh don't be silly. I hope you are ok," says the customer.

She sniffles. "I was just having a moment. I haven't had a night out in a long while and it just got to me all this work." She raises her hands. "Why am I even telling you this?"

"If I'm being totally honest, I could use a night out as well," he says and smiles his pearly whites at her. "I'm Elliot by the way."

She smiles. "Arabella. I'm Twenty-Three." She raises her hands again. "Once again… not sure why I'm telling you that."

"It's ok ha-ha. I'm Twenty-Six." He pauses for a moment. "Did you know that Arabella means answered prayer in Latin?"

I hope this isn't a chat up line. "I did."

He puts his hands in his trouser pockets. "Maybe you would answer my prayer of accompanying me later for a drink?"

She giggles. *Wow.* She looks him over again. *Well educated, smooth and sophisticated. I like it.* "You don't waste time do you."

He grimaces his lips; the gentleman in him doesn't wish to put her in an uncomfortable position. "I apologize, I hope I didn't overstep."

Well that's not attractive. She turns around and returns to her seat. "Anyway, what can I do for you?"

With his cheeks bright red, he reaches into his jacket pocket and retrieves a folded piece of paper. "I'm an event's organizer for the City Council. Our provider can't accommodate this year, so I've been tasked with finding a suitable replacement to cater for the yearly, Winter Wonderland ball on December 1st." He hands her the long list of flowers and turns around, as Clarissa enters.

"It's freezing," says Clarissa, and looks him at him. "Well hello, who is this fine catch?"

He smiles at the blonde diva. "Why hello. I'm Elliot. I was just telling Arabella here about the Winter Wonderland ball."

"Oh yeah, I know the one." she says, walking past him with her hands carrying her new Autumn wardrobe. She turns into the open longue and places her shopping bags on the couch before joining Arabella behind the glass counter. "Nice to meet you, Elliot. I'm Clarissa. I know the event well." She looks to her brunette friend. "Father always makes me go but this year I won't be," and looks back to him, "because I'm in Paris. I've heard the location changed this year though?"

He nods. "Yes. It's being hosted in the new manor built on Pier 40. I don't personally agree with tearing down a baseball pitch myself as an avid sports fan, but what can you do."

Arabella hands her the long list. "What do you think? He wants us to supply the flowers. He works for the council."

Skimming the list with the only thought on her mind being a business opportunity, she looks up to him. "Yes, we can."

His face lights up with a smile. "Great." Reaching into his pocket, he pulls out the taxpayers' credit card and hands it over.

Glancing over his empty ring finger and tired of Arabella's depressive state, she gives him a shifty look. "So, a councilman." She leans on the glass and stares into his stunning complexion. "How would you feel about a date with a florist?"

He casts his eyes to Arabella with a cheeky smile. "Oh boy, you don't waste time do you."

Arabella bursts into a giggle. *Yeah, he's funny.* She grabs a pen and writes down her number for him, as Clarissa looks flustered.

"Fineeee," exaggerates Arabella and passes him the note.

He smiles and locks eyes with her highness. "My apologizes, Clarissa, but it appears I have a date with your lovely friend tonight. I do know a guy if you're interested?"

"Like a double date?"

He looks to Arabella, who nods to him, before turning back to her. "Yes, a double date. How does eight pm sound for some drinks?" They both nod to him. "Great. I'll give you a text with the location once I have confirmed everything."

"What's his name?" asks Clarissa, as she hands his card back to him.

"Why ruin the mystery? I best be going now." Pocketing his card, he smiles his pearly whites at them and heads for the door. "See you both later," he excitedly says and exits into the cold.

Sitting in the workshop, Arabella looks at her vibrating phone; the anticipated text has finally come through. She opens it. *A nightclub. God that isn't a bit of me.* She looks to Clarissa sitting opposite her. "I've got the text. He said to meet him at outside Devil's nightclub at eight. His colleague has managed to secure us a V.I.P booth. He knows the manager."

Clarissa's eyes light up. "So, we're going clubbing. Yes!"

Oh why not. "I've been like once. What do you even do?"

Sliding the seat along the hard floor, the blonde queen stands. "Come on, let's go. I'll tell you in the car."

Exiting into the early darkness of Autumn, they make their way to the Range Rover. Throwing the excessive shopping bags on the back seat, they both enter the front and set off to the Campbell residence on East 72nd St.

"What do you think his name is then?" asks C.

Oooooooo. I like this game. She plays with her chin. "I think he will be quite posh. I'm going to say, Brandon."

Clarissa's screws her face up. "Brandon? Oh no. I like the name Hunter. I'll be his catch." They both break out into laughter.

Turning left onto 5th Avenue, Arabella stares out at Central Park; hit with a dose of nostalgia of her and Clarissa spending countless times after school with their friends. She spots the James Michael Levin playground and looks at her. "Do you remember when you kissed Taylor over there?"

Clarissa screws up her face up again. "Don't remind me. Have you seen what he looks like now? Didn't age very well that one," she says and turns left onto East 72nd.

Cruising down the street, Arabella scales the luxury building complex she once called her second home. *It hasn't changed a bit.* Reducing speed, they turn left into the driveway, watching and waiting as the white garage door slowly reveals the private underground car park. Entering the grey pillared room, she observes the wealth of the residents, as they pull up next to a lime-green Lamborghini Aventador. Unfastening her seatbelt, she carefully opens the door, not wishing to scratch it. Hit by the strong car fumes, as she squeezes out, she walks around the back and joins her, holding out her hands to assist the shopping queen.

"Thanks," says Clarissa, and slams the door.

Following behind the blonde queen, they turn right and reach the residential elevator. She presses the call button. They wait. "Nothing's changed at all," she says, as she inspects the room. The doors open. Making her way into the cove lit brown box, she checks herself out, as C hits the number 50 on the panel. Turning around on the chocolate marble floor, she says goodbye to the wealth with her excited eyes, as the gap starts to close.

With a protruding smile, she follows behind Clarissa as they step into the Campbell penthouse. *This hasn't changed at all.* She sniffs the penthouse air. *Mmhhmmmm. Vanilla.* "This hasn't changed one bit!" she shouts, as Clarissa carries her shopping bags and scurries through the kitchen and around the left corner towards her bedroom.

"I know!"

Moving inwards along the polished laminate, her arms spike with goosebumps as the memories flood back. Entering the kitchen, she stands in the center on the modern white tiled flooring and glances straight ahead into the square, open lounge, looking at the red brick fireplace. *Oh my god.* Racing past the couches and along the Persian rugs, she grabs the silver frame and widens her mouth, filling with flutters as the picture of her and Clarissa from their joint twenty first, spring birthday party sends her on a trip down memory lane. *I look so young.* Putting the photo back on the mantlepiece, she retraces her steps and re-enters the kitchen. *Why do I have to get old?* Staring at the black marble kitchen top, she's spirals into a flashback frenzy; recollecting the intense summer parties and copious amounts of liquor bottles and cocktail bowls that once consumed it. She hears a sliding door behind her, and spins around. *Oh I forgot about that.* She follows Clarissa out onto the wrapped terrace. Approaching the edge, as her brunette locks fly around her glowing face, her trip down memory lane is restored as she absorbs the mesmerizing nightlife of Roosevelt Island across the river. *Gorgeous.* Hearing the flick of a lighter, she raises her eyebrow and looks to her right. She widens her eyes. "What the hell!"

With a premium cigarette hanging from her scarlet red lips, Clarissa shrugs. "What? It's just a phase."

I can't believe her. Watching her inhale, she shakes her head and attempts to enjoy the view. "You do you." Gazing up at the twinkling display, she struggles to block out Mr. P. *Why did you have to do that to me?* With the wind carrying the smoke around her precious nose, she plays with her hands. "Do you think Elliot is worth pursuing?" she asks and faces her.

Clarissa exhales, as she joins her on the white cushioned couch. "Maybe. He seemed a bit too nice for me personally. You know I like a good bad boy." She exhales the smoke and flicks the ash. "Yeah, actually I think you would probably be suited, as you're not really wild."

I am very wild thank you. "I suppose."

She flicks the ash again and exhales a cloud of smoke. "Something like that. What do you think this guy is going to look like?"

Fanning the smoke from her face, she grimaces her lips. "I think he will be blonde."

"I don't know what I want, usually I'm a blonde but ever since Mr. P, I just haven't looked at them the same way."

The pit of her stomach sinks. "Should we get ready?" Watching Clarissa stand and flick the half-lit cigarette over the edge, she trails behind as they head for the bedroom.

Dropping their clothes on the light grey carpet, Clarissa goes the extra step and removes her bra. Arabella widens her eyes in awe at the blonde goddess as she watches her bend over into the built-in wardrobe; her ass is on fire in that white thong.

"Christ C, I just want to grab your ass," giggles Arabella.

"Go on then!"

Is she actually serious? The room claps.

"Ha-ha," laughs Clarissa, and turns around. She throws two pairs of black heels onto the bed and observes her brunette guest observing her breasts. She waves her hand. "Hello? Do you want to suck them?" she asks and cups them. They both burst into hysterics. What are they like! Clarissa stands over her king size bed and reaches into her shopping bag, whipping out a new black midi short cut silk dress. "Try this on," she says, and throws it to her.

Sliding it over her, Arabella turns around to face the mirror, brushing her hands down her silky hourglass. "What do you think?"

"So hot!"

She bites down on her finger and turns around, looking over her backside. "I do look pretty good."

"Pretty good? You look like you should be on a catwalk."

She flutters her lashes. "Thank you. I do consider myself humble though." She turns back around and continues to gaze over her humble self, as Clarissa rummages through the bag.

"Well don't be staying humble tonight," winks C and pulls out a white dress and white laced bra. She rips the tags off and puts them on before joining her bestie in the mirror.

Arabella's jaw drops. "If you think I belong on a catwalk, I don't even know where you belong."

Clarissa flicks her flaxen hair and turns around. "This should be fine for some hard grinding," she says and wiggles her peachy bottom.

The room claps again. "Naughty girl."

"Easy, Harper," she says and grabs the black heels. "Can you book us a cab?"

She nods grabs retrieves her smartphone from her bag. "What time?"

"Book it for half seven," she says and steps into her heels. "Right, time for pre drinks."

DEVIL'S NIGHTCLUB

With pre drinks flowing through them, the kinky duo wait outside Devil's nightclub along the sidewalk, watching the clubbers in front form an orderly queue behind the red rope.

Clarissa looks left. "Where are they?" she asks, as she crosses her arms and shivers.

Flicking her brunette hair against the wind, Arabella looks right. *Oh isn't he looking handsome.* She taps her on the arm; their pearly whites revealing in sync as their stunning dates near.

"You look very pretty," says Elliot; his muscles teasing her through his tightly wrapped light blue shirt.

She blushes. "You look good yourself," she says, as she lets him in for a hug. *Mmhhmmmm.* "You smell nice."

"Beat me to it." He unwraps himself from her silk short cut dress and places his left arm behind her curvy waist before looking right with his hand out. "Allow me to introduce your date. This is Joshua."

Clarissa locks onto his intense oceanic blue gaze, as he steps closer; her lashes fluttering as the blonde, Norwegian prince with his spiked ashen blonde hair, leans in for a hug. How could she possibly resist those screaming muscles! Opening her arms wide for her short sleeve, white shirt of a man, she boldly stops his attempt at a French kiss and catches his soft lips, exchanging her scarlet red lipstick with him; their instant attraction burning a wild flame.

What the hell? Arabella rolls her eyes, watching as the filthy couple seem to have forgotten there's an entire queue observing them. She looks up to Elliot. *Are you going to do anything?* She looks back again. *Ewwww.* "Should we go in now?"

"Good idea," says Elliot, and breaks up the display. "Let's go."

Showing their I. D's to security, Josh leads the entourage through the double doors; swapping the sound of chatter for electric club music as they enter the dark, L shaped venue. Turning left, they make their way along the black tiled, crowded dance floor; the flashing lasers and slut drops lighting up the atmosphere. Reaching the V.I.P area, he stops at the red rope and waves to the brunette goddess in the red booth.

Uncrossing her slender legs, she stands in her tight black cut out mini dress and approaches. "Nice to see you again," she says, and unhooks the rope.

Standing behind with Elliot, Arabella squints her eyes at her. *Why do I recognize her?* Ascending the 2 steps, she follows Clarissa and sways left around the L shaped VIP area, guided to their own red leather booth in the middle. Sliding in first, followed by Clarissa and then Josh, with Elliot sitting to her left, they wait for the brunette to return, as they listen to the climaxing beat drop its bass. The fire goddess returns. *She looks so familiar.*

With her hands full, she places a golden bucket full of ice and two bottles of premium vodka in the middle of the table. She smiles her professionalism. "Please enjoy. I'm the manager here. If you need anything just let me know!" she shouts over the music. She looks at Josh. "Have fun!"

Clarissa leans into Arabella's ear, as the manager returns to her booth across from them. "She looks like your twin!"

Grabbing the ice-cold bottle, she lines up four shot glasses and pours. "She does doesn't she!"

Cheering to a good night, they all look up and throw it back; the vodka working its burn against their throats as they slam the empty glasses down. Clarissa nods in agreement before turning to Josh.

Running her right, black, and white tipped acrylics through his thick hair, she leans in and parts her lips, finding herself caught between his burning moisture as their steamy breath collides. Raising her left hand, she places it on his warm cheek, fluttering inside as their sinking lips vaporize their vodka cocktail.

Elliot leans into Arabella's ear. "They look like they're having a good time!"

This is a bit extreme. Watching the blonde king and queen eat away at each other, she taps her. *Please stop.* They don't stop. She rolls her eyes and slaps her peachy bottom. "Stop!" Met with a dirty look amidst the drunken giggles, her and Elliot watch them both vacate the booth and descend onto the dance floor, observing the filthy queen grind against the king. Elliot looks away, as she continues to observe, watching as his hands travel up her bronze legs, higher, and higher; her hands around his neck as she grinds her sweat against him. *You are so dirty C. Then again, maybe it's fun. Yeah, live a little. Why not.* Turning to Elliot, she giggles and leans in, running her dainty fingers down his hardened abs as she parts her moist pink glossy lips and closes her eyes. Sliding their burning warmth, a wavy sensation flows through her; the flashing lights and loud music carrying her into a euphoric heaven.

With a pretty boy smirk on his face, the owner enters the L shaped club, accompanied by two gorgeous brunette models. Making their way across the spicy dancefloor, they pass the dirtiest duo in the room, and reach the V.I.P entrance. The red rope drops. Taking off his black suit jacket, he slides from his left side into the center of the red leather, with the manager to his left, and the two models sliding in from his right. Sitting comfy, he looks out at the dancefloor straight ahead, before casting his eyes right, over to Arabella and Elliot.

He leans into the manager. "They look like they're having fun. Why don't we ever do that?" he asks, attempting to keep a straight face.

"Say that again?"

He leans back in and prepares his strong voice. "I said, we should—" But for the club music, a clapping noise would have just been heard. He chuckles with a red mark across his right cheek. "Fine. You're not really my cup of tea anyway." But for the club music, another clapping noise would have just been heard.

"Behave." She looks over at the kissing duo, as he shakes off his red imprint. "They're getting a little bit too much." He taps the brunette model on the edge and sends her to the bar for a bottle of gold champagne. Returning with the bottle, he directs her with his eyes to the erotic pair.

Stepping along the black tiles, the model approaches. "Compliments of the owner!" she shouts, interrupting the show as she buries the expense deep into the ice bucket. Smiling at them, she turns around, blocking their view as they try to thank them.

Watching her slide back into the booth, Arabella's flushed face freezes. *I don't believe this!* Burning her glare deep into his green eyes, as Elliot puts his thumb up, a scorching fire brews within. The intense showdown doesn't go unnoticed as Dakota casts her eyes back and forth between them. Arabella watches as Mr. P smirks and turns to the nearest model. *You do that and I swear to god!* She watches as he locks his lips with the brunette. *Wow! Ok. Two can play at that!* Shotting back the vodka, she slams the glass down and climbs on top of Elliot, clawing her nails through his light ash hair; her red laced thong on full display as her short cut dress rides up her.

Dakota raises her eyebrow, constantly flicking between them as the show unfolds. "What the hell is happening here?" she murmurs. She looks to the devil and digs her pinch deep into his muscly waist. "Whatever you're doing, stop it!" It doesn't work.

Clarissa and Josh make their way back to the booth, looking at Elliot's uncomfortable face peek left at them in embarrassment as he holds his hands in the air. Spotting an opportunity, Clarissa returns the favor and slaps Arabella's bare cheek, leaving a naughty red print. "How do you like that you filthy slut!" she laughingly shouts and makes her way into the booth.

With a glowing red cheek, Arabella continues to eat away at Elliot's gentlemanly composure, keeping her right eye on Mr. P as he abruptly stands and shimmies past Dakota. *Where are you going?*

Clarissa's jaw drops. She looks to Josh. "I can't believe it's him!" she drunkenly shouts, watching as her fantasy drops the red rope and U-turns left into the bathroom hallway. Josh sticks his thumb up and draws her attention to the champagne. Does that man ever talk? Too focused with attempting to open the bottle, they miss Arabella's abrupt departure as she storms onto the dancefloor and U-turns left, leaving both Elliot and Dakota with raised eyebrows.

Bursting through the black door, she stares at the back of his white shirt, as he stands at the end of the small hallway; the club music fading behind her as the door swings closed.

"Quite the show you put on out there," he says, and turns around to face her.

Seeping her fiery glare into his smirking appearance, she steps closer. "What cologne are you wearing?" she asks, moving closer, and closer, as she sniffs the small air space pretending to indulge herself in his powerful woody scent to feed his ego.

"Well, well, well, I knew you wouldn't—" She unleashes an almighty powerful slap across his right cheek. He shakes it off. "That wasn't very nice," he says. She slaps him again. He shakes his red face and smirks. "Third time lucky?" He leans into her; her hand failing to deliver the fatal blow as it meets with the back of his head and grips on, as he lifts her up and pins her against the wall.

Tightly wrapping her thighs around his muscly waist, she squeezes tight. "Fuck you!"

He leans into her right ear. "That would be the dream right."

She leans into his right ear. "You mean nightmare," she devilishly whispers back, and squeezes her legs tighter.

He slams his hands above her, either side, and presses his forehead against hers; their green eyes creating a ferociously hot firestorm as their explosive lust builds. "You have yet to see this nightmare."

With the sexual tension looming, she lightly claws down her alpha's face and smirks before leaning into his left ear. "Then show me," she whispers, and bites down on his ear lobe, slowly scratching her teeth along.

"Oh, I'm going to do a little more than that." He leans into her ear. "I'm going to send you into fucking sin," he dominantly says, and spins her around, slamming her through the women's bathroom door; the two girls at the sinks vacating, as the room echoes a loud bang. Carrying her through into the middle cubicle, he swipes the door behind him with his left hand before turning around and slamming her against it; the row of cubicles shaking like an earthquake, as she lowers her right hand and locks the door.

"Corrupt me," she says and pulls on his wild hair.

Moving his right hand from underneath her, he spreads her legs and creates a gap between them before sliding it inside her red lace thong; his knuckles dipping in her warmth as he clenches his fist. He tears the thong from her with one intense pull; both side ribbons torn as he dangles the red lace in front. "Now where should I put this?"

"Wherever you—"

He stuffs it inside her mouth. "Don't moan too loud."

Moaning away as the bathroom shakes to its limits, she hears the door swing open. She places her hand over his wrist and listens to heels step along the tiles.

"Arabella? Are you ok?" asks Clarissa, as she looks at herself in the mirror and fixes her sweaty blonde hair.

She widens her eyes. *Oh please not now. Not now.* She begs him to behave with her horny eyes, as she removes her gag and drops it to the floor.

"Yes!" The cubicles start to shake again, as he turns up the heat with additional fingers. "I'm just… feeling… a bit woozy. How's Josh?" She bites down on her bottom lip, shutting her eyes to the shooting pleasure, relentlessly holding in her desire to moan. *Please be too drunk to hear.*

"He's alright. Mr. P was here, I should have said something to him." She checks out her teeth before turning around. "The things I would do to that man. He could go as hard as he wanted on me."

Don't you dare! She feels his speed increase, as his eyes light up. Caught between a state of panic and a desperate need to release her drowning pleasure, she says, "Clarissa, Mr. P is out the front. I passed him in the hall and mentioned your name, he wanted a chat with you."

"Aww, you did that for me," she says and blushes; too drunk to notice the obvious. She turns around and does one last check. "So sweet, where would I be without my bestie."

Listening to the door swing shut, Arabella pulls him in closer, exhaling her gasping moan into his ear. "You did this to me," she breathlessly screams, dripping in sweat as she gazes into his fresh look face. He hasn't sweated a drop!

"We're just warming up."

She gulps. *I can't do this. This isn't right.* Clouded with betrayal, she enters an anticlimax. Wrapping her right hand tightly around his penetrating wrist, she stops him and shakes her head. She feels his muscles relax as she guides his fingers out of her. "I'm sorry, this isn't me."

He lowers her to a standing position. Watching her unlock the door, he remains silent as he listens to the bathroom door swing shut. Looking down at her torn thong beneath him, he crouches and grabs it. Holding the ripped ribbons either side, he loses himself in the red lace pattern. He sighs. After six weeks of trying to forget her; he can't. Her quirks and stifling beauty triggering dangerous emotions within him that could have major implications for his secret plans. It's for her own protection. Scrunching the thong in his right hand, he shuts his eyes and shakes his head, releasing her from his catharsis as the soothing sense of calmness takes over. He opens his eyes and stands, pocketing the thong and exiting the cubicle before staring into the mirror. Washing his hands, he glares into his reflection; his devilish appearance protruding as he tilts his head forwards. Smirking his dangerously charismatic complexion, he regains himself before rejoining his brunette goddesses.

Stepping outside the club, Arabella listens to the chattering crowds as their cigarette smoke strongly lingers, looking around for the rest of her entourage; her sweaty flushed face hit by the strong winds as a cold sensation tingles up her dress.

"Over here, Arabella!" shouts Elliot.

She looks left and smiles. Making her way to him, as he holds out his left arm, she sneaks under and side hugs him, wrapping herself tightly around his waist. Warming her right cheek against his rippled abs, she stares at her own doing, watching the blonde damsel in distress struggling to find Mr. P. "You and Josh should go have fun!" shouts Arabella, as she pats Elliot's chest. "We're going to go!"

He looks down. "We are?" he whispers.

She gives him the look. "We are," she says, with a pearly smile.

He looks up to Josh. "We will catch you two later." Leaving the blonde king and queen behind, they begin making their way towards 1st Avenue; the nightlife fading in the background as they venture off to an unknown destination.

Crossing her arms, she brushes up and down her goosebump. They reach Elliot's apartment located on East 49th street. *Is that his?* Listening to him insert his key, she stares at the black and yellow 69 Camaro parked out front. "Is that yours?"

He turns the lock. "Yeah, that's my pride and joy," he says, and pushes open the white door; hit by the toasty warmth as he hits the light switch of the L shaped apartment. He throws his keys into the woven fruit bowl on the modern white chester draws to his right, as she enters the cream wall apartment. Walking inwards along the brown laminate, he removes his light blue shirt and drops it beneath him before turning left and looking left at her with a smile and one dreamy athletes body. "Make yourself at home. I'm going to take a shower."

She takes her eyes off the fruit bowl and looks straight ahead at him. *Very hot. A bit pale though.* She smiles. "Ok." Listening to the bathroom door close, she enters deeper inside the spacious apartment; her body defrosting as the showers running water echo's under the gap in passing. *Well he seems normal.* She gazes straight ahead at the king size bed positioned at the end and makes her way to it. Turning around, she throws herself onto the bed with her arms spread out, as her rosy skin tightens. She leans her head right and raises her eyebrow. *Typical.* Inspecting the living room from afar, she looks over at the cream leather couch propped against the right wall, facing a flat screen mounted against the shower wall with his clear obsession for ice hockey obvious from the custom black designed hockey puck table in the center. She looks up at the ceiling spotlights and closes her eyes; the warmth and wavy combination flowing through her as she listens to the water. *I wonder if he wanted me to join him. Should I?* Well I don't… oh too late!

Kicking her heels off, she sneaks towards the bathroom and grips the silver handle. Making her way inside without a trace, the soles of her feet step along the moist tiles. Dropping her black dress, she looks at his light ashy hair through the foggy glass and bites down on her lip. Gripping the handle, she slides open the entrance and steps into the sauna heat; her skin softening as she turns around and quietly traps them in. She turns around in the large walk-in shower. *Mmhhmmmm.* She watches innocently, fluttering inside as he flexes his arms under the steamy water dripping down his godly physique; his muscles working their weight as he combs his veiny hands through his thick hair.

"Feel free to join," he laughingly says.

She presses her tongue against her cheek. The cheeky devil must have heard her! "I hope you don't mind."

"Not at all." He listens to the light splashing behind him as she treads the black tiles towards him.

Wrapping her arms around his muscly torso from behind; she presses her warmth against him and lightly claws her way down his rippled abs. Painting his back in pink gloss as the water trickles from above, her fingers continue their journey downwards over his smooth V line.

I think it's best if we extend this gentleman the curtesy of a little privacy.

A BLOSSOMING ROMANCE

Separating the bacon from the eggs, Elliot picks up the tray and exits the kitchen, hitting the light switch as he walks past the hockey puck table; listening to his restless queen snore away as he approaches the bed.

"Good morning beautiful," he softly whispers, and places it on the bed side table before leaning over Arabella.

Groggily rolling onto her back, as the sweet bacon air caresses her nose, she squints her eyes; her stomach grumbling as she props herself up. "Thanks," she half smiles, as he passes her the tray. He's forgotten the drink!

Rushing back into the kitchen, he grabs the fresh orange juice from the blue counter and returns, placing it on the side table before propping himself on the edge of the bed, watching her cuteness devour his cooking skills.

She looks up to him as she swallows the last bite. "That was so good. I could get used to this," she says, as she wipes away the grease.

"You've had this for the last six weeks," he laughingly says, as he takes the empty tray from her lap.

Has it actually? She raises her eyebrow. "Has it been that long?"

Leaving her to count the days, he returns to the kitchen and walks straight ahead to the sink. He turns the tap and begins to scrub. Staring out the small window into autumn's darkness, he gets lost in his reflection; the kitchen's yellow glow shining in the background of his warn out image, as the sponge squeaks away. As the water splashes from the plate onto the white tiled floor, a smile sweeps across his face. Hit with a spontaneous idea, he rinses and places it on the silver rack before drying his hands. Turning around, he steps to the entrance and pauses, watching her sip away on the juice, as he bolsters up the courage.

Filled with nerves, he steps out. Here he goes! "Will you move in with me?"

Arabella spits out her drink; the acid seeping into the Egyptian sheets as her eyes widen. "You're crazy."

He moves to the end of the bed. "I mean you've been here for what? Six weeks now. We clearly enjoy each other's company."

She looks at him. *Why are you so lovely and sweet?* "It sounds great, but aren't you forgetting something?" She watches him raise his eyebrow. Rolling her eyes, she points at him, and then her, and creates a love heart with her fingers and thumbs.

He facepalms. Turning right, he walks over to the bathroom and enters, closing the door behind him. Did she scare him away? He comes back out; his face glowing a gorgeous smile as he approaches her. "Will you, Arabella Harper, be my girlfriend?"

With a glowing face as the blushing intensifies, she throws the cover from her warm body and stands on the cold laminate in her matching black lingerie. Fluttering her lashes, she moves to him and takes hold of his soft hands; the sparkle in her green eyes glistening as she looks up into his majestic brown gaze. "Yes, I will be your girlfriend." Taken back by his magical kiss, she breaks their lock. "I would love to live with you," she passionately whispers, unable to contain her bright white smile, as he sighs a huge relief.

Swept in her beauty, he gets another spontaneous idea. "What are you doing today?"

She pauses and grimaces her lips. *What do I have today? Winter ball?* "I have work to do." She pokes his white vest. "Your flowers."

He looks up at the ceiling, planning a schedule in his head before looking at her. "Do you think you could finish midday?"

"Whyyyy?"

"I think it's time I introduce you to my mother."

She gulps; her stomach sinking as the thought of not being good enough clouds her. "Oh wow! What will she think of me?"

He brings his right hand up to her rosy cheek, gently caressing her soft skin before twirling her brunette curls between his fingers. "She will be thinking, how have I managed to get so lucky with a beautiful angel."

Awwwwwwwwwwww. Melting away inside to his perfect words, she wraps herself around him and squeezes tight. "You are so sweet." Releasing him, she throws her hands in the air. "What the heck. Let's do it. Can you drop me off at work though?"

He chuckles. "I've been doing that every day anyway," he says, and teasingly taps her peachy bottom. "Go get ready."

The roaring horsepower of Elliot's black and yellow Camaro shreds through the cloudy morning peace along East 90th. Arabella looks at him from the passenger's seat, as he drives with two fingers on the wheel. *Such a bad boy.* Pulling up along the sidewalk opposite Campbell, and Co, she leans over the handbrake. "Thanks for the lift. I will see you at twelve," she smilingly says, and pecks him on the cheek before unfastening her seatbelt. Opening the door, she climbs out and slams it behind her.

Watching her step-in front of the bonnet, he rolls down his window as she looks left and right to cross. "Those jeans really do you justice."

Lathering up his compliment, she blows him a kiss and crosses the street. *Life is good.* Passing under the shops sign with a smile on her cupid lips, as the Camaro's roar zooms off behind her, she enters.

"You look rather glowing this morning," says Clarissa, as she exchanges smiles with her from behind the counter.

"So do you. Morning sex perhaps?" she asks, as she walks into the open lounge and chucks her black fur coat and bag down before sliding behind the counter to take her seat.

Clarissa jokingly slaps her arm. "You are so horny these days, my god! What has Elliot done to you?"

She leans into her ear. "He asked me to be his girlfriend." The shop floor explodes with excitement of a joyful scream and clapping.

"Oh my god! We need to celebrate."

"Well, it can't be today, I'm meeting his mom at half twelve, so I'll have to leave at twelve if that's ok?"

Clarissa slides the seat from under her and makes her way under the arched doorway into the workshop. Inspecting the mounting workload, she shrugs her laziness off and reemerges with a smile. "Screw it, I can't be bothered today, so yes you can." She retakes her seat. "I can't believe you have a boyfriend, and I don't."

God here we go. "Well what about Josh?"

C rolls her eyes. "We broke up. He doesn't speak, and when he does, it's all about him. He was great in bed but that's about it… so I broke it off."

She puts her hand on her blonde besties shoulder. "Well I'm sure you will find someone else. These things just happen." She slides the seat from under her and brushes past her golden locks, shimmying past and moving into the open lounge. Standing in front of the shop front window, she gazes out into the busy street with her hands on her hips. *Hmmmm.* Hit with a sudden reality check, she sighs. *I mean maybe being taken isn't such a bad thing.* She grimaces her lips. *Is it bad if I say I don't see myself with him? Oh god, why have you done this. Jesus.*

"You know who I want," says C, and spins around on her chair to face her brunette bestie. "Mr. P."

She closes her eyes and deeply inhales. "Clarissa. In the nicest way possible, he doesn't want you."

Clarissa screws up her face. "Excuse me? Listen, you might have a boyfriend but that doesn't stop you from clearly being jealous."

Oh she didn't just say that! With a face painting red, she turns to her. "This needs to end now. He doesn't like you," she says sternly, as she walks in front of the glass counter.

Met with confrontation, Clarissa gulps; her pale cheeks turning bright red as she turns to face her and looks up, feeling small as the devil's green eyes singe their dominance. "How would you know?"

Slamming her hands either side of her on the glass, she towers her. "I said he doesn't like you."

Clarissa stands up, keeping a calm composure as the bad bitch attitude simmers on the tip of her tongue. "Just because he would never go with someone like you, doesn't mean he wouldn't with me!"

"He's already been with—" She gasps, placing both hands over her mouth as she snaps out of her possessed state.

"Already been what? Go on!"

Why did I just say that? She looks up at the clock. It's only 10:30. *I can't do this.* Racing into the open lounge, she grabs her fur coat and bag. "Doesn't matter," she says, and throws the coat over her, before storming towards the shop door.

"Don't come back. I will hire a team to finish off these flowers. Maybe you will have changed your attitude when I'm back in January!" she shouts, as Arabella exits the shop.

Flagging down the nearest cab, she opens the yellow door and slides into the back seat.

"Where to?" asks the driver.

"Hotel L'Amour on Fifth Avenue." Placing her head in her hands with her arms shaking uncontrollably, she holds her breath; her heart racing as she exhales through her nose. *What am I doing?* Shaking her head, her parent's divorce rushes back; her mother's affair with her personal assistant tearing up their family when she was a teenager. She could never understand betrayal, and now she feels just like her mother; unable to get him off her mind as the deceit to her best friend and now boyfriend spirals. It's like he's cast a spell over her, no matter the length of time apart, she remains trapped in his web as he eats away.

Pulling into the red cobble lane of the hotel, she pays the driver, as the red coat approaches. Taking his white gloved hand, she steps out, listening to the door slam behind her as she takes a deep breath and allows the soothing flow of the fountain to take over. Leaving her anger behind, she takes a slow walk up the white stairs, playing with her hands as she gives the doormen a blank look. Saying nothing as they open the gold framed door in line with her snail's pace, she steps inside the white marble lobby and turns left towards the brown mahogany reception desk. Oh look, it's Chloe.

"Welcome to Hotel L'Amour. What is the nature of your visit today?"

"I'm here to see Mr. P."

Chloe looks to her left and stares at the other receptionist; their eyes signaling an unknown form of communication. She looks back to her. "One moment please." The other receptionist picks up the phone before signaling Chloe again. She nods and turns to her again. "I'm afraid he isn't looking for flowers today, Arabella."

She raises her eyebrow. *How does she know my name?* She taps her acrylics along the desk. "Oh, you know exactly why I'm here," and looks down at her nametag, "Chloe!"

Chloe smiles. "I'm sorry, I don't know what you're talking about."

She rolls her eyes. "Bitch," she snidely mutters, as she turns around and walks to the waiting area. Taking a seat on the brown leather couch, she grinds her teeth, seeping her burning glare into the evil blonde. She takes out her smartphone and browses through social media. She sighs; a request to change her relationship status pending from Elliot. Just want she needs! Hearing the penthouse elevator doors open, she peeks out her right eye, watching as three gorgeous brunette girls in their mid-twenties exit. She bites down on her tongue, watching as they light up the marble lobby in their stunning dresses from the night before, their heels echoing the sky-high empty reception as they proceed towards the exit. Shaking her head, with a sour red face, she fights her spasming eyes lids as the urge to cry strikes. *You really know how to hurt me.* Burying her face in her smartphone, she presses her tongue against her cheek, feeling like a complete and utter fool, as she loads up her messages and constructs a text to Elliot. Nothing but lies leaving her fingers as she pretends to have delivered a bouquet to the hotel and asks that he picks her up.

Hearing the Camaro's roar pull up into the lane, she stands and makes her way to him. Opening the passenger door, she climbs in with a fake pearly smile.

"Hello beautiful," says Elliot.

She leans over the hand brake and sinks her pink gloss into his cheek. "Hello to you too," she says, and fastens her seatbelt. Exiting left onto 5th Avenue, she sits in silence; the only thing she wants to do right now is crawl up into bed.

Passing East 48th Street, she looks to him. "Where are we going?"

Elliot raises his eyebrow. "Have you forgotten? Lunch? Mother?"

I don't need this right now. She totally forgot about it to be fair between being fired, falling out with her best friend, and chasing another man in the space of three hours. "No, of course not, silly."

With two fingers on the wheel, he glimpses over. "How was work?"

Don't ask that. She sighs. "It was good, your flowers are keeping us busy."

He nods. "Interesting," he says, as his inquisitive mind wonders about any other gossip they may have discussed. "Anything else?" he asks, and turns right onto West 43rd St. "Did you tell Clarissa about us?"

She looks away from him and gazes out the window. "She screamed with joy."

Slowing down for the 6th Avenue traffic, he smiles and looks at the back of her brunette hair. "I am so pleased to hear that. I was worried she had me down as a bad boy for stealing her away from you ha-ha."

Oh you are about as far away from a bad boy as possible. Hang on. Yes! She spots an opportunity to play on his words and turns to him. "Actually, it was the opposite. She was so happy that I found

127

someone, she decided to give me until January off to spend time with you. Isn't that amazing?"

Filling with concern, he widens his eyes, as he crosses over 6th Avenue. "What about the flowers?"

She flicks her hand. "Oh, she has hired a team for that. She doesn't need me."

"Wonderful." He turns left on 7th Avenue and continues for a bit before pulling up along the sidewalk. "We're here," he says, and turns off the engine.

Leaving her morning in the car, she climbs out; the reality of meeting his mother kicking in as she looks over to him across the roof of the car with grimacing lips. "What if she doesn't like me?" she asks, whilst playing with her hands.

He walks around the back of his beauty, inspecting the paint for scratches, as she makes her way onto the sidewalk. "You'll be fine, what's not to like? She will think you are an innocent angel." With no scratches detected, he joins her side, only to be met with rolling eyes. "I know you're not though," he says, and winks.

Gripping the long black handle, he holds the black framed glass door open for her. Letting the door swing shut behind him, he trails behind her, making their way through the orange tiled waiting area; the lunch time diners chatter piercing their ears as Arabella pulls opens the second set of doors. Making their way into the crowded, Italian themed restaurant, they approach the desk in front.

"Welcome to Alphonso's. Table for two?" asks the Italian manager.

"Table for three please," says Elliot.

"Certainly." The waiter grabs three menus from the stand. "Follow me please," he says, and walks to the entrance's right, leading them down the dark orange tiled floor through the black leathered booths of their fellow diners. Both inhaling the mouthwatering smell of Italian cuisine, their stomachs rumble as they turn left down the aisle. The waiter stops, and turns around, directing them with his left hand. With a smile, he patiently waits, watching the indecisive duo take a moment to decide their seating. Finally sliding in either side of the black leather, with Arabella having her back to the entrance, the waiter places the menus on the light brown tabletop. "Can I get you both some drinks?"

"I'll have a sex on the beach," says Arabella.

"Excellent choice." The waiter looks left at Elliot. "For the gentleman?"

"I will have an orange juice since I'm driving. No pulp. Oh, can we also get a jug of iced water for the table?"

"Certainly," the waiter replies, and heads for the bar, as Elliot's pocket vibrates.

Retrieving his smartphone, he opens the text from his mother. "Well my mother is five minutes away."

I hope she will like me. Twiddling her thumbs, she looks to him. "What is she like?"

He puts his phone back into his pocket. "I'll leave that a surprise."

Shooting with nerves, she spots a bathroom sign dead ahead. "I'm going to freshen up. I'll be right back." Sliding out the booth, as he nods, she makes her way down the aisle and turns left into the women's bathroom.

Leaning against the sink, she closes her eyes and exhales. *She's not going to be that bad. I'm sure she's lovely.* Standing up straight, she rehearses her smile. *Ok, breathe. Let's do this.* Gripping the door handle, she pulls it open; swapping the smell of cleaning products for garlic bread as she peeks around the corner. She opens her eyes wide. *You can't be serious.*

Releasing the door, she returns to the mirror. "What the actual?" *I can't. What?* She turns the tap on. "Is this real?" She cups her dainty hands and splashes the cold water over her face. "This can't be real." Shaking her dripping face, she bursts into hysterics. Hearing the door open, her heart races as she looks left, watching as a customer enters. *It's not her. God I can't.* Well unless you want to remain trapped in a bathroom, Miss Harper, you're going to have to. Closing her eyes again, she takes a deep breath and exhales her nerves away. Here she goes! Taking hold of that handle in this soon to be life changing event, she swaps the smell of cleaning products for something Italian, and exits, holding back the laughter as she makes her way down the aisle.

Hearing her footsteps from behind, Elliot turns around with a smile and slides out the booth, guiding her into his side, as his mother sits opposite them, before retaking his seat. "Mother, this is Arabella. Arabella, this is my mother, Barbara."

"Can you give us a moment my dearest son."

Listening to his mother, he looks at them both. "Well sure," he says and slides out the booth. He points to his left. "I'll just pop to the bathroom whilst you both get acquainted."

Arabella leans out the booth and watches him walk down the aisle and enter the restroom. Turning around like lightning, she looks the wild cougar up and down in her usual attire. "What the hell Barbara?"

Closing her purse, Barbara rests her hands on the table. "Yes, I am as shocked as you are dear. I have to tell you sweetie that I am thrilled for you both, but I must tell you that Elliot thinks that my young lover George is sixty-three. He couldn't handle it if he knew his real age."

Taking out her smartphone, she opens her messages and scrolls, finding the long list of filthy messages she keeps receiving. "Oh, you mean George who text me, "Dearest Barb, your riding skills can't compare to these young girls," that one?"

Barbara starts blushing. "He really said that. He is such a sweetheart." She reaches into her bag for a picture of him. "Would you like to see him?"

She raises her eyebrows and leans in. "I don't think this is the time to be showing me pictures of your filthy toy boy when your son will be out any moment," she loudly whispers.

Barbara adjusts her hearing aid. "Sorry sweetie, can you repeat that? This old thing needs replacing."

Oh my god. Rolling her eyes up, she sighs and shakes her head before looking back at her. "I think it's best if we don't tell Elliot where I live. He hasn't been to my apartment."

Elliot exits the bathroom and returns, sliding into the booth with a cautious smile. "I hope the two most important ladies in my life got to know each other well," he says, as his girlfriend violently sips through her straw whilst staring at his mother.

"Yes dear. Me and Arabella have met before," says Barbara, as Arabella wonders where the hell she's going with this.

"You have?" He casts his eyes to Arabella. "You have?" Met with silence, his question is paused as the waiter returns.

"Are you ready to order?"

Elliot looks at the hungry pair. "Yes, we are. Can we have three garlic breads with margherita, two calamari and one stuffed meat feast calzone." He passes the menus to the waiter. "Thanks."

Watching the waiter vacate, Barbara smiles to her handsome son. "We do know each other. This is George's niece."

You are joking. Dropping her mouth in disbelief, she looks to Elliot. "I, I…" She sighs. "Yes! Good old, George. Me and your mother have shared some stories in our time."

Elliot can't believe it; he's absolutely thrilled. "Well I'm pleasantly surprised, I still have to meet George. Me and him sound like we would enjoy a few rounds on the golf course."

Arabella's face lights up with a cunning smile. "He loves swinging. Swinging that club and he doesn't stop talking about riding," she says, whilst staring at Barbara.

A look of puzzlement sweeps his face. "Riding?"

Barbara interrupts. "Riding his golf cart dear."

Arriving with his hands full, the waiter places the dishes in front of them with a professional smile. "Please enjoy."

Smiling back, Elliot says, "It looks great," and picks up his fork; his first bite interrupted as his smartphone vibrates in his pocket. Placing his fork down, he retrieves it and glances at the incoming call. "It's my boss. I'll be right back," he says, and slides out the booth before making his way out front.

Putting her fork down, Arabella swallows the tender sweet calamari and glares at the liar chewing on her meaty calzone. "What the hell did you say that for?"

Barbara swallows the meaty delicacy. "You asked me not to say anything about where you lived sweetie."

She raises her hands. "You could have said you buy flowers from me? Now I'm stuck in your love—" *That doesn't look good.* Watching Elliot race back down the aisle with a fearful panic swept across his face, she asks, "Is everything ok?"

"I have to go." He puts money on the table to cover the bill. "There's been some sort of elaborate robbery at work. You two can share a cab." Leaning into the booth, he pecks her on the forehead, before kissing his mother. "Love you. I'll ring you some time," he says, and rushes for the exit.

Finishing their meals in silence, they both wonder about the robbery.

Barbara looks over to Arabella. "Could you ring George please sweetie? Ask him to pick up his sugar plum."

That is so disgusting. Scrunching her face, she picks up her smartphone and dials the toy boy. The lines dead. "There's no answer." She opens the local cab app. "I'll book us a taxi instead."

The waiter reappears. "Oh no, do we have an unhappy customer?"

Barbara places her hand on his arm. "It was lovely dear. Tell the chef he did a fantastic job. My son had to rush away but he's left the money on the table for you."

He smiles. "I will pass on your compliments." He pockets the money and collects the dishes. "You both enjoy the rest of your day."

Leaving the smell of Italian cuisine behind, they exit, breathing in the Manhattan fumes as they step onto the sidewalk, looking for their cab through the lunch time crowds. There it is. Approaching the cab; Arabella takes the back, as Barbara enters the front.

Pulling off from the side, the driver turns left onto West 40th before looking over at Barbara. "Did you hear about the robbery at the City Council?"

She places her hand on his navy blue, fleece jacket. "Why yes dear. My son had to leave our lunch date due to it."

"They're saying it was four Italians. I think the chase is still going on as we speak."

Arabella perks up in the back. "What are they going to steal? Pens and paper?"

The driver's detective hat comes on, as he turns left onto Madison Avenue. "Four Italians, City Council? Hmm... Nope I can't think." He chuckles and looks to Barbara. "I guess that's why I never made it as a detective ha-ha!"

Barbara lightly slaps his arm and chuckles in sync with him. "Quite true dear, unfortunately not all of us have the brains for that. When Elliot's father left, I had to take care of us by any means," she says, as Arabella screws up her face, wondering how she ended up as a third wheel.

"Absolutely. This generation will never know how lucky they have it, especially with technology these days."

Sitting in the back disturbed, she rolls her eyes and browses her smartphone in an attempt to zone out. She opens a text from Elliot. *Guns?* "Elliot has text me. He said, "It was four Italians with guns, and no one was injured, and a forensic team was at the scene," so I guess that's good news."

"Guns! What could they possibly be stealing that requires guns?" says Barbara, as the driver widens his eyes. Arabella shrugs, and zones out again.

Pulling up behind the wreckage on Cypress Avenue, the driver drops his jaw. "Woah! That car needs urgent scrapping."

Barbara places her left hand on his arm. "That's my car dear, someone crashed into it, but they were never caught. I might have to scrap it."

The criminal in the back rolls her eyes, as he reaches onto the dashboard and grabs a pen and sticky note before writing down his number. "Here." He passes it to Barbara. "My names Enrique. If you need anything, let me know."

Enrique? Arabella raises her eyebrow at this overweight, Caucasian male in his mid-fifties. He must have left his Spanish side in Texas. "You don't seem Spanish?"

He looks behind to her. "I'm not." Listening to her laughter, as she undoes her seatbelt and opens the door, he looks to Barbara with flushed cheeks. "I changed my name because I was going through a midlife crisis. Now all the women seem to scream down the phone every time I give my name."

Barbara unfastens her seatbelt and places her arm on him. "You are Enrique to me," she says, and opens the door. Climbing out, she turns around and leans back in. "I will ring you my sweet, Enrique." She slams the door and turns around, making her way to the black gate, as she listens to her potential daughter in law gasp for air through her dying laughter. "Now, now. Let's go inside dear."

Wiping away the streaming tears from her hysterics, she continues to giggle as she waves goodbye to Barbara in the communal hallway. Retrieving her keys, she opens her apartment door and steps inside, throwing her bag on the dusty couch to her right; that home sweet home smell faded as her eyes turn cold and empty. *This seems different.* Walking further into the gloomy apartment, she takes a seat on the edge of the bed and looks to her right, staring through the half open bathroom door. *Wow that seems so small now.* Laying back, she closes her eyes and sighs; everything she has built independently escaping her as the inevitable change casts over her crumbling kingdom. *I need to decide… this is too much. Mr. P or Elliot?* Placing her dainty hands over her face, she can't help but think about how Mr. P stimulates her in ways no one else can. *I wish you was just normal. Why can't you just be you, but not you?* Tearing up, she thinks back to the rejection earlier, feeling trapped in a void; all she can do is wait and see how this plays out. *Elliot it is, I guess.*

Sitting up, she wipes her wet cheeks. Reaching under the bed, she slides out a brown box before working her way around the apartment, collecting only necessities. The rest of her stuff can go into storage when she hands over the keys. Placing the box onto the bed, she grabs her bag from the couch and retrieves her smartphone. She books a cab with her BookShib. Throwing her bag over her, she makes her way to the mirror. Staring at her dusty reflection, she puts on a brave face; the reality that her life will officially change the moment she exits the apartment lingering in the back of her mind. Looking over her shoulder, she gazes into the box, and turns around, reaching for the picture of her and Clarissa on top from her 21st birthday. *I shouldn't have said those things earlier.* Overwhelmed with regret, she wipes the dust off and places it back inside. Lifting the box, she moves to the door and opens it, gulping as her heart races. *The start of a new life I suppose.* Casting her eyes back over her shoulder, she captures the moment and grimaces her lips. With a deep exhale, she lets the door slam behind her.

GEORGE

Wearing her fluffy socks, Arabella snuggles tightly with Elliot on the couch, watching the grand opening of the winter games, the last day of November.

"Want a drink?" asks Elliot. No response. The toasty apartment has sent her to sleep. Leaning forwards with her wrapped around him, he hits the secret button on the hockey puck table, and watches as the lid raises. It's a hidden mini fridge! Reaching inside the chilled space, he grabs a cold beer and sits back in comfort. It's like nothing could go wrong. The apartment starts hissing; his eyes widening as the foam sprays onto her beautiful locks. Oops! He looks down at her. Still asleep. Phew! Bringing the can to his chapped lips, he looks up and chugs the crisp, cold beverage before facing the flatscreen. He widens his eyes; spraying the beer all over her as he chokes.

"What the hell!" she screams, and pulls herself up, as he places his can on the table and grabs the remote.

"Listen to this." He turns up the volume.

"This is New York Live with your latest updates. This just in moment ago. One of the four, City Council heist members has just been captured in the early hours of this morning as this long manhunt continues. We're currently standing outside the precinct here at the New York Police Department where the suspect is currently being held. We have been informed the suspect is a twenty- three- year-old, American Italian male by the name of George Russo. We will update you as soon as we get further information."

Oh my god. That sounds like... no, surely not. The door knocks. She looks to him. "Are we expecting someone?"

He shrugs his shoulders and stands, walking across the laminate in his grey sweatpants and white tee. Gripping the handle, he opens the front door; his heart racing as two FBI agents flash their badges.

"Elliot Smith?" asks the Agent, on the right.

"Yes?" he nervously replies.

"I'm Agent Cody."

"And I'm Agent Sanders! You work for the City Council?"

"Ye-Ye-Yes."

"Can we come in Elliot?" firmly asks Agent Cody. He directs the plain clothed men through; their badges capturing Arabella's attention from the couch as they flash them to her.

"And who do we have here?" asks Agent Sanders.

Arabella stands in her white top and black lingerie. She points to her wardrobe. "I'm Arabella. I'm just gonna…" She races over to it and slips on a pair of grey sweatpants.

Agent Sanders sits down in her seat and looks to her. "Hope you don't mind," he says, patronizingly.

"Not at all," says Elliot. "Please have a seat as well, Agent Cody."

Taking a seat next to his partner, he looks up to Elliot. "Agent Sanders and I are here, as you might have suspected because of the heist at the City Council. We have reason to suspect the captured individual today by the name of George Russo might have been trying to get close to you." He reaches into his pocket for a mugshot and holds it out for him. "Does this man look familiar to you?"

Taking the picture, Elliot observes it carefully. "No. I have no idea who this guy is. What do you mean get close to me?" He passes the mugshot to Arabella. "Do you know?"

Jesus Barbara, he's jacked up. Shaking her head at the tank in the picture, she grimaces her lips. "No, I don't," she softly says, as the Agents observe her.

"Let's try this again," says Sanders, and passes Elliot another picture. "Is this your mother?"

His eyes widen. "What on earth is this?" he shouts. He passes the picture to Arabella as his face turns red. "Explain this at once!"

Agent Cody's observational skills notice her widened eyes. "Arabella, what do you see on his neck in the first picture?"

Wishing she hadn't seen Barbara naked; she swaps to the first picture and bites her bottom lip as she inspects it closely. "Umm...some sort of tattoo. SM?" She hands both pictures to Elliot. "What does that mean?" she asks.

Agent Sanders looks at Elliot. "Do you know what the S and M means Elliot?"

He raises his hands.

"No, I don't? Now can you tell me why there's a picture of my mother in your fucking hands please."

Agent Sanders stands up. "Cue the language. They're technically in your hands." He turns to Cody, as they share a moment of laughter, before looking back. "Ok. Sorry for that good cop, bad cop routine. It's clear you have no idea."

"Get on with it!" shouts Elliot.

"We believe they may have been following you for a while. We believe your mother's picture has been stolen from somewhere and George Russo has somehow obtained it. It's possible they were planning to use her as a ransom if their initial plan failed. We simply do not know at this time."

Elliot's heart starts beating, as his breathing heavies. "Who... who... who is they? What is this tattoo?"

Agent Cody continues. "We would call them the mob, but you would know them as the American and Sicilian Mafia."

His eyes widen in fear as the hairs on his arms spike. Arabella hugs him as she looks to Agent Cody. "What would the Mafia want with Elliot?"

Both Agents look at each other, before Sanders looks at her. "As of right now, we are unsure. Sensitive information regarding investors and property owners were compromised. Having found the picture of his mother on the suspect, we can only speculate they used Elliot."

Agent Cody looks to Elliot. "Unless of course your mother just happened to be sleeping with him and this is all just a huge coincidence?" They look at him with blank faces.

"Ignore my partner. He's a little insensitive," says Sanders. "Just to add, we believe you are no longer in danger, nor your mother. Might I also mention that we can't officially confirm he is part of the Sicilian Mafia at this time. Most members do not have tattoos."

"So what makes you suspect he is? It could be anything?" asks Elliot.

"Previous intel. This guy is likely a fresh recruit who got in way over his head," replies Agent Sanders.

Taking back the photos, they make their way across the apartment and head for the door. Agent Cody turns around to Elliot, as Agent Sanders exits. "Are you going anywhere soon?"

Elliot pauses and rolls his eyes up. "We have to go dress shopping around the corner in a bit for the Winter ball tomorrow."

"I see. We will have you followed for the rest of the week just to be safe. Thanks for your cooperation."

Watching the two enter their black unmarked Chevrolet Tahoe, he closes the door and turns around. Placing his hands over his stressed face, he deeply exhales and takes a slow-paced walk to the couch, shaking in fear and worry.

She observes him from the edge of the bed. "Should we go dress shopping now to take your mind off this?"

He releases a heavy sigh as he sits. "Are you sure it's safe?"

She stands from the bed and makes her way over to him. Sitting on his lap, she wraps her arms around him and combs her fingers through his ashy hair.

"You heard them. They have someone tailing us. I wouldn't worry. Think about the positive things like tomorrow night."

He takes comfort in knowing she's stronger than him and smiles. He looks up to the flatscreen to check the time. It's 13:30. "We best get ready."

Elliot gazes over at her from the front door, watching as she checks herself out in the mirror. "I love the outfit. Your ass looks great in those jeans."

She shakes her curvy hips. "You think?" *I do look hot to be fair.*

He chucks her a black coat before wrapping his scarf around his neck. "Always," he sweetly says, with a smile. "Ready?" he asks, and holds the door open for her.

She nods and exits their Midtown East apartment and turns right, as he locks up.

Walking along East 49th together hand in hand, as an unmarked black, Ford Crown Victoria tails closely behind, they turn right onto 3rd Avenue. "What color dress do you want then?" asks Elliot, as she shivers away.

"Pink," she says, as the cold captures her breath.

Elliot looks at her. "Pink? You realize this is a masquerade ball, right?"

Maybe I should have researched this. "What does that mean?"

"Each color indicates what sort of person you are. Pink is friendly."

She screws her face up. "Well that's boring. What about red?" she asks and lets go of his hand. *I should have worn gloves.* She rubs her purple hands together and blows her warmth through her chapped lips. She probably should have worn Vaseline as well. If it's like this tomorrow, she's going to need a cardigan.

"Red? Oh, you don't want that. It signifies risk. You're hardly risky ha-ha."

Ummm.... I definitely am. "Well I'll have red then," she stubbornly says.

Entering the small square boutique shop, Sewing Queen, Elliot waves to the owner blonde Sally stood behind the glass desk, left of the entrance. She is best friends with Barbara, having both met in sewing school before he was born. She's like an auntie to him.

"Hey Sally, same time of the year as always. Only this time, I've brought a surprise."

Sally emerges from behind the counter, stepping along the white and black tiles and inspects the brunette beauty. "Oh my Elliot, she's gorgeous. Who are you then my pretty?"

Arabella starts to blush. "Well, I'm Arabella. Elliot's girlfriend."

"Girlfriend?" She looks to Elliot. "You must spoil this one."

He nods. "Yes, I intend to. Arabella wants a red masquerade mask so—"

"Say no more." Turning around, Sally struts her devil red heels over to the silver stand and removes her latest design: a custom silk, strappy sweep train, sleeveless rouge red dress with a split front. "I think this will give you some flair," she says, and hands it to her with a scarlet red smile.

She widens her eyes. "It's beautiful. Be right back," she says, and walks along the tiles, turning left at the end of the square room into the dressing rooms.

Sally returns behind the glass counter and reaches underneath for a white box. Bringing it to the countertop, she removes the lid. "Usual for you."

He leans over and looks down at the black tuxedo. "I love it."

She places the lid back on top. "You always look sharp in them every year." She looks left, as Arabella makes her way out. "Well would you look at that. I knew that dress had an owner."

Elliot leans against the counter. "Wow," he says, blown away by her glowing soft skin and curvy thighs and legs showcasing her stunning complexion, as she twirls for them both; her beauty bones complimenting the elegance of the dress.

She smiles like a princess. "I love it!"

Elliot looks at Sally. "How much for your favorite, and longest customer?"

Sally taps on the glass and looks up, crunching numbers in her head. "I had planned to sell that at twelve-hundred, but I will do it for a thousand, and you can pay me one-hundred over ten months to help you out." She leans over the counter into his ear. "Use the money to take her out. You don't find many as high quality as her," she whispers.

He smiles and nods before looking to his sparkling princess. "You honestly have no idea how beautiful you are. There is no word to describe it."

I'll give him that. He knows how to make me feel good. With a smile on her cupid lips, she rolls her eyes, too humble to take the compliment, and returns back into the corridor of the dressing rooms, as Elliot hands Sally his credit card.

"Tell your mother I say hello. I spoke with her a few weeks ago," says Sally.

He enters his pin. "I haven't seen her in a while. How's she doing and how's George?"

She rips off the receipt and hands him the card back. "Oh, she didn't tell you?"

He can't handle any more bad news today. "Tell me what?"

Staring into the long mirror, Arabella listens from the end of the hallway as she relishes in her own beauty.

"She left George. She has a new man now," says Sally.

He widens his eyes. "What!"

She smiles. "It's all good, this new one sounds like a dream. She said his name was Enrique and he writes serenades and sings them to her as he cooks his special paella for her."

Oh for Christ sake. Arabella places her petite hands over her mouth, trying to contain the urge to break out into dying laughter.

Elliot grimaces his lips. "I never took my mother as the type to go for a Spanish man… but… as long as she's happy, I'm happy."

"Exactly Elliot. Sometimes the universe works in mysterious ways and takes us on paths we never imagined. We can't help who we fall for."

Removing her hands from her mouth, Arabella's world turns upside down, as Sallies wise wisdom sweeps her ears. *Why did you have to say that?* She gulps; her smiling reflection flipping as a raging storm of regret throws her into a hurricane; her pent-up emotions for Mr. P exploding inside of her, as single tear drop streams down her rosy cheek.

"Tears of happiness?" asks Elliot, as he appears in the reflection.

What am I doing? Staring helplessly back at him with a blank look, her heart turns cold – nothing but feeling trapped and alone clouding her as she starts to hallucinate. *I thought you didn't want me.* Watching him step towards her, she feels his muscly arms wrap tight around her waist.

"He's not for you," whispers Mr. P, as he rests his jaw on her right shoulder.

"Why do you this to me?" she weeps.

"Because I love you," says Elliot, as her distorted vision ends.

What just happened. With her ears ringing, she blinks rapidly, met with Elliot wrapped around her. "Sorry? What… did you say."

Gazing deep into her teary eyes, he smiles his pearly whites. "I said… I love you."

She gulps, as her stomach sinks. *Why did you have to say that?* Wiping her flushed wet cheeks, she exhales through her nose as his innocent eyes await. "I, I... love you too."

Melting inside with a sweeping smile across his handsome complexion, he reaches into his pocket and takes out his smartphone. "Smile," he says, and takes a picture, capturing their romantic milestone. "Remind me to have that framed." He kisses her on the cheek and turns around, leaving her to finish up.

With the dress over her arm, she turns the corner and passes it to Sally, before joining Elliot in front of the counter.

Sally hands her, and Elliot their white boxes. "I've put a red mask and a black mask in your boxes. I hope the event goes well for you both tomorrow and I hope to see you both next year. Take care now."

"Bye," says Elliot, with a smile and opens the door, holding it like a gentleman for his brunette angel. Exiting behind, he takes hold of her hand; the cold winds hammering against them as the FBI tails closely behind. He looks back at them. "Do you think I should ring my mother?"

Strolling along in silence, her chest drowns in guilt, eating away at the meaningless words she said moments ago, as the icy wind eats away at her purple hands. "Huh? Oh, I feel really weird today, so I think I'm going to just sleep it off. Do whatever."

"Good point." Arriving at the apartment, he passes her his white box. "I'll see you later then."

Entering the toasty apartment, she slams out the world behind her, as her face and hands start to defrost. Throwing the keys into the woven fruit bowl, she kicks off her brown boots and carries the white boxes over to the wardrobe. Placing them on top, she strips down before climbing into the sheets. Drifting into heaven, she lets Mr. P consume her.

WINTER WONDERLAND

Standing in front of the mirror, as Elliot fusses behind her in the reflection in search for his watch, Arabella clips her brunette hair up, showing off her beauty bones as her red dress wraps tightly around her hourglass figure.

"Found it!" shouts Elliot and wraps it around his wrist; the final piece to his attire. He looks like a true gentleman.

Turning around to him, as he approaches from behind, the florist in her adjusts his black bow tie. "Perfect." She pats down his custom black suit jacket and smiles her pearly whites at him. *No don't.* Met with parting lips, her scarlet red lipstick smudges, as their lips slowly slide their moisture. *Grrrr.* She places her right hand on his white shirt. "Right, enough of that." Sending him on his way, she walks over to the apartment door and looks down at her collection of heels. *Too many to choose.* With the stilettos of her past screaming at her, she sighs. They do seem the best fit for this outfit. *Fine.* Stepping into them, she turns around, practicing her catwalk skills up and down the laminate as she wears them in again.

Elliot emerges from the bathroom and watches her from the doorway. "Are you sure you're fine going just like that? Even the car had ice on it earlier."

She rolls her eyes. "I was made for the cold. Do you have everything?"

He does one final check in the mirror. "Yes. Yes, I do." His eyes widen, as his heart races. "Oh sweet Jesus. I haven't even checked to make sure the flowers arrived. Can you ring Clarissa?"

She looks away from him. *What am I going to tell him?* Grimacing her lips, she reaches for her silver clutch bag on the bed as she thinks of an excuse. *Oh Paris duhh.* She turns around to him. "She's in Paris. Don't worry, we have a great team. They will be there. I promise."

He sighs his relief. "I trust you." He walks over to the fruit bowl and takes his car keys. "Ok, let's go," he says, and opens the door for her.

Hugging herself tightly as the cold winter winds attack her bare legs and arms, she races to the Camaro and climbs into the passenger side seat, chattering her pearly whites away as he walks in front of the bonnet and makes his way into the driver's seat. She looks to him. "You look very handsome in that tux," she says, as the smell of his strong woody cologne and her sweet perfume fuse in the small space.

He smiles and turns the key, soaking up the sweet roar of the engine as he starts to pull away from the sidewalk. Looking in the reverse mirror, the headlights of the unmarked car shine as it starts its tail. "Words can't describe how you look."

Reaching the end of West Houston Street, they turn right, following it around as they slowly cruise along, looking for a spot amongst the line of luxury sportscars; his pride and joy gaining attention from the arriving guests. Finding a space, he shuts the engine off and brushes his hand against her glowing legs as he goes to pop the glove compartment. "I have a surprise gift for you," he says, and retrieves a small black box.

Acting surprised like she's reading a birthday card, she takes it from him. "Aww." She opens the lid - a white gold amulet, encrusted with diamonds shining back at her. She removes it and turns it around; the back engraved with the initials 'A.H & E.S'. "I love it," she smilingly says.

"Open it up."

She unlocks it. It's the moment they exchanged their romantic milestone; he spent the morning getting it custom made. She hands him the necklace and looks to her right, observing the guests congregate near the staircase of the manor, as the amulet dangles in front of her. She feels the thin silver chain caress on her beauty bones; it's elegance drawing attention to her upper beauty, as he links it together. *That's so beautiful. Hope he likes mine.*

Turning around with a pearly smile, she retrieves his surprise from her clutch bag. "Close your eyes and give me your wrists."

He follows her command. "I'm not being hand cuffed, am I?" he laughingly asks, as he places both wrists out.

She takes his right wrist first, using her sleight of hand to carefully remove the white button before threading a platinum cufflink through. She repeats on the left wrist. "There."

He opens his eyes and looks down; he has never owned a set of cufflinks. "These are amazing! Where have these been all my life," he says, as he flicks his wrists back and forth.

She places her hand on his shoulder. "Women know best," she says, as he leans in for a kiss, met with her cheek as she turns her head. She doesn't need them smudging again thank you! She opens the door and climbs out. Standing on the sidewalk, she crosses her arms as the winters ocean breeze sweeps its cold spike against her. *Brrrr. Why didn't I wear a jacket? Brrrr.*

Locking the car, he makes his way around the back, checking for paint scratches before making his way behind her. "Ready?" he asks and puts his mask on before wrapping his arms around her. Both looking across the street, they observe the winter theme manor in all its glory.

She puts her mask on, as she breathes the ocean air. "Let's go," she says, and takes his left hand.

Hand in hand, they ascend the four concrete white steps, passing under the elegantly curved wooden garden arch connected to a hedge wall either side surrounding the fortress in front of them. Stepping onto the lit pebbled path with the winter themed, white manor dead ahead, they venture along the Lyon red carpet, gazing left and right; their eyes absorbing the square front gardens exquisite beauty, as the pebbles crunch underneath their feet.

This is so beautiful. She turns her attention to the lined-up banquets either side of the path. She taps him, as he smiles and waves at the other guests stood on the lawn. "See! I told you Clarissa would pull through."

He looks ahead at the line of vibrantly welcoming colors. "They look fantastic." He breaks their joining hands and places his left arm out for her; her right arm linking around him as they reach the entrance. They both smile at the white gloved, red coat doorman.

"Good evening. Welcome to the Winter ball. Your names please?"

"Elliot Smith and Arabella Harper," says Elliot. The doorman glances down his list and spots their names. He smiles and grips the large gold handle, pulling the brown door open as he directs them inside with a courteous bow. Walking through, they step onto the black and white tiles, scaling their eyes along the beaux art hallway in awe as they pass through the overarching white pillars.

Elliot breaks their linked arms as they reach the end, pushing open the mahogany dark brown door; their ears blissfully caressed by the heavenly keys of a grand piano as they make their way into the crowded, extravagantly large winter themed ball room. They smile to the classy, dressed guests as they make their way under the icy tiered, center crystal chandelier.

Following the wide red-carpet staircase in front with her eyes, she reaches the top; fluttering inside as the giant stain glass window depicting two lovers beams its fairytale magic at her. With her rosy cheeks aching from the constant princess smile, she looks left, as he looks right, their linked arms saying goodbye as they slowly turn 180 degrees, scaling the white balcony landing before meeting in the middle as they stare up at the overlooking finely dressed guests.

"I feel like I'm in a fairytale and I just don't want to leave," she says, as she drools her heart out over this dreamy palace.

"Soak it up, it's real."

The white coat waiter approaches. "Champagne?" They both smile and take a glass, sipping on the fresh, crisp, fruity delight.

"I probably shouldn't be drinking since I'm driving."

She rolls her eyes. "Oh, lighten up and enjoy the night."

He chuckles. "Ok." Looking up, he throws it back; the dry flavor overwhelming his palette.

"Calm down, my boy. The evening has just started," chuckles Mayor Wilson, as he approaches in his tux and black mask, with his light brunette-haired wife, Melinda; the woman in red a fitting title to match her stunning dress and mask.

Elliot laughs. "Good point."

"I would take my hat off to you but then I would be bald ha-ha. Well done on organizing yet another spectacular event."

"Thank you, Mayor. The pleasure is all mine," he says, and guides his eyes to Arabella. "Let me introduce you to my girlfriend, Arabella Harper."

The Mayor looks her up and down. "Hello Arabella, you are stunning." He takes her hand and kisses it. He looks to Elliot. "A lucky man you are."

Melinda slaps him on the arm and looks to Arabella. "My apologies Arabella, I'm Melinda. His wife."

She giggles. "It's absolutely fine. Nice to meet you both. It's an honor."

Melinda looks at the men. "Why don't you both go sit upstairs by the bar and talk about whatever men discuss whilst us ladies take a stroll in the garden?" She watches as her husband puts his arm around Elliot's shoulder and guides him up the stairs before looking to her. "Men," she says, and rolls her eyes through her red mask.

I like her already. She swallows the extravagance. "Tell me about it."

Entering the grand hallway under the stain glass window staircase, they take a slow stroll along the black and white tiled long corridor; the tap of their heels echoing behind them as they enjoy the sky-high ceiling beaux art beauty with their champagne glasses wrapped in their hands.

"Men darling, they're so predictable," says Melinda.

"I know." *Actually, that's not true.* "Although… there's this one guy who is the complete opposite. Every word he speaks or action

161

he does, it's like its done with extreme confidence and a lack of care. It's not a cocky rich boy attitude either. I don't think even the word mysterious can describe truly just how mysterious he actually is."

Melinda looks intrigued. "And this guy is what in your life?"

Oh shit. I shouldn't have said that. She's gonna tell Elliot. "How well do you know Elliot?"

Melinda senses where she's going with this. "I see. You have Elliot but you like this other guy? Don't worry, we've all been there."

Reaching the end, they proceed through the double glass doors, holding their champagne glasses firmly as the ocean's cold breeze sweeps their glowing skin. Stepping along the pebbled path, Melinda guides her into the gardens labyrinth. Following it around, right, then left, Arabella runs her left hand against the freshly trimmed hedges, lavishing up her first touch of anything botanical in weeks. Finding themselves in the center, they step along the grey slabs and approach the maple bench in the corner.

"I love the dress by the way," says Arabella, as they both take a seat.

"We're twinning."

Taking a sip of her champagne in silence, Arabella listens to the gale ocean winds blow against the hedges. She grimaces her lips.

Maybe I should ask her for advice. She looks to her. "So, what would you do in my situation?"

"That's for you to decide," says Melinda, and takes out a pack of cigarettes. "Want one?"

Hmmm. "I've never actually tried one."

Melinda flicks the lighter, hovering the end over the burning flame; the smoke overpowering the ocean as it rises around them. She exhales her stresses away and looks to her. "It smells good, looks good and tastes good."

Fooling for her marketing campaign, she says, "Go on then," and takes a cigarette. Putting it between her scarlet lips, she grabs the lighter and attempts to light it.

Melinda swipes it from her mouth. "Silly girl."

She gulps. "You just offered me one?"

Throwing the lipstick-stained cigarette on the floor, she gives her a stern look. "You knew it was bad for you, yet you wanted to try. Now apply that to your situation."

Oh wow. That was so clever. She smiles at her creativity. "So, stick to the good one? Not give into the temptation. What about you? Why are you smoking?"

Melinda exhales and gives her a naughty look. "Because I'm a bad girl." She stubs the cigarette out on the side of the bench and stands. "Back to the public eye, I go," she sighs.

"I'll see you back in there. I'm going to have a moment."

Leaning back with her arms crossed, she stares up at the cloudy night sky, unable to see her favorite stars, as Melinda's pebbled steps fade in the background; the smell of smoke still lingering as she contemplates her feelings for Elliot. *He's a great guy. A true gentleman and kind. God stop already.* She shakes her head; feeling torn as she looks down at the stubbed cigarette. There's a reason she doesn't smoke; she knows it's bad and addictive, so she doesn't do it. Melinda is right. Stick with the good one! *Christ it's cold.* With her arms and legs in danger of frostbite, she stands, her teeth starting to chatter as she proceeds out of the labyrinth.

Emerging from the archway, she re-enters the winter ball room; her goosebumps fading as the toasty warmth soothes her glowing skin. Looking through the large crowds of masked guests preparing for the first dance, she tries to spot Elliot. *Where is he?* The guests take their positions under the dimmed lighting, as the slow music starts. *Oh there he is.*

"There you are. You've been ages," says Elliot, as she approaches him under the center chandelier.

"Sorry. I was just enjoying the garden." She takes his left hand and curls her fingers between his, feeling his other hand behind her back as she rests her right hand on his arm and relaxes her jaw on his shoulder. Starting to slow dance in sync with him, she catches a glimpse of the Mayor and Melinda with every slow turn. *This feels magical.* Pulling away from his shoulder, she draws her full attention to Elliot, gazing into his chocolate eyes; her tunnel vision slowing everything around her as she taps into her emotional catharsis. *Oh, why do I not feel the way you look at me.* She gulps. Nothing's coming to her, as she stares at his pale, sweaty face. The spark seems so lost in her. Can't say the same for him as he soaks up her glowing beauty; twinkling inside, as if he's been touched by an angel.

With the first dance steadily grinding to a halt, the slow song cuts. Letting go of each other, as the Mayor and Melinda approach, they face them with their backs to the red staircase.

"End of the first dance. You know the routine Elliot," says the Mayor, as Arabella raises her eyebrow.

Elliot nods. "Yes. Time for the organizer photo."

Melinda looks at Arabella in front of her. "I hope you've had time to consider your little dilemma," she says and breaks eye contact with her, as her attention is drawn to the top of the red staircase in front of her, watching as an unknown guest stands at the top; his divine beauty overpowering the stain glass window. She continues to observe as he signals goodbye to the crowd of Italian men behind him before slowly descending in style.

Arabella looks at Elliot. "Did she hear me?" she whispers, as Melinda stays locked in her dreamy gaze; the unknown man locking onto her before casting his dreamy gaze left to the Mayor. Elliot turns his head to Melinda, as the unknown guest recasts his eyes to the side of Elliot's face. Arabella follows Melinda's eyes and looks behind her. *Huh? Nothing there.* She turns back around.

Melinda snaps out of it. "Sorry. What was we talking about?"

"Organizer photo," says Elliot and looks to his girlfriend. "I forgot to mention, every year the organizers have a photo with the Mayor and Melinda to hang in the City hall. It will take about five minutes. Are you ok to wait here?"

She rolls her green eyes and shrugs. "I guess I'm going to have to."

Standing alone under the chandelier, Arabella sips on her champagne, looking to her left as an older gentleman approaches. *Please don't hit on me.*

"May I escort the pretty lady to the garden for a stroll on this fine evening?" She is grossed out; his wrinkly face suggests he's at least Barbara's age.

The unknown guest emerges from the crowd behind her; the heels of his penny loafers tapping against the black and white tiles as he signals for the older man to vacate with his scorching glare through his black mask.

She raises her eyebrow as the gentleman abruptly leaves. *What the hell! Am I that boring?*

"Your hair would look better down you know," says the seductive voice, behind her. Good lord. Elliot goes for one moment and she's been hit on twice in 30 seconds!

Great. Another one! I probably shouldn't have worn this red mask. Rolling her eyes, she slowly turns to face him. "Sorry, I have a —" Frozen, she stares up into his mystical green eyes, her heart racing as he towers his charm.

Gently caressing his smooth fingers along her blushing cheek, he continues his feather touch above her ear; the tingling sensation shooting through her, as he leans into her right ear. "Miss me?" seductively whispers Mr. P.

Frozen, she stares up into his mystical green eyes, her heart racing as he towers his charm. "You are so—" Catching him between her soft cupid lips, time slows down for the magical moment, her temple entering a fairytale meltdown as a sensational warmth and burning desire ignite inside. Closing her eyes, as their hands hold on to one another's cheeks, this kiss shows no sign of slowing down as she holds her breath; willing to suffocate to keep this euphoric moment alive. Everything she couldn't feel for Elliot erupting inside her.

He peeks out his left eye, spotting the organizers proceeding to re-enter the ballroom. Keeping the passion alive, he reaches into his inner jacket pocket and retrieves a white card. Using his sleight of hand, he maneuvers through the front slit of her dress and slides the card onto the side of her hip; held in place by the elastic waistband of her thong.

She gasps the ballroom air, as his lips pull away. *That was some—*

"You look a bit flushed. Ready for another round of dancing?" asks Elliot, as he approaches her from the right.

She slowly opens her eyes, looking at him in a dazed state, her entire body being thrown into a hurricane of chaos as a swarm of guilt, confusion, lust, and deception cloud her. She takes the champagne glass from him. *Where did he go?* Drowning out Elliot's words, she casts her eyes to the crowd in front; her heart racing as those devilish green eyes stare out at her from the crowd in front. Elliot walks in front of her, blocking her vision as he repeats her name for the fifth time. She looks up at him with a blank face, unable to process his moving lips; his voice bouncing off her ears as the bubble effect takes over. "Huh?" she says, as Mr. P exits the crowd and listens to the commotion, as Elliot starts to wave his hand in her face. She spots him to her right, and watches as he approaches the Mayor and Melinda from behind.

He taps the Mayor on the shoulder. "She's going to faint. Think how good you'd look in the re-election as a hero," he whispers. The Mayor looks behind him; too slow as Mr. P vanishes. It must be a message sent down from the heavens. Listening to his angel, he rushes into savior mode and approaches Arabella, as her ears begin to ring to the spinning room, watching as Mr. P approaches Melinda from behind. "I know a naughty girl when I see one," he seductively whispers, and slips a white card into her hand from behind. "Hotel L'Amour." He winks to Arabella, and turns left, heading for the exit, as Melinda palms the card.

Arabella's heart races. "I, I, I—" Her trembling hand drops the champagne glass; the shards covering the black and white tiles as her vision fades black, her knees giving way as her ears flatline. The ballroom fills with gasps as they watch her drop - their gasping turning to clapping, as the Mayor catches her.

Tucked away in a private room around the corner, Elliot sits on the brown couch; his fainting queen's head resting on his lap as he fans her with a magazine. He notices her arms twitch. "Arabella," says Elliot.

She slowly opens her eyelids as the makeshift wind cools against her flushed face. Staring up at him with a flustered look, she swallows the dry air as the room spins. "Where… are we?" she groggily asks.

He looks the square office over. "We're in some private room. You fainted."

Owww. She slides her hand down her leg, irritated by something digging into her hip. She slides her dress up and pulls out the white card. *Mr. P.*

Elliot looks at it. "What's that?"

She palms it. "Oh, just the tag. New pair." Bringing her hand to her chest, she stuffs it under her right breast before sitting up. The room starts to spin.

Elliot holds her, as she attempts to stand. "Easy now."

"I'm ok," she says, and finds her balance.

"We should probably go."

She yawns. "I think that's best. How long was I out for?"

He looks at his watch. "Roughly half an hour."

"Yes, ok let's go." She stretches her arms. "I'm exhausted."

Holding hands, they exit the room and turn right, following along the black and white tiled hallway before swinging left, catching the final keys of the slow music to the third dance as they enter the ballroom. The Mayor approaches with Melinda.

"Good of you to rejoin us, Arabella. You gave us all quite a scare out there," says the Mayor.

She smiles at him. "I'm not sure what happened."

Melinda reaches into her clutch bag. "If you ever need anything, here's my card darling." She passes it to her before looking at Elliot. "Now, please take your queen home. She needs her beauty rest."

Elliot surprise sweeps his brunette queen off her feet. "I will do exactly that. Thanks for the evening, it's been a great night, and thank you Mayor for saving this one." With Arabella wrapping her arms tightly around his neck, he carries her in his arms towards the exit. "She likes you."

She looks up to his sweaty face, blushing and smiling as they walk under the overarching white pillars. "You think?"

Reaching the entrance, he lowers her to the ground; his arms burning, as she finds her balance. "I do," he says, and opens the door for her. "Time to go home."

DEVIL'S LAIR

Relaxing under the pressure of the hot water splashing against her soft skin, Arabella combs her dainty fingers through her brunette hair; her mind flickering back and forth as her devious kiss from last night replays over, and over. Raining the pink tutti-frutti shower gel from above, she softly cups her tight, and rounded breasts as the gel seeps, turning to foam as she caresses them to the vision of Mr. P. Biting down on her sultry bottom lip; the foam drips around her, floating towards the drain of the walk-in shower as her fingertips softly, and slowly draw circles around her hardening nipples. She closes her pretty green eyes and widens her mouth; the showerheads whirring drowning out the escaping pleasure. Luckily, Elliot's asleep! The bathroom door opens. Spoke to soon! Interrupting her chance to reach maximum satisfaction, he steps along the moist tiles. *God sake! Why can't I have some privacy for once.* Rolling her eyes, she listens to the electric whir of his toothbrush and shakes her head. Finishing up, she slides the glass door and steps onto the tiles; the cold air penetrating her skin like blades as the goosebumps set into her glowing skin.

He spits into the sink before putting his toothbrush back on charge and turning around, grabbing the soft towel from the heated towel rack. Gently wrapping it around her soaked hourglass from behind, he listens to her oozing sounds as the warm sensation smothers its heavenly pleasure around her. "How are you feeling this morning after last night?" They haven't spoken since they got back.

She grabs the corners from him and wraps it around her front tightly. "I'm good now."

Elliot smiles at her. "That's good. I was really concerned. Have you ever fainted before?" he asks, as he shimmies past her and exits the bathroom.

"No, it's my first time!" she shouts, as he makes his way into the living room and engrosses himself in the news, yet again!

"Maybe you should see a doctor then!"

Perfect. Like music to her ears, she dries herself down and throws the towel into the basket before exiting; the apartments cold air hitting her tight skin as she walks across the laminate to her wardrobe. *What should I wear? Has to be sexy.* There it is! She retrieves her infamous black dress; the one from her unfortunate Bahamas date and lays it out on the bed. "Yes, I think you're right. It's best to see a doctor."

With his eyes glued to the flatscreen, she reaches into her underwear draw and picks out a red laced lingerie set; the devilish red screaming naughty and playful, as she slips into them. Sitting crossed legged in front of the mirror, she turns on the hairdryer; the loud blowing air drowning out the apartment. Drying away, she hears the news reporter blasting in her left ear, as he turns up the volume to drown her out. *What is wrong with him?*

Leaving her stilettos on the couch from last night, she makes her way into the living room and looks above the flatscreen for the time. It's 11:00. She leans over him and grabs her heels, his nose twitching to her flowery perfume. She moves back, his attention too focused as he awaits an update about the heist. She returns to the mirror; feeling gorgeous as her loose thick brunette waves compliment her tightly wrapped black dress around her curves. She hears him moan and turns around to face him, chucking her stilettos on the hard laminate; his eyes casting towards her as the loud bang draws him in.

He looks at the time. "Where are you going looking like that at this hour?"

She steps into her shoes. "Well I have a thing with Beatrice. We're going to get drinks. I am going to go to the doctors first."

He stands up, looking her up and down. "Well, you look amazing. Beatrice is one lucky girl," he laughingly says.

She fake smiles and grabs her clutch bag from the bed. "Bye."

He looks at her neck. "Wait. Your necklace?"

She grabs it from the top of the wardrobe and places it around her neck. "See you later," she says and steps towards the exit; the tapping of her heels fading, as he focuses his attention back on the heist update.

Slamming the door behind her, she looks around in search for her cab. *Where is it?* She frowns. *I forgot to book one, fuck sake.* She sighs and pulls out her smartphone; her glowing skin turning red as the cold attacks. Walking right, towards 3rd Avenue, she opens the cab app before looking behind at the Ford Crown Victoria tailing her. *Hmmm. Maybe.* She turns around and approaches the slowing car, as Agent Sanders winds down the passenger side window.

"Hello Arabella."

"Could I get a lift? I'm awfully cold and poor Elliot can't drive today. He's feeling under the weather," she innocently asks.

He points to the back and closes the window, watching as she climbs into the middle leather seat with a smile. With Agent Cody in the driver's seat, Sanders looks back at her through the mirror, as they slowly cruise along East 49th Street. "Hello Arabella. Where are you off to this morning?" He looks at her dress. "Lunch party?"

"Actually, Hotel L'Amour." They pick up speed as they cross over 3rd Avenue.

"So, Arabella, what's at the hotel?" asks Agent Sanders.

"Just meeting a friend. Why?"

He reaches for the glove compartment and pulls out a photo. "This friend?"

Shit! She gulps; her face lighting up bright red, as a picture of her and Mr. P kissing catches her out. "Why do you have that?"

He turns around to face her. "We were doing some surveillance; the photographer couldn't resist throwing that in for us," he says and elbows Agent Cody briefly as they chuckle away. He looks back at her with a serious face. "What nationality is he?"

She gulps. *What do I do? I don't want to lose him.* Her protective instinct takes over. "I don't know. Why do you care?"

Agent Cody turns right, onto Maddison Avenue. "He must have an accent?" he asks.

She raises her hands. "His voice is deeply mysterious. I have asked him before."

Agent Sanders raises his eyebrow. "Appeal to me and Agent Cody here, Arabella, and you can have this photo. Why is he seen exiting a crowd full of suspected Sicilian and American mafia members moments before he kisses you?"

Ok, now they're just being silly. She laughs. "Do you know anything about him?"

"We just learnt of him last night, so feel free to enlighten us," says Sanders.

She sighs. "He's an investor. He owns the hotel. He's likely just working his way around the room. He's a charmer. It's what he does."

Agent Cody turns left onto East 61st. "What's his name?"

Technically I'm not lying here. "That one truly is a mystery. I have been asking him ever since," she says, as the agents give each other a raised eyebrow.

"I'll take your word for it," says Agent Sanders, and hands her the photo.

Turning left, onto 5th Avenue, they pull into the red cobbled lane of the hotel. Agent Cody looks back to her, as the red coat approaches. "We all have our secrets. Agent Sanders here collects rocks," he says, met with a sarcastic grin, as the door opens.

Standing under the glass roof, she fixes her hair as the fountains bliss unwinds her flustered mind. *Hope he's here.* Brushing her hands down her dress, she ascends the white stairs, smiling her pearly whites to the doormen, as they open the gold framed doors in line with her pace. Leaving a tapping echo behind her, she approaches the reception. *Oh, why don't you take a day off.*

"Welcome to Hotel L'Amour. What is the nature of your visit?" asks Chloe, with a professional smile.

Tapping away on the mahogany counter with her sugar cherry acrylics, she gives her an evil glare. "What do you think," she says, sarcastically.

The evil villain screws her face up. "Please go up, Arabella," she says, patronizingly. Well that wasn't very professional!

Awful cow! With a fake smile, she spins around and struts towards the steel doors; the guard hitting the control panel behind him, as she crosses the white marble. The doors open. She smiles and enters, watching the lobby light fade behind her. Reaching into her clutch bag, as the devil red lights illuminates the lift, she retrieves her pink lip gloss. *I want you to know... No, I want you to tell me why you...* Rehearsing what she intends to say, she coats her lips.

Reaching the top, she brushes herself down once more. "Welcome to floor one-hundred. The Penthouse," says the seductive recording. The door slowly opens; her eyes saved this time by the miserable grey clouded sky. Stepping onto the black and white tiles, her heart races into oblivion as a whiskey glass flies past her face and hits the wall to her right at full force, covering the table and floor in shards.

"FUCK!" aggressively shouts Mr. P.

She cautiously approaches the corner and watches him through the glass wall reflection. He's standing shirtless and watching the news on his new flatscreen between the coffee table and the long couch. He must have grown tired of looking at himself! Overhearing the news anchor repeat that the second member of the City Council heist has been captured, she raises her eyebrow.

He spots her out his left eye and hits the power button, turning off the flatscreen. Time for another show! "Just when I thought god was playing tricks on me, here you are. The biggest trick of them all," he says, as she moves behind the nearest small couch.

She looks him and down and raises her arms in the air. "Here I am. Once again," she says, dramatically.

He puts his veiny hands in his black suit trouser pockets; his muscly arms untensing as he turns right on the Persian rug and slowly walks around the coffee table, looking down at the rugs bordered pattern beneath his bare feet. He stops at the edge and closes his eyes.

"Tell me why you're here," he says, and listens to her heels begin their walk.

She slowly steps to the end of couch. "Why did you kiss me last night?" she asks, as she turns right, and right again onto the Persian rug; her heels now silenced.

Continuing to look down, he chuckles in silence. "Carpe diem." That would be 'Seize the day' for all those non-Latin speakers.

Standing between the front of the small couch and the coffee table, she steps out of her stilettos and places them, and her clutch bag, on it. "Do you want to tell me why you up and left me that evening?"

He smirks. "The flame burned too hot for me."

She veers left and takes a slow, silent walk between the coffee table and the long couch; the soft Persian rug caressing the soles of her smooth feet as his broad shoulders and shredded back tease. "What does that even mean?"

He looks up to the ceiling, carefully constructing his response as to not reveal his dark secret. "In my world…" He sighs. "In my world…"

"Spit it out," she says, and turns the last corner, coming face to face with the devil himself, as he spins around.

Sinking his cold glare into her, he moves towards her. "In my world, danger awaits those who let emotions distract them," he says, and towers over her.

She closes her eyes, the power of his woody scent teasing her in every way, as she feels his warm thumb run along her glossed bottom lip. "Mmhhmmmm."

Like the tease that he is, he removes his thumb and spins back around, turning his back on fate as he slowly steps off the rug; his godly body flexing its divinity, as he walks across the tiles towards the corner wall. "I can't have distraction."

Is he calling me a distraction? Oh he has some serious nerve. Biting her tongue as her burning secret brews inside, she steps to the edge of the rug. "You think giving myself away to you is a distraction now!"

Taken back in shock, he pauses and frowns. "What?" he asks, and spins back around to face her.

She raises her hands in the air and twists her tongue. "Exactly," she says, with a flushed face. "Now you know." She listens to him sigh and look up. "I also have a boyfriend now. Your fault!"

He releases a single, deep chuckle of disbelief and casts his deadly gaze into her, as he slowly steps towards her. Bringing his right hand to her cheek, he sweeps her dark tamed hair behind her ear; her body shivering to his tingling touch as he devilishly leans in. "Then you best know how to keep a secret," he temptingly whispers, and steps back, keeping his green temptation locked with a smirk, as their sexual chemistry and lusting desire becomes unbearable.

Why did you have to say that! Oh, no, no, no, no, no. This is wrong. With her insatiable appetite overflowing, she exhales heavily, her heart racing as the flutters shoot down her. "You really are—"

Racing towards him, he leans in and picks her up by her curvy waist; her arms and legs wrapping tightly around him as he finishes off her sentence, "Your fucking nightmare," and spins her around, slamming her against the wall; her passion fueled adrenaline blocking out the pain, as she digs her claws deep into his back.

"What's your plan with me?" she sweetly asks, as he grips the top of her dress.

"Well first of all," he says and tears the black dress from top to bottom with ease. "That's got to go." Watching her bite down on her sultry bottom lip, with her eyes widening, he reaches behind her with his left hand and unclips her red bra with one pinch before burying his right into her sweaty cleavage. "And now this," he says; the straps gliding so fast along her smooth arms as he rips it from her. Dropping it to the floor, her perfectly rounded breasts breathe the penthouse air, as he leans his parted lips towards her.

She stops him with her index finger and leans into her alpha's ear. "You forgot my panties," she seductively whispers.

Cupping her rounded breasts in his veiny hands, he squeezes them, twisting her nipples between his fingers and thumbs. He leans into her ear. "You're playing with me now," he says, dominantly, and licks her ear. Traveling his tongue towards her juicy lips, he feels her steam exhale its warmth as he nibbles down her neck; her nipples hardening to his soft twists. Reaching her parted lips, he stares deep into her flushed face, as she pulls his forehead to hers. Twisting her nipples hard, he catches her bottom lip, feeling her heat exhale against his top lip as she looks up and releases a sensational moan.

Time for her red thong! Releasing his bite, he trails his soothing fingers down her curvy temple, as she throws her arms around his neck and hugs him tightly; her hardened nipples pressing against his steamy chest, as his hands glide around to her stomach before journeying underneath her inner thighs. Gripping her cheeks tight, he lifts her up; her legs taking their new position as her thick thighs wrap around his neck. "You smell, exotic," he says, as his cock hardens against his suit pants. Feeling her grip his thick black hair, he lets go of her peachy cheeks and steps back, using his shoulders to hold her balance before removing his trousers; his erection escaping as he drops everything down and kicks them from around his ankles. Returning her to the wall, he raises her legs above his head. Sliding the red lace down her smooth legs, he ducks under and re-emerges.

She blocks his access with her hand. "I think you're forgetting something," she says, and looks to her panties dangling around her legs. Watching him drop them to the floor, she wraps her thighs tightly around his neck, as his hands palm her cheeks. Leaning against the wall, she spreads her pink lips for him, looking up as her mouth parts to his circling tongue. Gripping his wild hair with her left hand, she twists her marble nipple with her right and thrusts her hips; riding her come soaked lips up and down like a rodeo, as her thighs spasm in sync to her lustful moans. Feeling his buried tongue whisking up against her g spot, her temple spikes with intense waves of stimulating pleasure; the penthouse capturing her deep and loud moans, as the euphoric sensation shoots through her. Pulling his laced tongue out, he slides up her soft pink; her moans intensifying as the tip of his tongue draws heavenly circles.

With his neck burning, he brings her away from the wall and lowers her down; her arms and legs assuming their normal position as they wrap around his neck and waist. He pushes her back against the wall, and presses against her forehead, their majestic green eyes exploring one another's fiery blaze, as she bites his lip and tastes herself. Teasing with the tip of his cock, he brushes the outside of her tight and warm entrance.

Lightly clawing her alpha's shaven face, she feels his hands spread her inner thigh. "Gahhh," she gasps, as her moist entrance spreads to his thick tip. He releases a powerful thrust. The penthouse fills with a loud, sharp gasp, as he penetrates. She didn't do that with Elliot! Leaning her head over his shoulder, she squeezes him tightly, her cheeks flushed as her other cheeks smash against his wall, as he smashes against her wall. She digs her claws deep into his back; his thick skin enjoying the kitten scratch as his thrusts gain power. She starts to hyperventilate, her legs shaking uncontrollably as her moaning pitch changes; his ears enjoying her high pitch screams as the pressure around his cock tightens. She rolls her eyes up, drowning in heavenly lust. She leans into his right ear. "I want you to hear everything you've done to me," she moans, piercing his ear drum with her orgasmic screams as she enters the longest orgasm of her life, thrusting her hips as her pussy leaks around the tight gap; the black and white tiles drenched as he pulls out.

Resting against the corner wall, sweat drips down her flushed face as she catches her breath, observing Mr. P to her left as he searches through his wardrobe and retrieves a black tie. He slides the mirror door shut and walks towards her, locking his glistening eyes into her as he approaches. Their noses lightly graze. She watches him go around the corner. *What's he doing now?*

Listening to him tapping on something, she hears his footsteps come back. She looks up into his towering dominance. "Into BDSM are we?" she hornily asks, as she trails her fingers along his rippled abs.

He shakes his head sideways. "Do you trust me, Arabella?"

"I do." Biting down on her juicy bottom lip, she turns around; his semi pressing against her plumped bottom as he brings the tie over her face. She lifts her hair up and rolls her eyes up, her vision turning black as he loops the left end, over and under the right end, and pulls tightly before looping it again.

He puckers his lips and blows on the back of her left ear; her body shivering as she sweats away. He switches sides and leans into her right ear. "In my world, risk is part of the fun," he alluringly whispers.

She turns around. "Show me," she softly says. *Be careful what you ask for!*

Stood behind her with his veiny hands gripping her curvy waist, he guides her across the tiles; the smell of her strawberry shampoo hitting him, as they swing right, towards the elevator.

We're going right? Surely not. "You can't be serious?"

He chuckles as he leans over her and hits the call button. "Oh... I'm serious." The sound of the steel doors penetrate her ears. Aroused, and nervous, she lets him guide her inside, his half erect cock brushing against her peaches as her bare feet step onto the glossy floor. Reaching the opposite mirror, he turns her around and releases her. "Have fun," he says and steps back.

"What?" Silence sweeps the small box, as the doors close. *Unbelievable!* Darkness fills with the devils shade as the light breaches her blindfold, listening to the elevator start its 100-floor descent. *Why does this seem slower than usual? God, what do I do?* With her heart racing, she reaches for the knot; stopped as the swift force of muscles pin her wrists against the mirror.

"That's not for you to remove," he dominantly asserts, as their lips graze.

She exhales her submission, her breathing gaining momentum as they slowly free fall. "You're quite the devil," she breathlessly whispers.

He leans into her left ear, hitting her with the power of his woody cologne. "You have yet to see the devil," he says, and licks the side of her neck slowly; her wrists flinching as her body lapses into a sensational whirlwind.

"Why… are we going… so slow?" she asks, heavily exhaling against his cologne as his teasing becomes excruciating.

Sucking away on her neck, he opens the corner of his lips. "I slowed…," distracted by her moan, he releases her neck, "it down. We have ten minutes before this reaches the lobby," he says, and bites down again.

"That's… very specific, Mr. P."

"It is," he murmurs, and releases his clamp, pulling his neck away as her body spirals into a deep lust. Pressing his forehead against hers, he listens as her breathing consumes the small space between them.

"What are you wait—" Caught between his lips, she deeply exhales through her nose, her struggling desire to touch him becoming unbearable as she attempts to break free from his pin. He's too strong. Slipping and sliding, she looks up; the elevator drowning in heavy moans as he pulls down on her bottom lip.

"Gahhh," she gasps. Feeling his tightening grip loosen, she slides out and pushes his rippled abs.

"Feisty," he says, and steps backwards.

She smiles, wittingly. "My turn," she says, and blindly steps forwards; stopped as he inside swoops his muscly arms between her juicy thighs and lifts her up; her fingers gripping his thick, wild hair, as her back slams against the mirror.

"I don't think so," he says, and leans into her neck, right side; her chest raising as the elevator fills with a loud gasp.

Sitting on the railing, with her legs raised, she feels his hard cock pressing. "Put it in," she pants.

He releases her neck. "We have seven minutes. Not yet," he says, and starts his journey down her temple, leaving a wet trail as his knees get lower, and lower.

Squeezing his hair to his silver tongue flicking against her rosy tip, she moans to his euphoric tease; her growing pleasure overpowering his dominance as she pushes him down and buries his face. Rolling her eyes back, she wraps her legs tightly around his neck, her thighs beginning to tremble...

Meanwhile in the lobby, six and a half minutes later... Dakota smiles. It's the New York Live reporters and they're aiming their camera straight at her.

"We're here with the owner of Hotel L'Amour, Dakota. How does it feel to be the youngest hotel owner in Manhattan at twenty-three?"

"I haven't quite grasped that reality yet," she fake laughs.

"Mind telling us how you achieved your success?"

"Now that would be telling. Come on let's take a tour," she says, and turns around, waving to Chloe to her left, before turning back around to face the camera. "Oh, and if you're in Manhattan this weekend, all rooms are half price," she says, and turns around.

"You heard that folks, half—" The elevator door fling open. The camera turns to it, as the sound of intense orgasms leak out into the lobby. "Call me promiscuous, Jim, but this is another level," says the camera man, as Mr. P's thrusting power displays to the world; his face looking down with her blindfold not revealing their identities.

"I am soooo sorry," says Dakota, as she widens her enraged eyes, scorching her fiery glare into the devil himself.

SUSPICIOUS ACTIVITY

Sliding the steamy glass door, Arabella steps out; the water dripping from her glowing skin as it splashes onto the ocean blue marble tile floor. She looks around the penthouse bathroom in search for a towel, spotting a white door to her left. She opens it. Viola! Reaching inside the heated space, she grabs the warm white towel from the top of the pile before locking the heat back in. Turning back, she smothers her tight moist skin in the soft fabric; her steamy sensational wrapped moment interrupted as she steps along the moist tiles to the bathroom door. *What's he laughing at?* She presses her ear against the door; her jealousy kicking in as she hears the voice of another woman. She sounds British.

"You can't be doing that! We have an operation to run!" shouts Dakota.

"Oh, give it a rest. If you wanted any say on who or where I fuck, you should have thought about that in university." Arabella opens the door partially and peeks through the gap. She can't see her, only hear her.

"Are you insane? This isn't about university! This is about you having a job to do! Not fucking tarts on my time for the world to fucking see. It's called staying anonymous. Dickhead!"

"Where are you going now?" shouts Mr. P, as Arabella hears the elevator open.

"To run your businesses! Get a grip of yourself. Go sort out shit in Italy and I'll see you when you get back. And no, I still won't fuck you. Twat!"

Arabella widens her eyes in shock. *Goddd, she is scary.*

Exiting the bathroom, she turns left, wrapped in a towel as she glances over at Mr. P; his shredded arms spread across the top of the long couch, as he stares back at her, wearing nothing but black suit trousers.

"Italy?" she asks.

He frowns at her. "How much did you hear of that?"

Stepping onto the Persian rug, she drops the towel and climbs on top of him, biting down on her sultry bottom lip as she throws her arms around him. "Enough to know I'll miss you."

He looks up to her towering beauty. "What did you think about her tone?"

She combs her fingers through his dark hair. "She sounds rather jealous."

He places his veiny hands on her curvy waist and chuckles. "Imagine that every day through uni." He taps her bottom and rolls her to his left side. He stands. "You best be getting back to your boyfriend. I have to go to Italy," he says, as he walks towards his wardrobe.

What are you hiding? "Can I ask you something?"

He smirks as he throws the white shirt around his muscles. "You may find yourself not liking the answer if you do," he mysteriously says.

She takes a deep breath. "Are you a member of the Sicilian Mafia?"

He drops the black socks, pausing as he stares emptily inside the wardrobe. He spins around; his hands in his pockets as he locks his glaring eyes into her and slowly walks behind the small couch. "I like that. You are very brave."

She looks confused. "Brave?"

He veers right, walking towards the edge of the couch. "If I told you I was, you would do what?" he says, as he turns left.

She hasn't thought this one through. "Well erm... I'm not entirely sure. Nothing? That's your business."

He turns left again, his feet brushing along the Persian rug as he faces her. "Interesting. How did you reach that conclusion?"

She exhales. "Well... for starters, everyone apart from Chloe is Italian in this hotel. You have an Italian themed club house. You have money and lots of property. You throw a whiskey glass at the wall when they announce the second member of the heist was captured."

He towers over her and leans into her right ear. "You fuck better than your detective skills," he seductively whispers.

She bites down on her bottom lip, extremely turned on by his dominance and pulls his wrist towards her entrance. "Mmmmmm," she says, as he pulls out. "You're really good at changing the subject."

He laughs and widens his shirt, as he slowly spins around. "You see? No tattoo."

She shrugs. "Anyone could just not get a tattoo."

He smirks. "Very good. You are, however, missing one crucial piece to this wild puzzle," he says, and returns to his wardrobe.

Hmmmm. I have no idea. She stands up. "What is that then?" she asks and makes her way to the corner wall. *He's ripped my dress. Shit.* "Do you have a dress by the way?"

Throwing his black jacket on, he turns around and enters the bedroom. Dakota stays here on occasion. He returns with an identical version. "Here," he says, and chucks it to her, as the elevator door pings open. He walks towards her, as Gino turns the corner, and places his right hand on her rosy cheek, gazing over her stunning beauty. "Well isn't it obvious? I'm British. Fully British."

She grimaces her lips. *That's a good point.* "Hmmm. Suppose. When will I see you again?"

He leans in. "When you least expect it," he mysteriously whispers and kisses her forehead. "Gino is waiting for you. I have to go."

"Ready, Arabella?" asks Gino, as she watches her alpha enter the bedroom.

She turns to her chauffer. "Yeah."

Pulling up on East 49th street, Arabella climbs out the back seat and slams the door. Making her way towards her apartment, she smiles and waves goodbye to Gino. The agents in their unsuspecting tail observe her walk right on by and enter her apartment.

Agent Cody looks through the reverse mirror, noting down the registration of the Phantom. "Chauffeured around by some old guy in a luxury car. There's something wrong here. Check the registration."

"Way ahead of you." He presses the enter key on his laptop. "The car is registered to a Gino Ajello, fifty-nine-year-old, Italian male. He's clean."

Cody looks suspicious. "What about family?"

Agent Sanders clicks on the daughter; his face dropping as he reaches for his smartphone. "This just took a turn." He dials his boss. "Sir, we need another tail for Elliot Smith. We will update when we get back." He hangs up; his request was granted.

"What's up?" asks Agent Cody.

"His daughter is Angela Ajello, married to the one and only Francesco Agosti, a capo of the Sicilian Mob," he says, as Agent Cody starts the car.

Looking from her apartment window to avoid Elliot, Arabella watches as Gino drives past. Turning around, she sits on the bed and looks to her right, glancing over at him still glued to the couch. *What has happened to him? Maybe this heist thing has taken a toll.*

"Quickly, come here. You don't want to miss this," he shouts, as he waves his hand to rush.

Racing over, she looks at the screen. *Oh my god.* She gulps, as her cheeks turn red. It's her in the elevator on the primetime news again.

"Oh my god!"

Elliot laughs. "Best thing I've seen all year. That's cheered me right up."

She looks to him. "I didn't know you were unhappy?"

He grabs the letter to the side of him and passes it to her. "I've been placed on six months stress leave. Apparently, it's been noticed at work. It's fully paid but I need to keep busy, or I'll go crazy. Maybe I can come help at the shop?"

Absolutely not. She fake smiles. "Let's enjoy the holiday first, then we shall see what happens."

He raises his eyebrow at her neck. "Where's your necklace?"

She brings her dainty hands to her neck. *Did I leave it at the penthouse? I don't think I took it off. Hmmm.* She stays composed. Nothing is coming to her. "Oh, it's probably on the bed somewhere. I just took it off.," she says, and turns around before laying back on the bed.

"Did you see they caught the second guy?" he loudly asks.

"Yes, I heard about it. Good job." *Let's look actually.* She loads up the web browser and searches the history of the Sicilian Mafia. *Interesting.*

REKINDLING THE FIRE

With a new year, new me attitude, Arabella crosses the busy East 90th Street, as Elliot sits in his Camaro, unable to keep his eyes off her tight Demin jeans and black heels as they radiate her stifling beauty. Reaching the sidewalk, she turns around to him; her long and curled brunette locks fighting against the wind as she signals one moment through the traffic. *I'm sure she will be fine.* She takes a deep breath and looks up at the gold sign reading 'Campbell and Co', gulping as her stomach turns. She looks through the open lounge window. The lights are on. Clarissa must be behind the counter. She takes another deep breath and steps towards the entrance. *Breathe...* She grips the handle and pushes it, looking down at the grey carpet to hide the nerves as the warmth hits her flushed face. Anxiously peeking her eyes at the glass counter, as the door swings closed behind her, she peels her sad look up and locks eyes with the blonde flaxen queen. *What on earth is she wearing?* Her sadness flips, trying to maintain a serious composure as the desire to laugh imminent, staring at her in a black beret and a black and white striped mime top with a red scarf. She's overdoing this France thing a bit! It's like a wild west showdown as the shop lays silent; even tumbleweed makes more noise than this!

Clarissa reaches underneath her and whips out a delicacy. "Baguette?"

She bursts into laughter, as the tears stream down her face. She watches as Clarissa drops the bread on the floor and rushes around the glass counter, met with welcoming arms; their bodies colliding as they squeeze one another tightly. "I've missed you. I'm so sorry for being like that," she weeps.

Clarissa's red beret hangs on as they move side to side. "I've missed you more." They are literally not letting go at this point. Oh, finally!

Arabella makes her way along the grey carpet into the open lounge, throwing her bag onto the couch before taking off her fur coat. Moving to her bestie behind the counter, her white top matches Clarissa's white pants, as she shimmies behind her and takes a seat to her left. Resting against her left arm on the glass, she gazes over Clarissa's wild outfit with a pearly smile; the smell of France rising from below. *I knew this would be fine.* She moves her foot. The sound of crunching floods the shop floor. Won't be eating that I guess!

"How was Paris then?"

Clarissa looks like she's about to have an orgasm. "Take me back! Shopping down Champs-Elysees felt soooo magical," she says, dreamily.

"I'm jealous."

Clarissa slides the stool from underneath her and disappears into the back. "Shut your eyes!" she shouts, as her bestie listens to the creaking steps of her ascending. "Open."

Oh wow. Her green eyes light up as she's handed a Christian Dior bag. "Seriously?" She places the bag onto the counter and reaches inside, the soft silk massaging against her hands as she pulls it out. "I feel so spoilt right now. It's gorgeous. Thank you," she says, pressing the black slit dress up against her. Placing it back inside, she hugs her before placing the bag down to her left and retaking her seat in line with the blonde queen.

"I knew you would love it. How's Elliot?"

She sighs. "Good."

Clarissa knows her better than anyone; the one worded response isn't fooling her. "Just good? What's going on?"

She rolls her eyes. "He's just not as I thought, if that makes sense?" Clarissa gives her a raised eyebrow. "What I mean is... he's just not spontaneous. He's a nice guy but I need more." She spots Elliot approaching. *Oh I forgot about that. Christ.* "Oh, and he got put on stress leave so I told him he could come join us on the first day. Sorry!" The door opens. Clarissa faces him and fake smiles as he walks through, as she absorbs the unexpected bombshell.

He smiles back. "Hey Clarissa, it's been a while. I hope you don't mind me dropping by?"

She looks at Arabella for a split second with her mouth wide open as she tries to conjure a rapid response in the awkward moment. "Umm..." She looks down at her coffee cup. "Sure, I'll take a latte from around the corner."

Arabella stands and looks at him. "Make mine an iced coffee." The gentleman he is obliges and exits.

Clarissa immediately turns to Arabella. "What the hell was that? It's like he's died inside!"

She shrugs. "He's been put on stress leave. I thought maybe this could do him some good," she says, and stands, shimmying past and making her way into the workshop. *Mmmmmm.* She works her way around the table, her nostrils reconnecting with her dearly beloved flowers, lavishing up the heavenly scent.

Sitting behind the glass counter, Clarissa starts getting used to this, having taken advantage of Elliot for the past four hours. He's swapped event planning for delivery service, as she watches him re-enter for a third time; his hands holding three ham and cheese paninis for lunch.

Arabella ventures out from the workshop, her parched throat dying to be quenched as she gazes over at the glass counter. "Where's the drinks?"

He looks down. "Oh, darn. Let me run back."

She rolls her eyes and races to the couch, grabbing her jacket in a hurry and moving towards the glass counter as she throws it around her. "Don't bother, I'll do it," she rudely says, and storms out in frustration.

Clarissa smiles to him and taps on the stool next to her. "Take a seat.," she says, as he slips behind her. She stares over his tired looking complexion. "You know why she's like that right?"

He picks up the panini and takes a bite as he thinks about the question. He swallows and looks to her. "I think it's just that time of the month."

She shoves him hard on the shoulder. "Spontaneous!"

He gives her the blank look. "Huh?"

She rolls her blue eyes. "She tells me you haven't been very lively. She feels like the fun has gone."

He raises his right eyebrow. "You mean she's like this because of me?" He really doesn't understand women does he!

A cunning grin sweeps across her face as an outrageous idea comes to her. "I know what she wants."

He raises the panini to his mouth. "You are her best friend after all. I'm all ears."

Clapping in excitement, she leans into his ear, as he takes a bite, chewing on the delicacy.

"Two words. Engagement ring."

The shop floor explodes with coughing as he chokes on his bread, lowering the panini down his cherry red face looks at her in disbelief. "I'm sorry, what?" he sputters.

She slowly nods. "Yup! That's right. If you want her around, that's the way to her heart." He stands up. "You know what? You are right. I was planning on buying her a replacement necklace, but I think I'll just use the money for a ring instead."

She has no idea what he's talking about. "Necklace?"

"Oh, I bought her a necklace for the Winter ball and then she lost it." He sucks in and shimmies behind her. "When would you suggest I propose?", he asks and makes his way to the front of the counter.

Clarissa raises her index finger to her cheek, grimacing her lips as she thinks. "Well it's the end of January now. You would need to think of where to propose so I would say the first day of spring."

He walks towards the entrance, holding the handle as he looks back to her. "I'll text you if that's ok. I'm going to search for one now. Can you drop her back for me?"

She nods, watching as he exits in a hurry.

Arabella re-enters holding three different types of coffee with a puzzled look swept across her. *What's happened?* She look over at Clarissa tucking into her panini. "Where's he off to?" she asks and makes her way to the counter.

Clarissa swallows her bite, trying to keep cool with this burning secret. "He said he had to go do something. Asked if I could take you back later. I said no problem."

She places the coffee holder on the counter and grabs a white cup, quenching her thirst as she devours the first sip of her iced coffee. *Ahhh.*

Working away in the workshop together, the table vibrates. Clarissa grabs her buzzing smartphone and opens it up. It's a text from Elliot.

She notices her face blushing with excitement. It's like C's forgotten who's in front of her. "What's up?"

With a shifty look, Clarissa places her smartphone back on the wooden top. "Nothing, just B. She's back from Tenerife tomorrow."

She squints her eyes. "Oh, really? I spoke to her the other day. She's been back for two weeks."

Twirling her golden locks in her fingers, she contemplates an adequate response. "I can't tell you, it's a secret." Talk about digging a deeper hole!

Arabella stands and points behind her. "Do you mind passing me the red ribbon?" she asks, innocently.

Turning around, Clarissa grabs the ribbon; the sound of metal chair legs scraping along the floor behind her as her brunette bestie throws herself onto the table, stretching her arm out and stealing her smartphone. Gulping, Clarissa turns back around, watching as she reads the message. "Surprise!"

She puts the smartphone down and props her elbows on the wooden tabletop, placing her head in her hands as she shakes her head in frustration. *No. No. No. No. No. I can't. I just can't.* "I'm going to say no."

Clarissa frowns. "What!"

She takes a deep breath and stands. "Give me a moment," she says, and slides the chair from underneath her. Ascending the archway, she hits the light switch off and makes her way into the dimmed open lounge, staring out at the winter darkness; the sidewalk glowing yellow as the streetlamps turn on.

Laying back on the couch, she closes her tired eyes, enjoying the bliss silence as her imagination takes over. The thought of her and Elliot, hand in hand, standing at the alter in the ballroom of Hotel L'Amour takes over. She breaks their eye contact, and looks right, her eyes trailing along the long aisle as they follow the red carpet. There he is! Mr. P, standing at the end with a cunning grin swept across his face, as he locks his smoldering stare into her innocence. He spins around and slowly walks to the exit, turning right as he ventures towards the garden. She releases Elliot's hands and rushes down the aisle; her long white wedding dress trailing behind her as she follows the tapping of his penny loafers. Racing along the red-carpet hallway, she approaches the silver door as the voice of Elliot calls her name; his voice fading behind her as she bursts into the exquisite garden.

Looking left, then right, as the door swings closed behind her, she's taken by surprise as Mr. P comes from her right and swiftly picks her up; her legs and arms wrapping around his tuxedo, as her back slams against the door. Pulling him in closer, she sinks her scarlet red lips deep into his warm moisture; their romance flame igniting its wild sparks amongst their exploding passion. He runs his hands under her wedding dress, sliding along her smooth and thick thighs with his fingertips; his stimulating touch shooting through her as she gently scratches her pretty nails along his gorgeous face. Widening her lips, she lets her moans escape, as he brings his hands back to the surface, tearing the wedding dress from her chest with his mighty strength. She breaks their locked lips and pulls his face down to her chest, looking up to the stars as he dominates, releasing a deep moan to the sensation of his sucking pleasure. Hit with an intense force against her back, Elliot bangs repeatedly against the door, as he screams her name... *Arabella ... Arabel—*

She intensely gasps the floral scent in the open lounge, opening her eyes as she awakens from her lustful nightmare. Sitting up, she pants and shakes as an uncomfortable sense of guilt settles in the pit of her stomach. *I can't do it.* She stands up, inhaling, and exhaling through her nose to claim back control. Making her way into the back room, she's met with deep blue eyes as Clarissa gazes over her sweaty, flushed face.

"Made a decision?" asks Clarissa.

She starts to assist with the clearing up. "I think I'm going to see how I feel at the time."

Clarissa grabs her coat. "I knew you would. You have that new dress as well. Just don't let him tear it after."

She rolls her eyes, and turns around, walking back towards the archway before stopping and looking back to the horny blonde. "Always sex with you."

Returning to the open lounge, she grabs her coat and bag, throwing them around her as Clarissa turns off the lights and emerges from the archway. They both make their way to the shop entrance.

"It's so dark outside. Spring needs to come quick," says Clarissa, as she locks up; her red beret blowing off as she turns the key.

Arabella bends down and grabs it, laughing as she brushes the top and tries it on. "Bonjour," she giggles, and curtsies.

"Very funny," she says, and snatches it off her head, on route to the car. Arabella turns around and releases a sigh of joy, smiling as normality returns to her life.

BEATRICE

Stood naked in front of her white wardrobe, Arabella gazes out her apartment window, the clear crystal blue sky and blush pink blossoming trees a refreshing change as spring arrives. *Hmmmm. What should I wear?* She grabs two playsuits, white, and pink and turns around to Elliot on the couch. "Which one?"

He stands and walks towards her with a chirpy smile. "Definitely white."

She chucks the white playsuit on the bed, as he leans in for a kiss, feeling his hands swoop behind her and gripping her cheeks. "What's got into you," she says, as her nostrils devour his heavenly cologne.

"Have I ever told you how great you look?" What in the devil has happened to this guy? She presses her hand against his abs and looks up at his glowing face. "What's got into you all of a sudden?"

"It's the start of spring. What's the point of moping around," he says, and drops the pink playsuit from her left hand before gripping the back of her curvy thighs and sweeping her off her feet; her arms and legs wrapping tightly around him as her peachy ass presses against the wardrobe. "Tonight."

Oh god, this is actually happening. She shrugs her shoulders. "Tonight what?"

He leans into her, grazing his moisturized lips against hers. "Yes. Tonight. Me. You. Classy restaurant. My treat." He mistakes her guilt for blushing. "Your rosy cheeks say enough. Meet back here for seven." He leans in; she doesn't stop him, as he slides his lips between hers, slipping and sliding as their moisture builds; her stomach moving in and out as flutters take over. It's been three months since she's had any action. Give her a break!

She closes her eyes, running her hands down his pink shirt in a blind attempt to unbutton it. With her chest moving up and down amongst the sliding rhythm, she feels his right-hand caress down her temple, trailing down, and down, his middle finger spreading her lips as it slides. It's absolutely soaked!

He breaks their intense kiss. "Save this for tonight," he passionately whispers, and gently lowers her back onto the bed, letting her unwrap herself from his body before turning around. "I'll see you later!" Unbelievable!

Tilting her head forwards, she rests her chin on her collar bone; her breasts blocking half her view as she watches him exit the apartment through her raised legs. Keeping the position, she journeys down her soft and tight skin with her left hand; the tips of her acrylics lightly scratching along her stomach in passing. She creates a V shape with her two fingers and presses on the outside, spreading her lips with her widened fingers. She brings her right hand over the top and dips her middle finger straight inside, the stimulating brush against her g spot shooting through her goddess temple. Leaning her head back, she closes her eyes, her freshly washed hair resting against the playsuit as she bites down on her cherry bottom lip. She pulls out her soaked finger and slides up her soft pink lips, delicately applying pressure to her clit; her index finger joining in as she performs circle motions. Picking up the speed, her legs start to spasm, as she releases her trapped lip, drowning the apartment in her deep moans as the bed begins to wobble; her ass thrusting up and down as her arm burns to the intensifying pace. She introduces her third middle finger and swipes side to side as silky pleasure slowly drips. Panting heavily, she raises her lower back, faster and faster she slides as her mouth opens wide; the orgasmic scream escaping her lips as her legs rapidly tremor.

Laying on the bed covered in her own mess, her sex drive screams for more as she pants away. Dangling her feet over the edge, she sits up; her back imprinted with the threaded pattern of her playsuit as she stands. Moving to the wardrobe, she opens the top drawer and reaches inside; her fingers brushing against the lace fabric as she wraps her dainty fingers around her 12-inch rubber cock. Fucking hell! Placing it on top of the wardrobe, she reaches back inside to retrieve her lube. She flicks the cap, and stands the dildo on its suction cup, pouring the gel as she slides her left hand up and down.

With her endorphins going parabolic, she races to the bathroom; the tiles still moist as she approaches the walk-in shower. Stepping onto the wet black tiles, she turns around and slides the cloudy glass door with her left elbow. Making her way under the shower head, she hits the power button before sticking it to the black tiled wall in line with her hips. Spinning around as the hot water pressure builds against her tight skin, she bends over as the steam builds around her. Bringing her lubed hands behind her, she grips her red cheeks, the tip of the monster teasing its thick girth as she backs up. Gasping through her cupid lips as her damp brunette hair dangles around her flushed face, she looks down; the inside of her widened mouth catching her wet locks as her sultry moans bounce off the glass to the penetrating force, deeper, and deeper. Biting down hard on her bottom lip, she removes her hands; her cheeks clapping around the rubber as her right-hand pushes against the slippery steamed panel, as her left-hand rests against the wall behind her. She closes her eyes and replays her penthouse experience; thrusting away as her silky mess laces the penetrating girth.

Opening the apartment door, the dangerously sexy, black long haired, hourglass figure model enters, raising her shades above her head. Listening to the extreme orgasms echoing across the apartment, she makes her way inside; her scarlet red lipstick matching her ruby red playsuit as her heels step along the laminate. Walking past the half open bathroom door, she inspects the place over and grimaces her lips. Not bad! Reaching the bed, she turns around and takes a seat, checking out her red acrylics between the moans. The apartment falls silent.

Stepping onto the steamy tile, Arabella feels destroyed as her legs shake uncontrollably. Grabbing a warm towel from the heated rack, she wraps her exhausted body; her hardened nipples stinging from the constant twisting as the soft fabric presses tightly into her smooth skin. *That was so needed.* Regaining herself, she opens the door and looks down as she steps onto the landing.

"You are one dirty little devil!"

She looks left; almost slipping as her heart races to her other bestie, Beatrice. "How long have you been here?" she embarrassingly asks.

"Long enough to know you're obviously sex deprived."

She points behind her. "Pass us the playsuit behind you please."

Beatrice reaches behind her and grabs the damp white dress, screwing her face up at it. "You can't wear this? It's wet." She stands up from the bed and opens her wardrobe. Taking out a red playsuit, she throws it to her. "Here."

Arabella raises her hands; the towel dropping to the floor as she catches it. "Oh my god!"

Beatrice walks over to her. "They have got bigger," she says, before moving towards the door. She spins around. "Hurry up bitch. I'll be in the car."

Waiting in the Porsche, Beatrice taps her thumbs against the steering wheel to the club music as she looks over to her twin locking up, watching as she makes her way to the passenger side door and climbs in. "Isn't it funny how we always look like twins," she says, as she starts the engine.

Arabella fastens her seatbelt. "We were always twinning. Clarissa used to get so jealous."

Beatrice hits the gas and sets off down 49th Street. "She doesn't need a twin. Have you seen her body!"

She nods. "Mmhhmmmm, perfect ten." She looks out at the traffic as they cross over 3rd Avenue. "Where are we off to then?"

"I thought we would try that new place over on Madison Avenue."

She raises her eyebrow. *Madison Avenue?* "Oh… Clarity?"

Hitting the volume, B looks to her. "Yeah, why not," she says, and turns up the electrifying tune.

Touching their heels down on Madison Avenue, Beatrice walks around the back of her Porsche and joins her filthy twin on the sidewalk. Arabella gazes up at the electric purple potion sign, 'Clarity', as Beatrice scales the white LED exterior design. They strut side by side like a pair of sassy devils and approach the double black and gold handle doors. Arabella walks through first as A is before B. Letting the door swing behind, they stand in a clear glass box waiting area on a brown straw thick carpet; their legs starting to ache as they wait for five minutes. Hearing the entrance door swing open behind them, they both look as an older gentleman in a grey tight-fitting suit enters and passes through a second set of doors in front of him; the smell of his lingering cigar smoke hitting their noses as they burst into catastrophic laughter.

"Oh my god!" giggles Arabella.

"Fucking hell A, you are such a clutz!"

Arabella's eyes tear up; her uncontrollable giggling state disturbing the clubs daytime peaceful atmosphere as they pass through the doors. Stepping along the glossy black tiled square room, they approach the long bar in front.

"What can I get two of Manhattan's finest?" asks the bartender, as he stares B up and down.

Beatrice smiles her pearly whites at the cute dark-haired bartender. "We will have two, raspberry vodka mixed iced teas please." The bartender turns around to prepare the drinks.

Tapping her nails against the bar top, Arabella looks to her right. *Why does she look so familiar?*

The woman sat across the bar notices her and stands, brushing herself down before strutting towards them. Make that triplets! "I'm Dakota, the manager here. You both look like you're enjoying yourselves," she says, and looks to the bartender. "On the house." Met with a smile from Beatrice, she watches B take the drinks and approach a one-legged thick black table.

Arabella looks Dakota up and down, trying to place her British accent. She widens her eyes. *It's you… from the penthouse and Devil's nightclub.*

Dakota drops the fake smile. She knows all about Arabella. The midday drinkers carry on with their business as the two feisty brunette goddesses lock their burning glares, the club falling silent as their intense battle rages on; their eyes revealing the others' secret. Dakota breaks their showdown and leans her strawberry glossed lips into her left ear; her flowery scent hitting Arabella. "Don't test me," she threateningly whispers.

Arabella glides her candy pink glossed lips to her left ear. "You seem rather jealous for someone who refuses to fuck him," she whispers, with confidence.

"Run along now princess."

Picking up the raspberry delight, Beatrice watches her bestie return and takes a seat on the black leather stool in front. "This place is practically empty," she says, and takes a sip on her iced tea, squirming as the sharp vodka burns her throat. "Jesus. How much did they put in this?"

Arabella takes a sip of her own drink. "Mine's fine." She swaps drinks. "Take mine. I need a stronger drink anyway for tonight."

Beatrice places her shades on the table. "Yes, tonight. Let's talk engagement."

Chatting away, the hours pass as they deeply discuss the pros and cons of engagement, feeling tipsy as they continue to sip away on the never-ending variety of cocktails.

"When you enter into engagement, it's saying you want to spend the rest of your life with them," says B, and takes a sip of her iced tea. "So when Tristram asked me, I just knew he was the one." She stands up. "I'm just going to use the restroom. Watch my bag."

The rest of my life? God, no I can't. Resting her elbows against the table, she places her head in her hands, rolling her forehead side to side, as the liquor flows through her. She hears footsteps rapidly approaching from her left; her ear feeling a sudden heat.

"I can fuck him anytime I want to," whispers Dakota.

Arabella looks left, brushing her cheek against her nose before staring deep into her revealing eyes. "I think deep down, you know he will never want anything more," she says, with a sober heart.

Dakota presses her tongue against her cheek and glares silently, looking to her right as the bathroom swings open. She turns around and walks away.

Beatrice exits and makes her way back to the table. "I'm far too drunk to drive. Book a cab. I'll have to get Tristram to fetch the car later."

Unlocking her smartphone, she opens the local app; the screen spinning as she navigates slowly and finally books a taxi with her BookShib. "Done. This does make me laugh," and shows B the screen, "I've got this cute dog I can pay things with."

"Well that's cute. So, tonight... you might be engaged."

She shrugs. "I don't know. I'll consider it in the moment," she says, and looks down at her vibrating smartphone on the table. "The cab is here."

Beatrice puts on her shades. "That was quick." They both stand and make their way towards the exit. Arabella stares goodbye at Dakota, as Beatrice exits first; they're so drunk they've forgot their own A before B rule.

THE PROPOSAL

It's 18:00. The season of spring has yet to welcome the bright, warm evenings as Arabella turns on the apartment lights. Elliot messaged her earlier to meet him at the restaurant. All sobered up, she stares into the mirror, gazing over her Dior black slit silk dress from Paris, her loose wavy brunette hair dangling over her shoulders as she slides her petite hands down her hourglass figure. She can't even enjoy her own beauty in the reflection as her mind clouds with endless worry; the thought of saying no in front of a crowd is embarrassing. She sighs. *I guess I best continue packing.* She walks over to her wardrobe and packs the last of her clothing into her bag. She isn't expecting to come back after. Who would!

Looking down at the bed, she grimaces her lips. *It's for the best.* Glancing left, she exhales, soaking up the atmosphere for the final time. Taking a slow trip to the kitchen, she stands in the doorway, flashbacking to the morning of Elliot cooking her eggs and bacon before asking her to be his girlfriend. She sighs. Hitting the light switch off, she turns around, stepping between the hockey puck and the couch as she looks to her right at the flat screen; the glass screen reflecting her distorted image as tears stream down her rosy cheeks. *He's going to hate me.* Wiping her face, she bends down and hits the hidden button on the hockey puck before sitting back. She leans over and stares into the white cooler, reaching inside as the pit of her guilty stomach turns, her right hand turning chilly as she pulls out a green bottle of Dom Perignon. *I'm so sorry.* He must have bought it for the engagement celebration. Placing it back inside, she lays back; her black mascara running down her sobbing face. Closing her weeping eyes, she blindly reaches to her right, gliding her hand against the blanket; its smooth fabric flowing through her dainty fingers. Journeying off it, the texture changes to rough as she brushes against his jumper. Gripping it tight, she brings it to her face and deeply inhales, indulging in his woody cologne scent.

  After five minutes of me watching her sniff that stupid jumper, she finally gets up and throws it inside her bag. OMG!! I bought him that for Christmas! She zips it up and turns around to the mirror, flapping her hands in front of her face in an attempt to save her mascara. She turns around and grabs her smartphone from the top of her wardrobe. It's 18:20. She has 40 minutes! She books a cab with her BookShib through the app and places it back on top, swapping it for her scarlet red lipstick. Returning in front of the mirror, she paints her Cupid lips before writing, 'I'm So Sorry' across the glass.

Her smartphone vibrates. It's time! Taking one final look in the mirror, she flicks her hair back into position, releasing a huge sigh as she steps into the center of the room. With her clutch bag in her hand, she does one final spin, absorbing the interior of her last six months. Approaching the door, her stilettos echo behind her as she grips the white handle with her right hand, as her left-hand rests on the light switch. She sighs and looks behind her, capturing the final image of a once peaceful home. It's done! Slamming the door behind her, she walks right; her hair lighting blowing around her flushed face as she makes her way to the back of the cab. Gripping the door handle, she looks back one last time. Oh, not this again! Finally climbing in, she slides comfortably into the leather and fastens her seatbelt.

"Where to?" asks the driver.

She opens her smartphone and reads the message. "Napoleons over on Fifth Avenue please." The cab sets off down East 49th Street, as she silently stares goodbye to the apartment. She looks down at her lap and closes her eyes, gulping as she rehearses the dreaded no in her head. He isn't Mr. P. She can't just be blunt; he's a delicate flower.

Full of confidence, she opens the door, her heels touching the ground as she climbs out and slams the door behind her; the spring breeze playing with her hair, as her pearly whites shine through her glowing smile. *Everything will be fine… this is so nice.* She captures the mystifying beauty of the realistic Arc De Triomphe artwork above the overarching stone doorway. *Here we go.* She takes a deep breath and approaches, walking inside of the red ropes as she makes her way down the red carpet, leaving Manhattan behind as the white gloved, red coat doorman smiles and grips the long gold handle, pulling open the oak brown and glass door towards him before guiding her through with his white glove.

"Merci," she smilingly says, and steps inside. Taking a slow stroll down the rouge carpeted hallway, she widens her eyes, mesmerized by the carved, long stretching timeline depicting the battle of Napoleon beautifully. She reaches the end of the hallway, smiling at the doormen either side, as they open the double brown doors in sync with her pace, her ears hit by the piercing chatter from the dining guests as she enters the dome shaped white marble room. Waiting patiently behind an elegantly dressed couple, she casts her vision left, scaling the circle room in awe to the napoleon timeline as it stretches all the way around; her stomach rumbling as the divine smell of French cuisine teases her.

"Bonjour. Welcome to Napoleon. You look exceptional tonight Madam."

Snapping out her dreamy state, she faces front, her eyes looking the bald, handsome, grey suited Frenchman. "Why thank you," she blushingly says.

He looks down at his clipboard. "Do you have a reservation?"

"I do. Arabella Harper."

He glides his pen down the list. He looks up, shining his pearly white teeth at her with a suspicious smile. What does he know that we know? "Arabella, you're in for one very special evening. Please follow me." He turns around and leads the way.

Trailing behind, she gazes up at the crystal glass dome top in the center; her hunger distracted by the magical tingle shooting through her as Orion's belt twinkles back at her. Walking down the aisle, the classy guests dressed in tuxedos and extravagant dresses stare out from their cream white leathered booths; her divine beauty blinding them. Still following, they turn left and continue towards the center. There he is, sat directly under the clear night sky. She looks to the side of Elliot's face; his light ash hair freshly trimmed.

He hears heels tapping and looks right, sliding out his seat, as the Frenchman gestures her to approach. "Oh wow," says Elliot, as she steps towards him with an anxious smile.

Surrendering herself to his gliding touch across her rosy, dimpled cheeks, she parts her scarlet lips; tasting his warm champagne breath as she softly brushes her smooth fingers along his jaw.

He breaks their passion and presses his forehead against hers. "I love you, Arabella," he softly whispers, as their noses graze.

Too caught up in the princess moment, she flutters inside, losing herself in his romance. "I love you, Elliot," she softly whispers, as he takes her hand and turns around, escorting her into the creamy leather booth, her right-side seat facing the dome entrance. She looks up to the glass top, as he retakes his seat, her stomach sinking in guilt as a replica marble statue of the famous Eternal Springtime depicting two lovers kissing watches over her.

The Frenchman approaches, holding two champagne glasses filled with Dom Perignon. "Please enjoy," he says, and places them on the graphite marble table before walking away.

She wraps her dainty fingers around the stem and raises it to her parted lips, the crisp and fruity luxury swishing around as her scarlet lipstick sinks into the rim. "So, what's with the fancy occasion?" she asks.

Elliot lowers his glass. "Well I haven't been myself these past few months, so I thought I'd make it up to you."

She draws circles around the glass rim, as she sinks her devilishly, seductive eyes into him. "I've been pretty naughty myself."

"Oh, I could imagine."

She removes her index finger from the glass and teasingly bites down. "You have no idea!"

He places the rim of the glass around his mouth. "Perhaps you could show me later," he flirtatiously says, and sips.

She brushes her stiletto up his grey trouser leg. "How about now?"

He nervously chuckles. "Very funny." He stands up. "I'm just going to use the restroom. Be right back."

Watching him vacate, she waits before slouching back, sinking into the leather with a blank look. She looks up to the statue. *What did I do that for? God, I'm so stupid.* She shakes her head. "Why would you say you love him," she mumbles to herself. Glad everyone's on the same page! She decides to abandon her poor attempt of imitating Mr. P. Leave it to the pros!

Sipping away on the flowing extravagance with an empty stomach, the white coat waiter finally arrives with their starters.

"Baked Camembert with olive oil toasts for Mademoiselle," says the waiter, and places it in front of her before looking to Elliot, "and for Monsieur, Queens scallops with sauternes butter." He looks at them both. "Bon appetite."

Arabella pinches the toast and dips it into the molten cheese before guiding it to her deprived lips, her stomach growling as she crunches on the creamy rich buttery goodness. She looks over at Elliot, listening to his lips slurp the floating scallop on butter sauce, as it slides from its shell.

He swallows the delicacy and looks at her. "Did I tell you how pretty you look tonight?"

She hovers her hand over her mouth, still chewing away. "You told me with your eyes."

He leans forwards. "Well I'll tell you with my voice. You look very pretty tonight."

She puts the toast down and smiles. "Aww. You look handsome yourself." *God.* She slides out the booth and stands. "I'm just going to pop to the restroom." Turning around, she strolls down the aisle, glancing at all the romantic couples dining. Picking up her pace, she swaps her artificial smile for a look of panic and bursts through the black bathroom door; the chattering guests fading behind her as the door swings closed. *Oh god...* Feeling sick, she rushes left along the long stretched white marble tiled floor and looks left into the wide stretched gold framed mirror; her face blushing a guilty red in the reflection.

With her chests tightening, she crosses her tremoring arms on the granite marble sink top edge and rests her forehead against them, sliding backwards on her stiletto soles. Staring down at the water splashed tiles, she deeply inhales, and exhales, as her loose brunette waves dangle either side. *I need a miracle.* Her right ear perks up as the far end cubicle unlocks. Listening to the tapping of heels stepping out and walking to the sink in front, she slowly pulls herself back up to standing position as the unknown washes their hands. She peeks to her right, missing the dark brunette woman's face as the sound of the air dryer whirs. *Right… stop being such an idiot and just go back out there.* Listening to her inner voice, she turns left and proceeds to the exit as the whirring stops. Gripping the door handle, she takes a deep breath. *You've got--*

"Not even going to say hello, Arabella?"

She widens her eyes and lets go of the handle, turning to face the identical looking older version of herself, dressed in a tight slit front black dress. "Hello, Elizabeth," she says, patronizingly, and retraces her steps to the sink with a fierce glare locked into the older woman.

"Don't call me by my first name. I am your mother!"

She fake laughs. "What are you even doing here?"

Elizabeth walks over to her. "Not even going to give me a hug. After all these years."

She stares at her through the reflection. "There's a reason for that," she says before turning to face her. "Now, if you'll excuse me, I have to go tell someone I won't be marrying them."

Elizabeth widens her almond eyes in shock. "What do you mean? I've missed so much," she says, and gently rests her left hand on her daughters shoulder. "Do you love him?"

Bursting into frantic laughter, she raises her hands in the air, removing her mother's warm felt hand off her shoulder in the process. "You are unbelievable!" She turns to the mirror and looks at her. "It's not about love. I can't marry him I've done exactly what you've done. Like mother, like daughter," she says, spitefully.

"Arabella Harper!"

She flicks her hair and aggressively turns to her mother. "Don't give me that. You have no right to judge me!"

Elizabeth sighs. "Well, what about this other one. Do you love him?"

She looks down at her feet, trying to not to show weakness as her eyes starts to tear. Feeling her mother's soft hands wrap around her, she breaks. "I gave myself away to him. Of course I love him," she weeps, as her mother hugs her tightly.

"You need to chase what feels right, even if that means hurting another. You are my daughter afterall. Fierce, independent and strong willed."

Regaining herself, she escapes her mother's arms and faces the mirror, wiping away the ruined mascara from her flushed cheeks. "What are you doing back here anyway?"

Elizabeth faces the mirror and fixes her hair. "I'm just catching up with an old flame. I'm heading back to Miami in the morning."

Taking a deep breath, she uses her dainty hands as a fan to dry her eyes. "Maybe, just maybe, I'll come visit you sometime. Maybe even bring the other guy."

Elizabeth smiles. "That would be nice."

She smiles back before approaching the exit. Gripping the handle, she looks over to her. "Goodbye Mother," she calmy says.

"Goodluck with your situation my beautiful baby."

Returning to the table, she smiles and slides in, as Elliot looks down to his watch. "You've been twenty minutes. I was about to send someone to go check on you. Is everything alright?" He notices a woman exiting the bathroom and points. "Is it me or does that woman look identical to you?"

She looks down at her Lyon-Style chicken with vinegar sauce, grabbing her knife and fork as she nods. "Yep," she says, and cuts into the succulent chicken. She takes a bite, pointing her fork at him as she chews. "This is good."

"Who is she?" he asks, puzzled.

She swallows the tangy chicken before reaching for the champagne glass. "The one and only, Queen Elizabeth," she says, and throws back the Dom Perignon.

His eyes widen in disbelief. "That's your mother?" He stands up, looking across the room in search for her. No luck! He sits back down. "Well, what did you discuss?"

She raises her hands. "Who cares." She looks around for a waiter. "I need a drink."

Leaning on her left hand, as she sips her fifth drink, she watches Elliot slurp the final spoonful of his Marseille-Style Shrimp Stew.

"Ahh! That was delicious," he says, and puts the spoon down. He looks to her. "Are you ok? You seem rather depressed. I hope your mom hasn't spoilt your evening." She ignores him and throws back the champagne; the guilt becoming unbearable. The waiter approaches.

"Did you enjoy the meal?"

Elliot looks to him. "It was magnificent." The waiter collects their empty dishes. She turns to the waiter and signals her hand back and forth for another drink. He casts his eyes to Elliot, who shakes his head side to side. He looks back to her and smiles before vacating with the dishes. She hears tapping underneath the table and looks to him, watching his shoulders move up and down as sweat drips down his face. He must be getting nervous! She gulps as the champagne and food dishes mix inside, the pit of her stomach becoming unsettled as the proposal lingers.

The Frenchman approaches with a smile. "Are we both ready for dessert?" he asks, as he winks to Elliot's sweaty, cherry looking face.

Elliot yanks the collar of his tight white shirt. "Is it me or has it suddenly got a lot hotter in here?"

The Frenchman laughs as he pats his back and looks over to her. "I think it's the sparkling diamond in front of you."

Please don't. She nervously smiles. "Yes, it's time for dessert," she says.

He removes his hand from Elliot. "Excellent," he says, clapping his hands before walking away.

Elliot stares at the Frenchman's back before looking to her, quietly observing her tap her matt black and white polka dot nails against the tabletop, with her shoulders moving in line with her deep breaths and eyes closed. He casts his eyes above, staring in astonishment as the white coat waiter looks back at him through the glass top. They exchange acknowledgment with a thumbs up. He raises his index finger up to signal one moment and looks to her, as he slides out the booth; her lips trembling, as she hears him stand. "I'm just going out the front for some air."

She closes her eyes and leans her elbows against the table before placing her head in her hands; the rooms chatter enhancing its volume as she tries to simmer her nerves. With her lips parted, she takes a deep breath and holds it, hearing and feeling her beating heart race, as the champagne effect takes over. She exhales her problems and repeats, unable to control her shaking.

The Frenchman approaches with his hands full, looking down at the back of her head before casting his eyes with fear at the empty seat in opposite. With his heart now racing, he scales the room for Elliot, cracking a smile as Elliot paces back down the aisle. "Had me worried for a moment," whispers the Frenchman, as Elliot slides back into the creamy white leather. He places the desserts in front of them, sliding her dish in between her elbows; her eyes opening to white meringue covered in caramel; the sweet vanilla custard teasing her nose, as she slowly raises her head. "Nice of you to join us again

Mademoiselle, please enjoy our famous Floating Island, a French favorite," he says, and turns left, patting Elliot on the back as he walks down the walkway with a gleaming smile.

Oh of course you would put it in the dessert. She picks up the silver spoon and slowly breaks away the meringue, gulping to what's hidden inside.

Placing the silver spoon in the empty dish, she enjoys the final piece; her mouth oozing with sugary goodness as the crunch of the meringue mixes with the rich and creamy vanilla. She swallows. *Where's the ring?* She looks up to him, as he places his spoon down. The white coat waiter comes over and collects the dishes.

"Merci," says Elliot, and looks over to the kitchen, nodding at the Frenchman. She braces herself as the looming event nears, tapping away as they both watch the Frenchman approach with two glasses of Dom Perignon.

"Enjoy," he says, and winks to Elliot, as he places them down and turns around.

She picks up the glass and parts her cupid lips around the rim. She tilts the glass back; her heart racing as the rooms chatter suddenly simmers mid sip. She brings the glass down, swishing the extravagance in her mouth as the domes lighting dims, as the keys of a grand piano release its elegant harmonic pitch. Here we go! Time slows down, her skin turns cherry red; unable to do anything as she watches him place his right hand above and behind him, placing his legs outside the booth as he rests his left hand on the tabletop and slowly pulls himself up from the creamy white leather seat. Only an earthquake can stop this! She raises her eyebrow, confused as he stops mid climb and retracts back to his seated position.

"Ooo, I love the heels," says a random diner, to Arabella.

She looks up to her left and smiles at the incredibly stunning brunette. So that's why he stopped! "Why thank you. You're so pretty." The girl blows her a kiss and continues down the walkway. I guess it's back to the issue at hand then! She looks back to Elliot.

"Oh, we will," seductively says Mr. P, dressed in a tuxedo as he trails behind the girl and looks back, sinking his smoldering green eyes and smirk into her.

Are you for real? Clenching her fists under the table, she sees red; her nervous guilt overpowered by extreme rage and jealousy, as her scorching glare sinks into the back of his tuxedo, watching him, and her, approach the exit. *Oh wait until I see him...*

Elliot stands, breaking her line of sight and gets down on one knee. "Will you marry me, Arabella Harper?" he loudly asks. The dimmed lit dome falls dead silent, as the guests watch from their booths in suspense.

She shuts her eyes and deeply exhales. Unable to rationally think through the intense storm, she responds, "Yes." The lights immediately glow again as the dome erupts with claps and cheers. Elliot takes hold of her hands and pulls her out from the booth.

Gazing deep into his innocent eyes, she notices his eyes roll slightly up with a sweeping smile, as a white banded single stone ring floats between them on invisible string. *What have I just done? Oh my god.* With her clustered mind cleared, she listens to the excitement around her. *I guess I have no choice now.* She watches him remove the ring and holds out her left hand, feeling like a princess as he slides the promise onto her fourth finger. *Ok, this does feel kind of good right now.* Raising her hand, she shows it off to the cheering room. She feels his soft hands glide her warm cheeks, parting her cupid lips as his wet lips lock; their vanilla and champagne flavors infusing as they slide, her chest fluttering as their passion spreads across the room, getting lost in the fairytale magic.

ARABELLAS'

Elliot mentally awakens to a warm, whistling snore in his left ear. He opens his eyes to the dark apartment, as his head pounds; his sweaty abs weighed down as her left arm lays across him under the thick duvet. Gently lifting her hand as he leans to his right, he lowers it onto the bed. Removing the cover from his steamy body, he rolls over her; his skin crawling as a cold spike hits.

"What the hell!" aggressively shouts Arabella, and flips over, her head pounding as she opens her blood shot eyes, catching his bare ass enter the bathroom. *What's the time?* Stretching her right arm out, the cold air swarms against her skin as she reaches onto the side table for her smartphone, brushing her knuckles against the empty bottle of Dom Perignon as she retrieves it. Flipping onto her back, she switches it on, the bright white light causing her to squint. It's 14:00. She sits up, as he exits the bathroom. "It's two in the afternoon," she groggily says.

"What!" He rushes over to the woven fruit basket and grabs his smartphone. "Jesus! I'm meant to be meeting my mother in an hour." He places it back in the woven basket and walks over to her, taking a seat on the edge of the bed before rubbing her leg. "What are you going to do today?"

Reading through the overwhelming number of congratulating messages, she breaks her focus and looks to him. "I'm not entirely sure. Maybe lounge around or go see Clarissa." A loud thud occurs. They both raise their eyebrows, her heart racing as they look to the bathroom.

Like the gentleman he is, he stands and goes to investigate this suspicious noise in the bathroom. "What the hell is that?" he shouts, as she panics whilst awaiting whatever it is. He hangs his head out the bathroom door and looks to her. "Why is there a ginormous dildo on the shower floor?"

Bahahaha. She breaks out in hysterical laughter. "It's just a toy," she laughingly says, gasping the apartment air with her face turning extremely red, as he looks back at it.

"There's toys and then there's that," he says and steps along the cold floor of the walk-in shower, standing above it with his eyebrow raised. He picks it up and exits the bathroom. He looks at her. "Do I pleasure you?" he asks, as he places it beside his flaccid penis.

"Yes," she says, with a serious voice, as he sighs. "Now put my dick down and go have a shower." He chucks it to her, his piss poor throw misses and hits the wardrobe, its girthy force knocking the Dom Perignon bottle on its side. She acts quickly, reaching over and catching it as it rolls off the edge. "Idiot!"

Listening to his footsteps exit from the bathroom, she pretends to be asleep, as he gets dressed.

He approaches the window and draws the curtains; the spring sunshine penetrating her eyelids as the room brightens. "Wakey, wakey," he says, and flicks his light ash fringe to the side as he steps in front of the mirror. He raises his eyebrow, turning to her, as he tucks his pastel blue shirt into his skinny black jeans. "Why is there writing on the mirror?"

Oh no... With a tightening chest, she tries to think. *Sorry for...* Opening her eyes, she sits up and looks to him. "I wrote it for making you feel small," she says, and looks at his trousers.

He awkwardly nods and turns around. "Right then. I'll be back around ten. See you later."

"Have fun." Hearing the door shut, she springs out of bed and retrieves her bag from underneath. Throwing it on the duvet, she unzips it and unpacks; sliding on a matching white lingerie set midway and a dress. All done. Turning to face the mirror, she checks out her strawberry red ditsy floral dress, spinning around as the bottom flows around her smooth legs. Turning around, she raises her dress and shakes her bouncy cheeks; her thong wedged high up her backside. *So hot.* With no time to waste, she grabs her smartphone, booking a cab on the app before heading to the bathroom to brush her teeth. Staring into the sink mirror, the electronic bristles brush away against her pearly whites as Mr. P consumes her. She hasn't forgotten his stunt last night; her anger getting to her as the red flashing signals she's brushing too hard. Exiting the bathroom with fresh breath, she sits back on the edge of the bed with her smartphone, scrolling through social media; the reality of her situation kicking in her single stone ring shines at her. *It wasn't a dream.* Her hands vibrate; the cab notification has come through. Standing, she reaches into the wardrobe and pulls out a cross shoulder bag and sandals; the light brown combo eloquently complimenting her dress.

Locking up, she approaches the cab and gets in.

"Where to?" asks the driver, as he watches her climb inside.

"Hotel L'Amour please."

Gazing left at the fountain as they stop on the cobble lane, she looks right, as the redcoat opens the door. Taking his white glove, she steps out onto the sidewalk; the spring breeze caressing her arms and legs as her ears absorb the fountains soothing shower. Wasting no time,

240

she rushes up the white stairs, smiling at the doormen as they open the doors to her fast pace. Tapping her sandals along the marble lobby floor, almost slipping in the process, she approaches the reception. Oh look. It's Chloe!

"Welcome to Hotel L'Amour. What is the nature of your visit?"

Arabella rests her arms across the wooden desk. "What do you think," she sarcastically says.

Chloe rolls her eyes. "Take a seat on the couch behind you. He will be with you shortly."

With a fake smile, she turns around, listening to the guests chatter as she takes a seat in the waiting area. Looking left at the entrance, she watches as guests arrive with their luggage. She forgets this is a fully operating hotel sometimes! Whipping out her smartphone, she buries her face in social media; her inbox showing no signs of stopping as the congratulation messages keep pouring in. She perks her right ear; drawing her attention away from her smartphone as the elevator door opens. She peeks out her right eye. *Wow… wow…wow… unbelievable.* Crunching her stomach as she looks straight down, she pretends to type away, listening to the queen of the city, Melinda, strut her heels in front. She looks up and catches the back of her light brunette hair as she exits. She stands. Racing towards the elevator, she hides her resent with a pearly smile at the guard and enters; the lobby light fading behind her as Melinda's floral perfume lingers. Glaring into the mirror, her reflection changes to devil red as she twists her engagement ring side to side. *Maybe I should keep it on to make him jealous! Yeah... oh for god sake... why am I so pathetic.* She slides it off her finger and places it in her bag. Raising her dress, she slowly spins around, checking out her glowing red thighs and peachy bottom from every angle. So vain!

"Welcome to floor one-hundred. The Penthouse!" The doors open.

Mr. P faces the wall to her right, lowering the hanging art to access his safe. He looks to her and gazes at her raised dress. "Now that's hot."

She lowers her dress and turns around, gazing over his flexing muscles with an unamused look swept across her, as he opens his safe in his white boxers. Stepping along the black and white tiles, she observes him in silence as the smell of cologne hits her, watching him grab three large white photo printouts from the silver table to his right and placing them inside the safe before slamming the black steel door shut; his secrets locked inside as he spins the dial and rehangs the fine art. Reaching the couch, she looks at his back, met with a smirk as he turns around before bending over and sliding his boxers down his shredded legs. *Gahhh.* Lost in the king of tease, she doesn't flinch as he kicks them past her head. Flutters shoot through her, all flustered as he turns around and heads for the glass door. The sliding noise breaks her dreamy gaze. *Right... enough of the bullshit.* She watches him through the glass walk left and descend into the swimming pool. Taking off her bag and sandals, she throws them over the couch and steps outside, onto the black glossy floor; the breeze flowing around her bare feet and up her dress as she walks straight ahead to the railings edge. She stares out at Central Park, listening to the busy 5th Avenue traffic from below, as the sound of water splashes behind her.

"Did you come here to stare at trees?" he chuckles.

She turns around, approaching the edge of the pool as the wind lightly raises her dress. Looking straight across and down to him with her arms crossed, she gazes over his broad arms spread across the third glass step, as the sun shines across his hardened pecks, his white teeth sparkling from afar with his rippled abs submerged in the clear water. *He's so smug.* "Why was Melinda here?"

He looks up at her towering dominance. "Politics."

"Mmhmmm. I see," as she raises her hands, "and you not telling that you were back, only to entertain another girl before me was what?"

He creates splashing as he raises his arms. "Entertaining," he laughingly says.

She slides her dress over her head and throws it on the black and white rattan sun lounger to her right. Reaching behind her, she unclips her lacey bra, gliding the white straps along her smooth skin. Dangling the strap around her right index finger, she gives him the look, as her rounded breasts breathe the open air. "Is this entertaining?"

He looks down and smirks. "It could be better."

She bites her bottom lip and sits on the edge, spreading her legs; the white lace teasing him as he starts to grow. "What about now?"

He tilts his head left and right. "Maybe."

She dips her toes into the warm water, creating mini waves as she draws circles. She places her hands on the black glossy edge and lowers herself in; the water line floating under her boobs as her lower body adjusts temperature. Cupping her warm breasts, she catches her rosy tips between her spread fingers and bites down on her plumped bottom lip, fondling them as she locks her fuck me look into his pretty green eyes. Treading the glass floor; her beauty bones catch droplets as tiny waves splash around her. Looking up at the clear sky, she parts her lips, twisting her hardened nipples as a loud and sexy moan escapes to the tingling sensation. Sinking her horny gaze into him, she submerges her upper body before re-emerging with her index fingers circling her areola's. "Now?" she seductively says, as the water drips from her goddess body.

He floats backwards, using his elbows to pull him back onto the second step; the sun shining on his golden abs as the tip of his cock floats above the water. "Nearly."

She parts her lips as she submerges her temple, the water splashing on her flushed cheeks as her feet touch the fifth bottom step, wrapping her drowned tits around his thick cock; her arms squeezing tightly as she lowers her glossy lips around his shaft. She slides up and down as she swirls her tongue, her jaw widening as he raises his ass.

He slowly sits up and pulls her along with his cock, her tight squeeze breaking as he perches his peachy ass on the black starry floor, as her feet grip the third step. He caresses his fingertips along the back of her neck, her body tingling from his feather touch, as she rests her arms against his thighs, wrapping her dainty hands around his weapon, finger by finger, she lets its penetrating force tests her gag reflex, deeper, and deeper. He brings his hands over her hands, releasing her tight grip and guides them onto his V line; her acrylics lightly scratching along his tight skin, as he reaches behind her head and gently grips her hair. Lowering her up and down, he listens to her gagging escaping the corners of her spread cupid lips.

She hits his toned abs, gasping the spring air as he pulls her up. Wiping her flushed face, she regains her breath and steps backwards, signaling him to come closer. She watches him slide into the water and raises her floating legs, wrapping herself tightly around his muscles, as he slides his hands under her and lifts her up; her creamy breasts pressing their softness against his hardened pecks as he carries her through the water. She parts her sultry lips and slides between his wet warmth, softly grazing her fingers along his fresh shave as he glides her to the pools edge; her back forming waves all around them.

Feeling the edge dig against her back, she pulls his forehead to her; sinking her lust into his dominance, as their warm, steamy passion collides. "You get me so flustered," she whispers and releases her grip, running her fingers down his golden chest before hopping to her laced front. Sliding the wet front to the side; his hands help as he pulls her wedged panties out from her cheeks. She applies pressure to the top of her pussy and pulls up, creating a V with her right hand as she spreads her pink lips wide, holding the position as she reaches for his cock with her left. Pulling him in closer, she looks up to the clear sky as she uses his hard tip like a toy, up and down her clit, deeply moaning to the waves of pleasure as waves splash around them.

He brings his hands to her chest and palms her full breasts, squeezing them as he parts his lips, whisking his tongue against her hard bead as he gently draws rings around the other with his wet fingers. Sucking goodbye, he switches, suckling on her rosy tip as he twists her other warm and wet teat; her chest rapidly breathing in and out as her legs spasm.

She places the tip of his cock in her tight entrance and lets go, bringing her elbows up onto the pools edge before cupping her breasts. Pinching her erect nipples, she twists to the sensational spike shooting through her as she feels his teasing girth against her g spot; the traffic below drowned out by her intense moans as she begs with her thrusting hips.

He raises her smooth legs and lightly trickles his fingertips along, journeying up her curves as he travels to her chest. He flicks her hands off and twists, as she pulls herself up from the water; his tongue sliding down her silky-smooth waist, as his hands move under her plumped cheeks and assist her onto the edge.

Laying back on black glossed floor hit, water drops from her temple as she raises her legs, feeling the tightening squeeze of his muscly arms wrap around her juicy thighs; the back of her curves tremoring as his tongue delivers its powerful strokes. Closing her eyes, she widens her mouth, tilting her head to the side as he buries his face deep in her soaking lips, sliding his face side to side as she drowns in his sensation. Feeling his tight grip loosen, she hears splashing as he pulls himself out, holding out her arms for her alpha. Catching her breath, as he slides on top; her dainty hands grips the back of his thick hair, as he places his hands under her head. She pulls him in closer; their dripping bodies pressing their beauty as she surrenders her bottom lip.

  He releases her hair clip, combing his wet fingers through her curly waves before gripping tightly, pinning her legs up with his muscly thighs and hovering the tip of his cock over her wet entrance. With his power, he hits her all at once, raising her neck as he pulls down on her hair, clamping down on her bottom lip as he penetrates his hard, thick, and long cock; the terrace filling with a loud gasp as her body explodes with intense heat.

  She wraps her legs around his waist, moaning into his mouth as her plumped ass pounds against the floor to his hard thrusts. She slides her glossy lips between his moisture, clawing her acrylics along his ripped arms as their pressed bodies sweat their steamy passion; their lust filled eyes exchanging their deep desire as her moans escape the corners of her panting mouth. She squeezes her arms around his neck, breaking their intense kiss and pulling his ear to her. "I'm close," she pants, as her hips rapidly thrust to the orgasmic explosion shooting through her; her legs shaking uncontrollably as her tight walls pulsate around his girthy cock…

Napping in pitch silence, Arabella opens her eyes, yawning as she peels her naked body from the penthouse long, main couch. Sitting up right, she rubs her eyes as she looks around the dark room; the white and purple fluorescent terrace reflecting through the mirror in front. She turns around, placing her knees on the leather and resting her crossed arms against the top of the couch. *That's so beautiful.* She gazes out at the crystal-clear swimming pool; the inbuilt white lights shining its waters beauty inside. *Where's my dress?* She scales the back of the terrace in search for her dress, enjoying the fluorescent purple lighting and fire lit beacons. Unable to see it, she casts her eyes up at the stars and sighs, releasing her catharsis as she loses herself in Orion's belt; her attention broken as she hears the elevator doors open. Listening to the taps of penny loafers walk along the tiles, she looks behind her, watching as Mr. P turns the corner, dressed in his usual attire. He claps twice. Blinded by the light, she turns around as her eyes adjust to the yellow glow.

"You're awake. Good," he says, as he moves towards her, placing a bottle of cold water and chocolate on the coffee table. "Get dressed. I want to take you somewhere."

She opens the bottle and parts her lips, watching him move to the bedroom as the cold crisp water soothes her dry throat. She places the bottle down and picks up the chocolate; the milky sweet flavor melting in her mouth as he reappears. She raises her eyebrow. *Not a chance.* "Do you honestly think I'm going to wear some random skanks thong!"

He slingshots Dakota's scarlet red lace over to her. "They're new." Suppose a white lie never hurt!

She throws the wrapper on the table and swallows, picking up the red panties from behind her and inspects them. Rolling her eyes at him, she stands and steps into them. Sliding them up her smooth legs, she watches Mr. P walks across the room, elevator side, and bend down behind the couch, reappearing with her strawberry red, ditsy dress.

"Where are we going to then?" she asks, as he throws it to her.

He puts his hands in his black trouser pockets and watches her slide the dress over her head. "You'll see."

She reaches down on the coffee table for her smartphone and opens it. *What?* Widening her eyes, she looks up to him. "Nine? You've let me sleep for five hours!" Shaking her head, she grabs her bag and sandals from the couch and makes her way behind it, throwing her sandals onto the white tile and sliding into them as she watches him open the elevator. Moving along the tiles, she approaches him, as he rests against the metal frame with his arms and legs crossed. She sarcastically smiles at him, and enters first, turning around, as he steps inside; the doors closing behind him as she looks up to his towering beauty.

Trapped in his erotic hell, she can't help but bite her bottom lip to his tempting devilish gaze, as the lights turn a devil red. Here we go again! Feeling his veiny hands reach behind her curvy thighs, she surrenders to him; her arms and legs wrapping around her alpha as he spins her around and slams her against the silver door. Closing her eyes, she parts her ice-cold lips, catching his sliding warmth between them; her lips melting as their steamy passion explodes, the taste of sweet chocolate and whiskey mixing as their tongues softly play. Widening her lips to his grazing touch above her ears; the back of her neck tingles as he flows his fingers through her wavy curls. She breaks their moist slide, looking up as he pulls her hair; his top lip steaming to her moaning warmth as the box drowns with deep pleasure. They gently press their foreheads together amongst the lust, brushing their noses as the doors starts to open behind her. He slides his hands underneath her ditsy dress and rests her plumped cheeks in his palms, saving her as he exits the elevator and carries her along the white marble floor.

She looks left and glares at Chloe. "I don't like her," she says, innocently.

He chuckles. "Who?" He looks over at the reception and turns back. "Chloe! She's a good girl," he says, as he carries her through the exit; the flowing fountains trickle bouncing off the glass top as they descend the stairs.

Gino stands with the back door of his Phantom open, raising his eyebrow as he focuses his attention on the bouncing brunette hair. "Since when did you and Dakota become lovers ha-ha?" Mr. P leans over the backseat and gently lays her onto the leather, kissing her forehead before closing the door and entering the front passengers seat, as Gino enters the driver's seat. He starts the engine and looks back through the reverse mirror at her. "Arabella!" He turns to Mr. P. "I thought that was Dakota."

"They do look alike don't they," he chucklingly says, as the Phantom pulls out of the red cobble lane and exits left onto 5th Avenue, passing an unmarked car with the two FBI Agents, Sanders, and Cody, hidden behind the tinted windows as they take pictures.

Arabella gazes out at the wild night life crowding along the sidewalks as they cruise down Broadway. She looks up and soaks in the vibrant colors from the electronic billboards; their magical glow making up the heart of Times Square.

Mr. P unfastens his seatbelt and looks over to Gino, as the car comes to a standstill. "Wait here," he says, and climbs out. Opening the back door, he holds out his hand for her.

Touching the sidewalk, as his strong arm pulls her out, she listens to him slam the door behind her. "So, what now?" she asks, as her hair blows around her face.

He places his hands over her cheeks and leans in; her chest fluttering as their lips share a romantic moment. "Now for business," he says, and spins around, undoing his second button on his white shirt as he maneuvers his way through the crowd, smirking his ego at all the gazing eyes, as she follows closely behind, rolling her eyes at his vain self. He's such a tease! The smell of fresh cigarette smoke clouds the air as they approach the glowing exotic blue sidewalk. She looks up, scaling the razer blue and red electric sign reading 'Exotic Bloom', with security either side of the square cave entrance, standing next to fire lit temples, as the chattering guests wait behind the red rope. He nods to the security; instant service as they walk straight through the double black entrance doors.

The door swings closed behind her; trading the sidewalk chatter for drowned out club music as they stroll the dim hallway. He pulls the silver handle, their ears exposed to the loud bass as they enter, their skin painted like a blueberry as they turn left, walking along the starry floor of the outer circuit of the neon blue lit strip club.

She looks right, raising her eyes as she stares into the center, watching as the naked busty stripper slides her oiled body up and down the pole; her feet lavished with piles of money as the guests throw their dollars from their red leather couches. *Ewwww. What the heck is this?* She turns to face him, as he turns around and leans his right arm against the black glittery bar top with a smile. "Why the fuck have you brought me to a strip club?" shouts Arabella. The bartender comes over.

Mr. P looks at him and signals his usual times two, before looking back to her, as she brings her ear to his mouth. "Do you like it?" he shouts.

She leans into his ear. "Why have you brought me here?"

He laughs and glides his hands across her face. "Do you like the interior?"

She looks to her right and screws up her face at the strippers filthy position. "This is disgusting!"

He laughs and leans in; their lips passionately sliding as she stands on her tip toes, wrapping her arms around him as he swoops her up and wraps her legs around him. She glides her hands around his shaved face, the smell of his fragrance teasing her as she gets lost in the moment. He breaks their lips, pressing his forehead against hers as his glistening gaze melts into her beauty. "Good. It's yours. Do what you want with it!" He puts her down and turns to the bartender, grabbing his Malibu and Coke, sipping as he looks back to her with a grin behind the glass. "What's wrong?" he laughingly asks. He sips on his drink as he waits for her to react.

Huh? She shakes her head and grabs her drink; the coconut rum swishing around her mouth, as she attempts to processes what he said before swallowing. "I don't understand. Repeat that!"

He leans in again. "I said... it's yours. Ignore the fact it's a strip club. Turn it into whatever you want!"

She frowns, shaking her head as she raises her hands. "Why?"

He puts the glass down on the bar, caressing his fingers across her flushed cheeks as he lavishes in her beauty. "I like to treat the ones who have a special place in my heart."

Fluttering inside to his melting words, she places her right hand against his chest. "Aww. Now that was sweet... and here I was thinking you were emotionless."

He chuckles as he lets go of her and turns to the bartender. He nods to him. The bartender reaches underneath the bar and pulls up a blush pink electric sign; her eyes widen as she reads 'Arabella's'. "Now it's official!" he shouts and winks at her.

She shots back the rest of her drink. *This can't be real.* She raises her hands. "How am I meant to tell people?"

"Oh, like your boyfriend!"

She doesn't correct him on Elliot's new title. "Sure… my boyfriend. How do I explain it?"

He places his hands on her warm cheeks. "Luckily for you, this place is being redesigned so it will be, give or take six months before we cross that bridge!"

"And what about us?"

He picks her back up; her arms and legs wrapping around him. He sits back on the spinning bar stool and pressing their foreheads together, as their burning green flames exchange. "Tell me why you gave yourself away to me first."

She sighs her coconut warmth against his lips. "This might sound silly, but I've always had this superstition about soulmates, and I don't know… I wanted to wait for this person… and then you came along out of nowhere." She starts to giggle. "I probably sound ridiculous!"

He raises her chin with his finger. "Do you want to know why I left you that night?" She nods. "Honestly, I didn't want to treat you like other girls. When I said that evening that you were like no one I had ever met… I meant it."

She releases a small tear and rolls her eyes. "I thought you said I was a distraction!"

He wipes her tear. "Well, that's true. It was part of the reason… but then you know me… a risk taker. You're the biggest risk I have ever taken; hence I kissed you that night. I couldn't let you go." He grabs her hands and curls his fingers between hers. "You're an angel that didn't fall."

Goddd…. You are so perfect. She tears up, as her heart races. She releases their linked fingers and throws her arms around him, sniffling as she parts her lips, squeezing his muscly neck as she slides her wet lips between his; their coconut passion mixing as tears stream down her face, fluttering inside as she scrunches her fingers through his spiked thick hair. She breaks their moment to catch her breath, brushing her wet nose against his as she giggles with a pearly smile.

Gino enters the club, looking around as the music penetrates his old ears. He spots them and races along the starry floor, interrupting the romance as he leans into his ear. "We've got to go. We're being tailed."

Widening his eyes, he looks to Gino. "What!" Gino nods to him and turns back around. Mr. P turns back to Arabella. "I have to go! I will come find you when the time is right," he shouts and removes her from him before standing. He looks to the bartender. "Make sure she gets home safe!" he shouts, as he points to her. He gently presses his lips on her forehead and sinks them in, his cologne teasing her nose; a parting souvenir as he releases her and turns around, looking back to her one last time before exiting.

MR. P

Resting her rosy cheek against her right hand, Arabella leans on the light oak rounded table, sipping on her iced latte through a thick green straw in the coffee shop, next door to Campbell, and Co. Gazing through the front window, she watches a romantic couple walk by, hand in hand, giggling away, as they walk their dog through the spring sunshine. She sighs, thinking about when Mr. P will next show up. It's been a month!

Slurping the final drops, she looks up to the clock. It's 14:00. Time to return to work. Scraping the metal legs of the brown chair along the small white tiles; the customers ears bleed as she stands, picking up the empty cup and walking to the front. Throwing it in the trash, she exits into the spring breeze; her hair lightly blowing around her glowing face as her emerald tea mini dress raises, showing off her smooth thighs. Approaching the shop door, she peers through the glass;

the sound of busy traffic moving behind her as she stares at Elliot, leaning over the counter in his grey suit trousers, chatting away to Clarissa. Bracing herself for boredom, she enters; letting the door swing behind her as she follows the grey carpet into the open lounge and throwing her maple cross shoulder bag on the couch. Turning around, she takes a slow walk to the counter and shuffles behind Clarissa to retake her seat.

"How about the public library?" asks Elliot.

Clarissa looks to her before looking back to him. "No, no, no! You can't copy B," she says, as Arabella nods in agreement.

"Well, we need to find somewhere soon," he says, and looks to his fiancé. "Any suggestions?"

She looks around for her smartphone. "One moment, I've left my phone in my bag." Shimmying past the blonde queen, she makes her way over to the couch and retrieves it from her maple bag, turning around as she unlocks it. Burying her face in her device, she loads up the search engine, moving slowly across the floor. Her right ear perks to the shop door opening. She breaks her engrossed search and peels her eyes off the screen, drifting her vision over to the customer; his penny loafers hitting her first, journeying up his black suit trousers before reaching his white shirt and black jacket. She widens her eyes; her smartphone entering a freefall as her grip loosens. The room falls

260

silent as Clarissa widens her eyes and mouth. Elliot looks at them both in confusion and turns around, still confused as he doesn't recognize the customer, as Mr. P casts his devilish gaze to Arabella, looking down to her feet and racing over to her, their souls sharing an unexplainable moment, as they both bend down to grab it. She rests her dainty fingers above his soft hand, as their green flames ignite. They both stand.

He hands her the smartphone with a smile, lavishing up her complexion before stepping back. "Hope I'm not interrupting anything," he says, as he looks Elliot up and down.

Elliot still has no idea who he is. "Not at all. How may we help you?"

Mr. P smiles to him. "Just browsing," he says, as Elliot turns to face Clarissa.

"That's Mr. P," whispers C. His eyes widen in shock; he's finally in the presence of the mystery that Clarissa doesn't stop talking about.

He turns around and smiles at the devil and holds out his hand to him. "Oh. I got what you mean," he laughingly says, as their hands lock and shake. Elliot points back to Clarissa. "You meant Clarissa ha-ha," he says, as Arabella looks down and shakes her head, feeling uncomfortable as it becomes too surreal for her.

Mr. P looks over to Clarissa blushing. "What's he like ay," he says, as Elliot makes his way back to the counter.

She jokingly slaps Elliot's arm. "I know. Fancy seeing you here anyway. Are you wanting flowers?"

He breaks their eye contact and looks to Arabella, before looking back to her. "Just one," he cheekily says, and winks to the blonde queen, as Arabella releases a jealous sigh.

Clarissa plays with her golden hair. "Well feel free to browse the list on the wall."

He smiles to her. "Will do. Pretend I'm not here and continue with whatever you were discussing," he says, and looks to his left, pretending to read the list of flower.

"So, do you have any other suggestions?" asks Elliot; his words falling on deaf ears as Clarissa leans against the glass in a dreamy gaze, watching her fantasy in front.

Mr. P peeks out the corner of his right eye over to Arabella, before turning to her. "May I use your bathroom?"

She smiles. "Sure. Follow me," she says, and turns around, descending into the workshop, as he follows behind, smiling at the blonde queen in passing.

Turning left at the end of the workshop, she walks the small hallway and turns around on the tangy orange tiled floor, standing between the men and women's bathroom doors either side, listening to the sound of his taps approach. Watching him turn the corner in style with a sexy smirk on his pretty face, she feels his dangerously seductive eyes lock into her. "What are you doing here," she loudly whispers.

"You're hard to resist!" he seditiously says.

She places her right hand over his mouth, pushing him through the women's bathroom door to her right; the hallway light fading behind her as the door swings closed; his hands gripping her curvy waist as he walks backwards, being guided through the dark room into the cubicle. She silently closes the door with her left hand and faces him; nothing but touch to guide them. "You can't just show up at my work." She feels his chuckling vibrations in her palm.

He removes her soft hand from his mouth, curling his fingers between hers and leans in, their noses brushing as his parted lips rest against hers. "You are funny," he passionately mumbles.

She deeply exhales; her warmth steaming against his ice blast breath, her lusting desire fluttering down her rapidly breathing chest. She lightly caresses her smooth hands along his clean-shaven jaw line, as his hands slide under her dress, picking her up from her thick thighs; her legs wrapping around him as he pins her against the door. She grazes her glossy pink lips against his and wraps her dainty hands around his cheeks. "I've missed you!" she softly whispers, gripping his thick black hair as she locks her parted lips, their moisture exchanging as he sweeps his fingertips above her ears, her neck tingling as she looks up; his teeth catching her bottom lip as she releases a soft moan to his feathering touch. He swoops his hands inside her dress from above, cupping her warm breasts; her lacy bra brushing against his knuckles as he catches her nipples between his fingers, her body sensationally stimulating as he squeezes his fingers and teasingly twists. She removes his hands from her bra. "I've got to get back, we've been away too long," she says, as he takes hold of her thighs and lowers her to a standing position. Turning around, she opens the door, holding his hand as she guides him to the exit. She rests her grip on the door handle, biting down on her plumped bottom lip as her juicy thighs tingle to his grazing touch. She bends over; the dark room sounding a loud clap, as his hand spanks her peachy bottom, her teeth sinking deeper as her sultry moan escapes the corners of her trapped mouth. She releases her bite and exhales, flicking her hair from her flushed face. "Maybe next time." She pulls back the handle; the hallway light shining through as she flicks her hair and exits.

Turning the corner into the workshop, she wipes her glossy wet lips, widening her eyes as Clarissa looks at her suspiciously flushed face from the other side of the wooden table.

"You took a while?" says Clarissa.

She walks towards the archway whilst looking back at her. "Yeah, I used the bathroom as well."

Clarissa's face lights up with a smile, as Mr. P turns the corner, gazing in his dreamy complexion, as he walks along with his hands in his pockets and ascends onto the shop floor. She makes her way back to the shop floor; she slides behind Arabella who's stolen her seat; the smell of mens cologne tickling her nose as it drifts from the suspicious brunette. Surely not she wonders and casts her eyes at Mr. P, as he looks at the list again.

Elliot leans his elbows against the counter. "Finally! Any other good suggestions for our engagement party C?"

She puts her suspicions to the side and looks to him. "I will have a think."

Mr. P's ear perks up and turns to face them. "Engagement. Who's the lucky couple?" he asks, as Arabella nervously sighs under her breath; the one thing she didn't want to reveal, as Clarissa points to her and Elliot. He pauses briefly to process, smiling at Elliot before casting his burning glare into Arabella. "Well, congratulations to both of you," he says, cunningly.

She looks down at his left hand, widening her eyes in shock as he dangles her lost necklace from his left pocket. *Oh my god. What are you doing?* She looks up to him, her anger intensely brewing as she bites down on her teeth, locking her glaring steam into him, as Clarissa taps Elliot's arm and hints with her eyes.

He turns around to Mr. P. "Clarissa wonders if you would like to accompany her to our engagement party?" he asks, feeling her slap him on the arm. "Sorry, Arabella and I would like to invite you to our engagement party. Maybe you would like to go with Clarissa?"

He pockets the necklace and looks to Clarissa with a smile. "I would be honored," he says, and casts his devilish eyes back to Arabella with a smirk. Watching her grind her teeth, he says, "In that case, we're going to need an engagement gift." He takes out his black wallet and walks to the counter, handing Clarissa a platinum business card registered to Hotel L'Amour. "Just bill the entire cost of the flowers."

She looks down in the hope to find out his real name. No luck! "Isn't he just the best," says Clarissa.

Elliot's looks to him in disbelief. "I don't know what to say. Thank you very much," he says, sincerely and shakes his hand, before looking back to Clarissa. "This guy is amazing." He lets go of his hand and looks over to his fiancé, raising his eyebrow as she glares at Mr. P. "Are you going to say anything?" That's the last thing she wants to do!

Arabella gulps. "Thank you," she mutters, met with a wink from the devil.

266

Elliot moves towards Arabella and takes her hand, guiding her towards the shop entrance before looking behind. "We're going to get a coffee. We will leave you two alone. Thanks again Mr. P, it's an absolute pleasure to have met you and we will see you another time, if not before the party."

"Any time," he replies and smiles to Arabella before turning around to face Clarissa.

ENOUGH IS ENOUGH

Sitting on the chocolate brown couch in a white laced dress, Arabella spreads her smooth legs spread across the hockey puck, clipping her hair up and closing her eyes before leaning back, attempting to cleanse her resentment for Mr. P's necklace stunt earlier. She listens out her right ear to Elliot rummaging through the cupboards in the kitchen, as he searches for wine glasses. She hears his footsteps and opens her eyes, putting her hand out and taking the red wine from him. She removes her legs from the hockey puck and scoots over for him, as he takes a seat.

"Cheers," says Elliot, their glasses ringing as they toast. They both take a sip. He lavishes up the taste, as she screws up her face from the bitter taste. "Ahh, that's a good one." He rests the glass on the table and turns to face her. "What's wrong?"

She leans forward and places the glass on the table before looking at him. "Nothing."

He gazes over her raspberry face and places his left hand on her warm cheek. "Are you sure? Since we've been back, you haven't said a single word."

She flicks his hands off her and leans back, placing her hands over her eyes and releasing a deep sigh. "I'm fine ok. Go get some paper and a pen and let's just do this."

He stands up and shimmies past her, towards the woven fruit bowl. He returns to his seat with his hands equipped. "So, do you want to write or me?" He receives cold silence. "I guess that will be me then." He leans forwards and places the pen and notepad on the hockey puck, rubbing his hands together before picking the pen back up. "Alrighty then, who do we have first?"

"Clarissa and Beatrice," she says.

He writes them down, tapping the end of his pen against his teeth, as he thinks. "Oh, my mom. What about yours?" She shakes her head sideways. "No thank you."

He closes his eyes, trying to draw names out of thin air. "Oh, of course. Mr. P. What a guy," he says, chuckling away as he writes it down. "Such a badass name." He feels the force of her, as she kicks the hockey puck in a burst of rage, the red wine spilling onto the cream rug.

"Jesus!" He jumps from his seat, rushing to the kitchen in a state of panic, as she stands and races over to the bed, grabbing her bag and smartphone before sliding into her brown sandals and exiting the apartment door. Returning with a wet sponge, he bends down, and scrubs away, too concerned with the forming stain to notice her sudden departure.

Walking under the yellow glowing streetlights along East 49th Street, she looks up at the clear night sky in utter despair; even the chilly evening breeze can't cool her down as it sweeps across her burning skin. She reaches into her bag and whips out her smartphone. It's 21:22. She clicks the cab app and waits for it to load and looks ahead. If it isn't a miracle! A cab pulls up in front. Steaming with rage, she races towards it and aggressively taps on the passenger side front window before opening the door.

"Can you take me to Hotel L'Amour please?"

The driver looks back to her. "Calm down lady. Get in," he says, and watches in the reverse mirror as she enters.

Pulling up in the red cobble lane, the driver looks back to her.

"That will be—" Dashing from the cab unpaid; she leaves the redcoat unable to perform his duty, rushing past him and bolting up the white steps, barging past the arriving guests at the top into the lobby. She puts her middle finger up to Chloe, and turns to face the guard, locking her enraged glare straight at the guard. He opens the elevator without a fuss. Stepping straight inside, the lobbies light fades behind her in the reflection; her eyes burning like the devil as the devil red lighting paints her skin, unable to recognize herself as her adrenaline pumps. Nothing but her fist in his face clouding her mind.

It's time! Reaching the dimmed penthouse, she steps along the black and white tiles with her right hand out, knocking over a vase on the silver table; the glass smashing into shards behind her as she makes her way behind the small couch. There he is! She glares at him, burning her green flames into him as he leans against the corner wall, shirtless, in his black suit trousers, as he dangles the necklace chain around his right hand.

He grins. "What did that vase ever do to you!"

She places her bag on the couch and slowly walks around the edge, turning right, onto the Persian rug and making her way around the coffee table, keeping her eyes on him, closer and closer. She clenches her fists. "You are something else."

Flexing his muscles, he blocks her attack, catching her wrists mid-air. "Feisty," he says, as she whips her wrists from his hands, breaking free of his muscly grip and tries again. He catches her wrists again and laughs. "You really are one wild ride." He lets go of her wrists. "Behave."

She turns around and walks behind the coffee table, staring out at the purple lit terrace; the reflection showing him opening the necklace. "Why the fuck do you have that?" she aggressively shouts.

He chuckles. "A souvenir!"

She turns around in disbelief. "Are you insane?" she shouts, as he raises his eyebrow. "You can't just play games like that!"

"Are you taking the piss?"

She turns back around, looking out at the clear water; her rage simmering as the shadowy waves soothe her. She sighs. "Why would you do that?"

"I like risk." He looks down at the picture of her and Elliot. "Imagine if we got caught…what would poor Elliot do then."

She spins around. "Keep my fiancé out of your fucking mouth!"

He tingles inside. "You just get hotter by the second."

She exhales and raises her hands. "Why are you being such an asshole?"

He walks towards her, his bare feet brushing along the Persian rug as he throws the necklace on the couch to his left. "I am the way I am."

She lavishes up his masculine scent; his hardened pecks inches away from her, as he towers over her. "What's that then?" she innocently asks; their eyes exchanging their green flames.

"One naughty devil," he says, mischievously, and spins around, her chest beating up and down as she flutters inside, watching him slowly step along the carpet. "So, here's your choice. I will give you the chance to walk away, my lips will remained sealed, and you can go about your life as if we never met."

She removes her sandals and sneaks up behind him. "And the other option?"

He starts to turn around. "I—"

She reaches behind his head and pulls him in closer; her dainty fingers gripping tight on his thick black hair as her glossy lips lightly graze his. "You are my only option," she passionately whispers, as her lust steams his upper lip. She pulls him backwards; his arms swooping around her curvy waist as he spins her around, lifting her up as he sits back on the main couch., her knees resting on the creamy leather either side of his muscly legs. She towers over him and locks her parted lips, running her acrylics through his hair, exhaling her passion to his stimulating touch along her smooth thighs. He raises her vanilla laced dress; her lips widening to his brushing palms. She pulls the dress over her clipped hair; her back releasing pressure as he unclips her white bra.

She looks behind her and throws the dress on the small couch, reaching her left hand to her right shoulder and gliding the strap off, gasping as he wraps his soft, moist lips around her rosy tip, her back tingling as he scratches his burning pleasure down her. She grabs his right hand and brings it under her legs, brushing his fingers against the outside of her wet lace. He trickles his fingers up; her body shivering to his feathering touch as he dips inside, the warm lace brushing against his knuckles as his fingers slide between her soft pink lips, whisking goodbye to her nipple and switches, suckling on the other as she throws her arms around his head, squeezing tight as her legs spasm to his circling fingers on her clit. She grips his hair tight and leans back, the penthouse drowning in intense moans as she thrusts her hips.

She listens to high heels tap along the tiles behind her, clamming up his moist lips with her erotic passion; his eyes peeking right, chuckling his lusting breath against her wet cupid lips as they continue to ride.

"Of course you would bloody come out now!" he shouts, as Arabella stops thrusting and turns around, widening her eyes as Dakota glares at him.

"I thought I would come watch."

Arabella turns her sweaty flushed face back to him. "Is she serious?" she whispers.

He nods and looks to Dakota. "Why don't you join us instead?" he laughingly winds up.

Dakota frowns at him, as she raises her eyebrow at him. "Not with you but…" says Dakota and looks at the beautifully rounded ass on top of him. Arabella's kinky mind runs wild; it's a new experience after all.

He looks to Dakota. "Well that's never—"

"Come on then," says Arabella, and turns around to Dakota.

He widens his eyes. "Seriously?" he whispers, as she bites down on her sultry bottom lip and nods. He watches Dakota smirk her scarlet red lips at him and spins around to the bedroom, before looking to Arabella. "Well this is going to be… interesting!" he says, as he lightly brushes his fingers against her g spot.

Leaning his head against the couch rest, bedroom side, he lays across the couch naked, as Arabella rests on her knees in front of him, her dainty hands twisting and sliding up and down his wet cock; her lips and tongue working his shaft. He hears high heels approaching and looks to his right, raising his eyes at Dakota's goddess body, as she makes her way behind Arabella, holding a range of sex toys and rope.

"Christ! This isn't uni," he says.

"Shut up you twat!" She places the toys to her right and gets on all fours, lavishing up her playmates arousing scent. Arabella releases his cock from her mouth and stares into his beauty with her mouth widened, releasing a deep, and long moan as the back of her thighs explode in an electric tingle to her icy tongue. Dakota grabs her first item and reaches around the front of her playmate, tilting her head up and strapping a ball gag around her mouth. "Can't be having excessive moaning now." Arabella rolls her eyes up; her ripe cheeks rippling their bounce from her hard spanks. Dakota flips her onto her back and looks to him. "Pull her onto your chest."

"So demanding," he says and rolls his eyes, trying to wind her up. Dakota ignores him and grabs her next item and steps off the couch. He swoops his arms around Arabella and lifts her onto his muscly chest, nibbling on the side of her neck as he listens to heels stepping behind him. Arabella looks up to her hands; her vision lost as the blindfold tightens behind her head. She listens to the walking heels out her right ear, her stomach breathing in and out as he cups her breasts and fondles. She releases a crying, muffled moan; her curvy legs intensely shaking, drowning in pleasure as her hardened nipples and wet clit, twist, and tingle. She hears a bottle cap flick open, followed by a squeezing noise. She gasps behind the ball gag; her tight entrance spreading, her chest and stomach rapidly moving as Dakota works her lubed fingers, in and out.

Dakota looks to Mr. P. "Don't get jealous now."

He laughs at her delusions. "Here we go again. We're not in university anymore."

She adds a third finger; her playmates muffled moans getting louder. "You're so inconsiderate."

He screws his face up, as the penthouse fills with muffled screams. "What are you talking about?"

She adds a fourth finger; twisting and turning, in and out, as her playmates legs spasm uncontrollably. "It doesn't matter prick!" She pulls her fingers out and grabs her third toy, placing it around her own waist.

He widens his eyes and leans into Arabella's ear. "See how crazy she is," he chuckles. "Oh, she also has a strap on," he quietly whispers, as she feels the cold rubber cock against her clit.

"Hold up one finger for nothing, two for my big rubber cock, three for that dickheads cock, or four for both."

Mr. P leans into her ear again. "I told you it would be interesting," he laughingly mumbles. He raises his eyebrows, as she raises four dainty fingers. "Christ!" He sighs, peeling her sweaty back from his rippled abs and wraps his left arm around her neck, lightly caressing her hardened nipple with moist lips. He looks at Dakota. "Well at least pop it in for me."

"Do it yourself," says Dakota, watching him roll his eyes. "Wanker!"

"Charming." Reaching between her legs with his left hand, he grabs his thick cock and shuffles into a comfortable position, pulling her ball gag slightly down with his right hand before slipping it inside; her orgasmic gasp pleasure to his ears as his girth slides her tight walls. Dakota positions her knees between his muscly calf's and leans over, as he pulls the ball gag under her chin. Arabella releases a breathless gasp across her playmates juicy lips; their pressed plumped breasts shaking together as her pussy stretches in orgasmic pleasure. She wraps her dainty hands around Dakota, scrunching her beautifully thick and wavy curls in her fingers as she pulls her parted lips closer, their lipsticks smudging as they exchange their icy warmth; her body scorching between the two alpha's as they pound away. She widens her juicy lips, panting away on Dakota's moist upper lip, her body spiking with intense pleasure as her moans become screams.

Dakota reinserts her ball gag and squints her glaring eyes at him. "What are you looking at?" Covered in sweat, he starts chuckling; Arabella's back feeling his vibrations through his shaking chest. "How the fuck you got your position, I'll never know," says Dakota.

"Wrong party, right time."

Dakota stops and pulls out. "Flip," she orders. He removes his cock and turns Arabella on her front; her dripping breasts pressing against his golden chest. She wraps her arms around his muscly neck, clawing the back of his head, resting her chin against his right shoulder and gasps through her ball gag, as they repenetrate. "Can you not look at my tits?" He takes both hands and makes binoculars, staring straight at her bouncing breasts. "You are so childish," says Dakota.

"Me being childish? You're in a double penetration and I'm not meant to look at your bloody tits?"

Dakota pulls out and removes the strap on. She lifts Arabella off him and chucks her behind her, throwing her arms around him as she climbs on top of him; the tip of his cock resting on his V line as she slides her teasing soft pink lips back and forth, pressing her forehead against his as their eyes deeply lock their emotional history.

"You infuriate me," she dangerously whispers.

"So they say... Dakota, you realize you're like laying naked on me, right?"

She grimaces her lips, as their noses brush. "I do," she lovingly whispers, and flutters her lashes.

"Oh god, look... I know how special I am, and yes, I am just absolutely amazing and stuff—" The penthouse fills with a loud slap.

"I was joking. Vain prick," she says, and climbs off him, as he laughs.

Watching Dakota return to the bedroom, he crawls along the leather couch to Arabella and lifts her blindfold; her eyes rapidly blinking as they adjust to the bright light. "I suppose you heard that?" He looks at her mouth. "Oh," he chuckles, as he reaches behind her and unties the ball gag.

She wraps her hands around his flushed cheeks and pushes him back, brushing her nose against his as their glistening eyes exchange their burning attraction. "Yes. You are very vain, but a funny vain."

"Thank you. I've been telling her that for years," he says, met with rolling eyes.

THE GRAND TOUR

Pressing her right ear against his sweaty peck, Arabella listens to Mr. P's heartbeat, lightly scratching her left acrylics up and down his rippled abs as she slowly widens her sleepy eyes, looking around the half-lit penthouse; the dusk grey sky reflecting onto the tiles as she clocks the Central Park birds chirping. She gently peels her sticky, naked body from him and stands, creeping along the Persian rug and behind the couch to her left. She leans down and grabs her bag, placing it on top of the couch as he rolls over, his peachy ass staring right at her as she retrieves her smartphone. She unlocks it; her stomach sinking as she stares at the bright screen. It's 05:00.

Shit. She stares at a dozen messages and missed calls from Elliot, gulping as she locks the screen. Moving silently along the tiles, she tip toes over to the opposite couch; the sound of faint snoring coming from the bedroom as she reclaims her dress. She silently slides it down her hourglass figure and grabs her thong, screwing up her face as she throws the wet fabric to the corner wall. *Yuck!* She looks at Mr. P and sighs a dreamy gaze. *You look so cute.* Sliding her feet into her sandals, she turns around and sneaks back over to her cross-shoulder bag. Throwing it over her, she closes her eyes for a moment, inhaling and exhaling as she prepares to start her journey. Attempting to be silent, she slides her sandals along the tiles and hits the elevator call button. The doors ping open, creating a loud noise. So much for silence!

Walking along the sidewalk of 5th Avenue, she lavishes up the freshly cut grass scent; the light breeze sweeping over from Central Park. *This is long.* Reaching inside her bag for her smartphone, she books a cab with her BookShib. She's only walked one block!

Standing next to the half-headed sculpture in Doris C. Freedman Plaza, she listens to the morning traffic as she grimaces her lips, struggling to conjure up an excuse for Elliot. She looks up at the yellow cab. Talk about instant service! Opening the back door, she smiles to the Italian driver as she climbs in. He doesn't smile back! She hears a click, and looks to the door, raising her eyebrow at the lock.

"You owe me money," he sternly says, and sets off.

She looks at the chubby, tough looking wise guy through his front mirror. *Oh my god.* It's the cabbie from last night!

"Sorry. I was in an angry state and totally forgot."

He turns left onto East 46th St. "Well, you're not getting out this car until you pay!"

She widens her mouth. *Who does he think he is?* "Excuse me?"

He turns left onto Madison Avenue. "You heard me!"

She deeply exhales through her nose. "Listen, asshole. You'll get your money but don't make threats to me."

He laughs and turns left onto E 49th St. He pulls up outside her apartment and turns around, glaring at her. "Money now."

She looks down and opens her bag, rummaging around. She gulps. "I have to go inside to get money." She watches him open his door and get out, looking at him as he opens her door. "Let's go."

She slides out the seat and stands; met with anger as he towers over her and grabs her arm. "What the hell do you think you're doing! Get your hands off me!" she screams.

She breaks free and huffs, walking to the apartment door as her heart races. *What do I do?* Panicking, she reaches into her bag, her arms shaking as she takes out her keys and inserts it into the lock, twisting it slowly as she tries to think. She doesn't want this man coming inside. She pushes down the handle and opens the door. "Elliot!" she shouts, sighing relief as he comes rushing from the couch.

He looks at her; his stomach turning as he's been up all night worried sick. "What's happened. Where have you been?"

"I went to Hotel L'Amour last night to see Mr. P and forgot to pay for the cab," she says, frightened and points to the driver, as Elliot reaches into his pocket.

The driver's lips start to quiver. "Mr. P?" he tremblingly asks, looking her up and down; her fiery attitude, gorgeous thick brunette hair and blazing beauty sending shivers down him. "Please forgive me, Queen Arabella."

Elliot stares at him with raised eyebrows before casting his eyes to her. "Queen?"

Queen? Mr. P? She twists her tongue and bites down, squinting her eyes at this Italian. "If you ever lay your hands on another woman, I will tell him." The driver nods and turns around, racing to his car, as she walks inside.

Elliot watches the cab drive off and turns around, closing the door behind him as he looks over to her dropping her dress. His tired brain doesn't even compute she isn't wearing any panties. "I'm sorry, do you want to explain what the hell that was? Queen Arabella?"

She gets into the sheets and lays back, watching as he moves closer. "He's crazy," she says with raised hands.

He sits on the edge and looks at her, shaking his head with a frown. "I've been texting you all night. What you mean you went to see Mr. P?"

This is it, I guess. It'll all be over soon. He's going to hate me. "I have something to tell you."

His engulfed caffeine blood shot eyes try to maintain their lock. "What is it?"

She closes her eyes, her heart beating as her lips start to tremor. "I… I…. I…. went to see Mr. P because I was angry with him."

He raises his eyebrow. "You've lost me."

She exhales heavily, her arms shaking as she looks down. "I went to see him because me and –"

"I am so stupid," he says, and stands, moving to the hockey puck holding his head over his hands as he looks down at the long list of names he's produced.

"I'm so sorry," she cryingly says.

"You're angry because he didn't offer us the ball room for the engagement party yesterday," as he grabs the list and walks over to her, "so you went to see to him to ask."

Wow! She wipes her tears and nods. "Exactly. I didn't get to see him. He was too busy, and I fell asleep in the lobby."

He passes her the list. "Check that out after you've had your beauty sleep," he says, and kisses her on the forehead, before turning around and heading for the kitchen; nothing but coffee on his mind.

She lays back and closes her eyes, inhaling, and exhaling as she tries to control her nerves.

Pumped with caffeine and a few hours of sleep on the sofa, Elliot makes some final adjustments in the mirror, rolling his blue shirt sleeves up to his elbows before tucking it into his white chino shorts and tightening his light tanned belt. He combs his slick fingers through his light ashy hair, as he slips into his brown suede driving shoes. He gazes at Arabella's boobs, as she sits up.

"Any plans for today?" he asks.

"Just spoke with C, we're going to go shopping for engagement party dresses. You?"

He grabs his car keys from the woven fruit bowl. "Maybe grab a bite to eat and search for some venues."

She stands and heads for the shower; his perked eyes following her sexy hourglass figure. "Sounds good," she says, and slams the door behind her. Left to his own devices, he throws his car keys in the air and catches them before spinning around and exiting the apartment.

The roaring engine of his Camaro tears through 5th Avenue; interrupting the lunchtime picnics in Central Park. Taking a sharp left into the red cobble lane, he removes his shades and throws them inside the glove compartment, as the red coat approaches. He gets out and turns around to him. "Take care of her," he says, watching his baby drive away. Turning around, he scales his surroundings; it reminds him of Vegas. He ascends the white steps; his ears soaking up the soothing fountain sprinkle as he smiles to the doormen who open the door in line with his pace. Stepping into the lobby, he scales the room in awe; the overhanging chandelier in the spacious white marble open floor catching his attention. He walks over to the reception, leaning his left elbow against the mahogany desk and looking over to the guard on the stool.

"Welcome to Hotel L'Amour. What is the nature of your visit today?" asks Chloe.

He stands up straight and faces her, looking the cute blonde up and down. "Well hello… I called earlier about a showing around the ball room for an engagement party. I was told to come in at midday. My name is Elliot Smith."

She looks at her sticky note. "Yes, I remember. You spoke to me. I'm Chloe, the manager here at Hotel L'Amour."

"Brilliant! Do I just follow you then?"

She looks to his left and right. "No fiancé?"

He puts both hands on the counter and taps away. "Afraid not. She came here last night in the hope of booking it and ended up falling asleep when Mr. P wasn't available? So I thought I would surprise her."

She knows that's not true. The lobby was empty! "Oh, I'm sorry to hear that. What's her name?"

"Arabella."

Her eyes widen. "Arabella, what a beautiful name. Will she be taking your surname?"

He laughs. "Funnily enough, we have spoken about this. You see, her surname is Harper and doesn't like mine as it's far too common, so she is refusing to change it."

She fake smiles and nods. "That sounds like a lovers dispute to me. One moment please," she says and walks over to the other receptionist. She whispers into her ear before moving back to Elliot. "My colleague, Maria, will be with you in a moment." She points behind him at the waiting area. "Please take a seat behind you, Elliot."

He smiles and turns around, taking a seat on the brown couch, watching Chloe as she picks up the reception phone. He looks to his right, wondering why there is a guard; his curiosity broken as the other receptionist steps along the marble in her black high heels.

"You must be Elliot? I'm Maria."

He stands and smiles. "That's me. Nice to meet you."

She turns around and starts walking towards the ballroom entrance, looking back at him to follow. "So, how long have you been together?"

He steps through the gold frame doors and widens his eyes in awe, looking left, and right, as they walk the walnut glossed floor. "Seven months."

She raises her eyebrow, turning around as they reach the center of the room. "That's great. Please look around and I'll be here if you have any questions."

He smiles and looks up, his chest pounding as he gazes at the three-tier crystal glass chandelier; concerned about the cost. What a tight ass! He spins around and scales the room, left to right, the spring mural wall depicting blossoming blush pink trees inside Central Park. He points to the mural. "Is there any reason for this mural?"

"This is called the Season's ballroom." Well that makes sense!

He continues along to the matt black marble topped bar, imagining all the guests piling around it. That a tick on his checklist. Turning 90 degrees clockwise, he continues along the next wall; the red leather long couches positioned around crystal glass square tables in a longue style setting will give the guests comfort. Another tick to his checklist. He turns 90 degrees clockwise again, tapping his right index finger against his lip as he looks at the stage; he loves a good speech. He turns around to Maria. "I love it. How much?"

"It's on the house!" shouts Mr. P, as he leans against the gold frame door with his arms crossed. He uncrosses his arms and walks towards them; the sound of his penny loafers echoing through the grand ballroom, as he snaps his fingers for Maria to leave. He gazes up, slowly spinning towards Elliot with his arms raised as he embraces his palace. "She's a beauty."

Elliot stands blown away at his generosity once again. "She is indeed. Are you sure about it being on the house? I can pay. You've already done more than enough with the flowers."

He brings his right arm around Elliot and slowly guides him towards the door. "I'm just full of surprises!"

Elliot looks to him as they approach the door. "Ha-ha, that you are."

Mr. P removes his arm and swings left to the elevator, looking left to Elliot. "Want to see another surprise?"

Elliot raises his hands. "Do I ever!" The elevator opens. Mr. P steps in first and turns around, watching as he enters to his right. The enclosed space turns dark. Elliot flinches: he wasn't ready for the devil red lighting. He looks at him through the reflection. "Has anyone ever told you that you look like the devil himself?"

Mr. P glares at him through the mirror. "It's my nickname in the mafia," he sternly says.

Elliot's lips explode with laughter, patting him on the back of his black suit jacket. "Good one," he says, as Mr. P starts fake laughing with him.

Stepping out, onto the black and white tiles, as the sound of Mr. P fades around the corner, his jaw drops, astonished by the exquisite luxury. Slowly strolling along the tiles, towards the glass sliding door, he gazes over the beautiful hanging artwork to his right, the smell of cologne and sex lingering. He grips the door handle, and looks left, watching Mr. P pour them a drink across the room. "Do you mind?"

Mr. P nods. "Go ahead, my man."

He slides the glass door and steps out onto the terrace, hit with a strong breeze across his face as he looks ahead at the approaching grey clouds. He walks along the black star floor, whistling at the stunning extravagant glass swimming pool. He crouches down; his legs clicking as he dips his fingers into the warm water. He hears the penny loafers approaching and looks left, shaking the water from his fingers as he stands and faces him. "This is awesome." He accepts the whiskey glass from Mr. P and turns around, following him to the railings edge, his stomach sinking as he looks out to Central Park, masking his fear of heights; he doesn't want to come across as a wimp. He takes a sip of the fine whiskey, swishing the sweet taste around his palette before swallowing it; the delicacy leaving his mouth feeling very wet. "That's very sweet."

Mr. P partially lowers his glass as he glances over his front garden. "That it is."

Elliot turns around, scaling the terrace, still blown away as he takes another sweet sip. He widens his eyes, lowering the glass and slowly looking over his shoulder to him. "Holy shit! You were the one on the news with that girl."

Mr. P lets out a single chuckle; his lips half parted around the rim of the glass as he looks to him. "Indeed. What about your love life?"

Elliot takes a sip. "It's nothing like yours. We don't even have sex anymore."

Mr. P finishes his drink and twists his right shoulder backwards, launching the glass across 5th Avenue towards the park. "How about a tour?"

Elliot downs the rest of his drink. "Of the bachelor pad? Hell yeah!" He looks to his empty hands. "Where did your glass go?" Mr. P points to the park. "Ha-ha, can I?"

Mr. P raises his hands. "Be my guest," he says, and steps back, watching Elliot as he attempts to pitch it like a baseball; his aim off target as it soars left, smashing against the brick building; the glass raining down on the sidewalk. Mr. P turns to the glass door, rolling his eyes at the idiot as he steps inside and moves to the main couch, looking left as he sits back; his arms spread across the top of the couch as he watches him look around. He points to the corner wall. "That's where a lot of action takes place."

Elliot walks in front of the coffee table and bends down, picking up a pair of white laced thongs. They're still wet! He looks to him. "I can see that."

Mr. P smiles. He's enjoying this. "I had a brunette up against the wall last night. I'm guessing those are hers."

He brings the wet thong to his face and sniffs; the lingering smell of his fiancé's pussy flaring his nostrils. He screws up his face and quickly pulls away. "Yep. I shouldn't have done that!" He drops them to the floor; feeling awkward as Mr. P looks at him in silence. "Well, I best get going anyway. Engagement invites to be sent out and all."

Mr. P stands from the couch, walking left around the coffee table. "Elliot, it's been a pleasure." He walks to the elevator and turns around, smiling to Elliot as he comes around the corner. "Tell Arabella I say hello."

Elliot smiles. "Will do. Oh, I forgot. When can we use the ballroom?"

Mr. P presses the call button.

"Anytime."

Elliot ponders as the doors open, stepping inside before turning around. "What about in two weeks' time?"

Mr. P nods. "That works," he smirkingly says, as the gap closes and turns around, chuckling at the fool and looks left to the white lace panties, shaking his head in disgust.

CLUB 33

Stepping out into the spitting rain with her hands full of shopping bags, Arabella turns around and shuts the Range Rover door behind her, smiling as Clarissa lowers the window and leans over the seat.

"I'll give you a message later," says Clarissa and blows her a kiss.

"See you soon," she says, and turns around, makes her way towards her apartment door as she listens to Clarissa drive off. She rummages in her cross-shoulder bag for her keys. "Oh my god!" she screams, as the weather suddenly turns torrential; her damp hair flying around her dripping face as her open sandal feet become cold and wet. Finally! She inserts the key, turning and pushing down on the handle. It doesn't open. The rain shower heavily intensifies as she twists back. It was never locked in the first place! Making her way inside, she drops the soggy bags on the floor, trailing water droplets along the laminate as she approaches the mirror, her goosebumps flaring across her shivering skin in the reflection.

"You look like a drowned rat," says Elliot, from the couch.

She puts her middle finger up to him and kicks off her dark tanned sandals, peeling the see-through white tee shirt from her sticky body and dropping it beneath her. She removes her dark blue denim shorts and slowly turns around, trying not to slip on her wet, slippery soles as she slowly steps towards the bathroom. "Can you put the heating on please?" she shouts and closes the bathroom door. He sighs and pulls his lazy ass up from the couch.

Wearing a creamy towel, pressed against her tight and warm rosy skin, she makes her way towards the bed, picking up her shopping bags along the way. She empties them onto the sheets, tossing the crispy bags behind her and looking down, smiling at her various accessories and engagement party dress. Reaching into her pantie draw, she pulls out a candy pink G-string and drops the towel, stepping into them and sliding the fabric along her silky-smooth legs; the string tightly sitting between her beautifully rounded cheeks. She moves to the mirror and sits crossed legged in front, leaning right for her hair dryer. Staring back at Elliot through the reflection, she rolls her eyes, as he sits with a stroppy face, listening to him grumble over his sports highlights being disrupted from the loud blowing noise. Turning it off, she places it down; the smell of burning lingering as her warm hair cools off.

"Thank god," he moaningly says, as she stands up and walks towards the bed. "Have fun today?"

"Suppose." She reaches for her new dress and slips it over her head, as he stands and walks towards her and sits on the edge of the bed, watching her slide her blush pink satin knee length dress down her curvy hourglass; his mind drawing a blank at what he was planning to say, too engrossed in her captivating beauty.

"Wow. Wow. Wow."

She slides her hands along the smooth fabric in front of the mirror, smiling back to him through the reflection. "I like it," she says, and moves to the wardrobe for her makeup bag.

"Very sexy. So, engagement, I have a surprise."

She sits on the edge of the bed and opens her pink lip gloss, gliding the bristles along her bottom lip. "I'm listening."

"So, after this morning, I went to Hotel L'Amour and managed to take a look around the ball room."

What? She pauses mid gloss, looking right, her attention fully on him, as her heart starts to race. "Ok? So, what happened?" She starts applying the gloss to her upper lip; looking left as her cheeks turn red.

"We're having the engagement there in two weeks," he says, as she rolls her eyes. "Oh, and it's free. Mr. P randomly appeared out of nowhere and said, "It's on the house!" and he also said hello."

Well that's not bad. She closes the lip gloss and throws it back in her bag, puckering her lips as her nerves simmer. She stands, as he stands, and looks to him, wrapping her arms around his neck as she rests her cheek against his chest. "Well, that's very kind of him. I hope you said thank you."

He brings his hands around her curvy waist. "I did. I do feel slightly bad for Clarissa though."

She looks up to him, raising her eyebrow. "Why?"

He looks up and chuckles. "Well… he's a bachelor. He invited me into his penthouse, we had a drink, and he was showing me his wall."

She unwraps herself from him, choking on her brewing anger. "Wall?"

He starts to laugh. "Yeah! He has a corner wall and was saying about how it's his favorite spot for you know."

She starts to slowly burn inside. "No. I don't know!"

He looks behind him to check the highlights. "You know. Sex."

Biting her tongue, she twists her lips. "Anything else I should know?"

"That's nothing. There was a white soaking thong on the floor from just this morning apparently. A brunette."

That son of a bitch. She clenches her fists, grinding her pearly whites as her cheeks turn red. Grabbing her cross-shoulder bag, she retrieves her smartphone and books a cab with her w. Inu before sitting back on the bed and putting on her rose gold strappy heels. She stands up. "I'll be right back. I have to go do something," she says, furiously, and storms towards the door.

"You're still wearing your engagement—" The door slams.

Pulling into the cobble lane, Pippo approaches with an umbrella; the torrential rain downpouring around him.

He opens the back door. "Hello Arabella, he is not here." The driver rubs his goosebump arms.

"Well, where has he gone?" she asks, resting her right hand on the center seat.

"Club Thirty-Three. You can come in and wait for him, but he might be a while."

She sighs. "Shut the door." He smiles and closes it, as she looks to the driver. "Change of location. Club Thirty-Three."

He doesn't like her tone. "I'm afraid that's the end of my shift."

She shakes her head. Sliding across the seat, she cracks the window open; the seat becoming wet as the strong wind carries the heavy rain inside. "Pippo," she shouts and waves her hand.

He reapproaches. "Yes?"

She looks at the splashing ground, taking a deep breath as she braces herself. "Cover me, I'm getting out," she says, and watches as he opens the door and holds out the umbrella for her; the gentleman that he is sacrificing his dry hair as her rose gold heels touch the sidewalk, slamming the door behind her and walking her under the glass roof. "Where is Club Thirty-Three?"

He points left on 5th Avenue. "Two blocks that way."

Swiping the umbrella from his white glove, she fake smiles and turns around, walking along the brick red soaked cobble floor towards the lane entrance; the hard rain bouncing on the umbrella top, as she turns left onto the sidewalk. Strutting along, she starts shivering; the gusts of wind sweeping the rain against her bare legs and open feet, as she listens to car tires splash through puddles.

Throwing the umbrella to the wet ground, she pulls on the dripping gold handle of the black framed glass double door and makes her way inside Club 33. Shaking the rain from her soft locks, as the toasty air attacks her dark pink dripping skin, she enhances her vision and scales the square room left to right; the meadow green pattern carpet with off-white nicotine-stained leather booths filled with classy snobs, topped with an old chandelier hanging in the center of the fine cigar club. She spots his spiked black hair peeking above in the right corner. She turns right and walks along before turning left, walking down the lane; the smell of old smoke lingering in the air as the dining guests stare out at her fierce frowning face.

"—will be ours. Run in the election, everyone drops out and I release the photos," says Mr. P, to the American Italian middle-aged male opposite him.

She shoves him hard. "How fucking dare you!"

He sits back up and looks to her. "Now that's hot," he chuckles, as the American Italian slides out the booth and brushes down his black suit down before nodding to Mr. P and walking away.

She slides into the warm seat opposite him, watching him sip on his aged whiskey; wanting to smash that glass over his head. "What do you think you're playing at?"

He lowers the glass from his lips. "Conducting business," he alluringly says.

She stands up, slamming her hands down on the brown table towers. "With Elliot, you fucking asshole!"

He places the glass on the table, gazing over her stunning attraction; her fierce glare is so goddamn sexy. "Harmless fun. Why are you so attractive when you're feisty?"

She sits back down and props her right leg between his spread legs. "Are you going to stop?" she pleasantly grins, as she pushes her right, pointy rose gold heel into his balls.

He brings his hands under the table, smirking as he massages her smooth legs. "Stop the fun? Never," he smirks, as she digs her heel deeper; his face isn't flinching. "It doesn't hurt, I have a high pain threshold." He winks.

She sighs and releases the pressure, resting her leg on his left thigh; his caressing fingertips shooting tiny tingles through her. She leans back and slides her bottom down, her chin in line with the table. "Where is this going?"

He smiles, drawing fingertips on her inner thigh, her sexual frustration building. "You mean the massage?"

She brings her hands to her face as her breathing heavies. "I mean us."

He grabs her other leg and rests it on his other thigh. "I think you already know," he says, as he runs his feather touch up and down her smooth skin.

"Do I… mmhhmmmm… how do you feel then?" she says, trying to stay composed.

He stops the tease and sighs. "If only it was so simple."

She presses her tongue against her cheek. "Right!" She grimaces her lips. "That tells me all I need to know then."

He gulps. "Wrong! When the time is right. I have things to carry out first. Also, you have a ring on your finger don't forget."

She rolls her eyes. "That's on you."

He raises his right eyebrow and tilts his head towards her with a smirk. "Then I guess I will have to fix your issue."

She shakes her head. "When will that be?"

He tilts his head side to side, twisting his lips as he thinks. "When you least expect it. Just carry on as we are for now. I'm doing this out of love."

She starts to blush; her eyelashes fluttering as her smiling cheeks turn rosy, pink. "Did you just say love?"

The waiter comes over. "Are you both ready for dessert?"

Mr. P stares at Arabella. "Nothing for me. My lover here, however, would love a classic New York cheesecake," he says, and winks to her. The waiter nods and walks away, as her cheeks start to hurt from the intense smiling. "Does that answer your question?"

She starts to giggle, placing her dainty left hand over her lips, tapping her acrylics across the table as her chest drowns in waves of flutters. "Maybe. Why didn't you get dessert?"

He picks up the silver spoon and holds it over the edge, the sound of ringing echoing across the chattering room as he releases his grip. "It's in front of me," he seductively says.

She looks around, her heart racing as he slips under the table, looking down to him. "Seriously?" she loudly whispers. She feels his soft lips against her inner thigh, her chest sinking as she exhales to the stimulating pleasure. She grabs his thick black hair. "What do I do if someone comes over?"

He nibbles his way onto her lace, brushing against the fabric; her divine scent trickling up his nose. He looks up to her through the small gap. "That's part of the risk," he seductively mumbles.

She positions herself properly, leaning back against the white leather and looking around. She bites down on her sultry bottom lip; his fingertips stimulating her curves as he reaches for the top of her G-string. She presses her hands on the seat and raises her body, the back of her pastel pink string peeling out of her peachy ass cheeks.

The waiter reappears with the vanilla cheesecake, smiling as he places the dish in front of her. "One New York cheesecake." He looks at the empty seat. "Where is the gentleman that was with you?"

She chokes on her moan, looking up to him with a smile as she feels his warmth steaming against her pussy. "He's just dipped outside." She raises her chest, as his tongue dips inside. "Mmhhmmmm..." She points at the cheesecake. The waiter smiles and turns around. She looks down, deeply exhaling as her thighs drown in stimulating pleasure. She tightly grips his fluffy spiked hair, her stomach moving up and down as she leans back, closing her eyes to his strokes. "I can't hold these moans."

"Why do you think I ordered the cheesecake?" he laughingly mumbles and slides up her soft pink lips. She brings her right hand up and grabs the silver spoon, her thighs spasming around his wet face as she breaks off the creamy dessert and brings it to her cupid lips; the rich vanilla biscuit base packing an oozing burst of sweetness in her mouth, as she releases a deep moan. The guests turn around. She points to the cheesecake for cover, failing to swallow as she gasps, squeezing her gripping hand harder against his hair, as his lips suck on her clit. She closes her eyes, exhaling out her nose as she closes her mouth, trying to swallow through the moan, her tight walls pulsating, as the bottom of her soaking entrance starts accumulating its silky mix.

She breaks off a huge piece of the dessert, tilting it on its side and removing the biscuit base. Putting the spoon down, she pants as her thighs tremble and pinches the cheesecake with her dainty fingers. She looks around through her aroused eyes for any peeking guests. The coast is clear! She releases his hair and pushes his face back, bringing the dessert below the table, as she bites down on her juicy bottom lip. Sliding down the seat, she spreads her legs wide; her curvy cheeks hanging over the edge as she creates a V shape with her left middle fingers. She presses her palm against the top and applies pressure, spreading her wet pink lips and inserting the delicacy inside. Releasing her hand, she lets the cream melt away. She pushes her left hand against his face and breaks herself off another piece, placing the rich, sweet treat into her mouth first. She drops the spoon and grips his hair with both hands, wrapping her thick thighs around him and pulling him in, shaking her thighs to his stroking tongue as they both enjoy their creamy experience.

    He pulls out, catching his breath as he brings his left hand to the top of her pussy. Spreading her come soaked lips wide, he leans back in and slides his white tongue up; her clit tasting of sweetness as he rapidly whisks, penetrating her dessert infused delight with his two right fingers and brushing her creamy infused mess against her g-spot. She bangs her knees against the tabletop, wrapping her thick thighs around his neck, her stomach intensely moving in and out as she squeezes her legs, panting as his fingers increase their speed to her thrusting hips; the banging echo from her knees getting louder, dragging his face up and down her pink vanilla as she moans. The customers turn around with dirty looks, staring at her closed eyes and widened mouth, watching as her shoulders and chest move up and down. She enters her climax, the banging getting louder as heavenly pleasure shoots through her, lost in the lust as she forgets where she is, her temple spiking with a sudden tremor as she raises her ass; the room filling with an extremely high pitch moan as her eyes roll back.

"Excuse me," says the waiter. She grips her teeth, blanking the waiter as her inner thighs explode in orgasmic sensation. She widens her mouth, hyperventilating as sweat drips from her forehead, drowning the room in a sultry orgasm and releases. The table bangs loudly.

"Fuck!" shouts Mr. P. She gently unwraps her shaking thighs from his neck.

"What in god's name are you two doing," says the waiter.

Mr. P reemerges holding the back of his head. She starts to giggle at his face. It's covered in come infused pudding. "Bit of fun. What are you doing?" he says, as he licks his creamy fingers.

"Calling the damn cops!"

He wipes his face, as the waiter turns around. "I wouldn't do that if I was you Zach."

The waiter turns around. "Excuse me! How do you know my name?"

He looks down at his watch. "Precisely twenty-four minutes ago, I became the owner of this place. So, if you want to keep your job, you will comply." He gets up from the booth and looks around at the disturbed guests with his dripping face. "Please order whatever you want. It's on the house. Enjoy!" He sits back down, listening to the guests clap as he shoos Zach away and turns to her.

She breaks out in a giggle, looking down to the leather seat and smiling; the way he takes charge is mesmerizingly breathtaking. "You are something else," she dreamily says. She sits back up and leans her elbows against the table, losing herself in his luminous beauty.

He takes hold of her petite hands and looks at her soft palms. "You wouldn't have me any other way," he charmingly says, as he curls his fingers between hers.

"I wouldn't want you any other way."

He looks at his watch and slides out from the booth, stretching his legs and walking around to her side. He pulls her out from her seat and towers over her, the power of his woody cologne masking the lingering cigar smoke. He rests his parted lips against hers. "I have to go," he passionately mumbles. She lavishes up his sweet breath, as she slides her pink glossed lips between his wet vanilla lips, her heart racing as he brings his hands behind her head, flowing his fingers through her thick, beautiful hair, as she wraps her hands around his sticky cheeks. She releases her soft lips, their foreheads pressing as she exhales her steamy passion against his upper lip, fluttering her eyelids as time slows down around her.

"Excuse me boss. I need you to give me a day off. I have a chess tournament in five days," says Zach.

She cracks a smile and starts to giggle. "Be nice," she whispers.

He turns around "Did you just interrupt a passionate moment for a bloody chess tournament?"

She slaps him on the arm. "Take a week off. Fully paid," she says.

Zach widens his eyes. "Well, thanks lady," he says, and runs to the back.

Mr. P turns back to her. "Why did you say that?"

"He just witnessed me orgasm. It's the least you can do."

He places his hands across her flushed cheeks and leans in. "I will see you at the engagement party." He kisses her on the forehead and brushes their noses together.

You are one of a kind. She sighs, as he lets go, watching him walk amongst the booths; her heart melting as he fades into the evening.

THE ENGAGEMENT PARTY

Twisting the white band around her engagement finger, around and around, as she counts one for every time the stone passes, Arabella sits nervously for a phone call, zoning out of Enrique's terrible karaoke attempt in front of her. Her legs start to vibrate, as her smartphone rings.

She stands from the vintage dark green couch and exits Barbara's apartment, pulling the door behind her and tapping answer. "Please tell me some good news?"

"They're all done. I'll see you soon," says Sarah and hangs up. She sighs in relief and leans over the bannister; the sound of a drowned cat singing echoes behind her, as the nostalgic aroma of her old apartment triggers her curiosity. Turning right, she walks across the landing and turns left, descending the staircase in her rose gold heels; her eyes gazing at her old white apartment door. Stepping towards it, she twists her lips at the unknown. *Maybe somebody lives here now?* She presses her ear up against it and closes her eyes. *Hmmmm.* Reaching into her cross-shoulder bag, she retrieves her old key. It still fits! Slowly twisting, she gently pushes down on the door handle. It's unlocked. *Oh my god.* Her heart races, as the door slowly creeks open. Her eyes widen. It hasn't been touched. Stepping inside; her arms and neck shiver as goosebumps dominate her glowing skin, staring at the shepherds sunset shining through the floating dust, her stomach sinking as her chest tingles to the flooding memories. The homely smell vaguely lingers as she steps along the light brown carpet and looks left at the half-opened bathroom. Glancing inside, her old bottle of pink shower gel still there. She sighs, her chest tightening as she closes the door and turns right, looking down at the imprints of her old bed still molded in the fabric. She gasps. Bending down, she picks up the dust covered, white gold encrusted envelope and letter from the silver paper waste bin. She blows her glossy lips against it, sneezing as the dust hits her. With no bed to sit on, she stands and removes the letter from its casing, brushing her smooth fingers, back and forth, over the bumps, as she reads the letter; her face turning strawberry red as her eyes start to water, her chest sinking as her tear hits the yellow paper. *To think I almost said no.* She neatly folds the letter and slides it gently inside the envelope, turning it front side up and caressing her thumbs over her italic black written name. Placing the sentimental memory inside her bag, she wipes her eyes and cheeks. Brushing the dust off her dainty hands, she fans herself, attempting to save her mascara from running.

"Arabella?" shouts Elliot, from the top of the staircase.

"Coming!" Spinning around the room one last time, she soaks it all in and never looks back as she moves to the door. Turning around, she pulls the door shut, and inserts the key, looking left at him as she locks up.

He looks down at her with raised hands. "Whose apartment is that and why do you have keys?"

Placing it in her bag, she ascends the stairs, pushing him along and back onto the landing. "It's one of our assistants apartment from the shop. That reminds me. The flowers have arrived and have been set up."

He turns around to her, as they reach the apartment door. "Should we go then?"

She checks him over; brushing his dark navy jersey blazer; the white shirt and slim fit brown chinos working their colors as his classic brown brogues look sharp. "Yes," she says, and lavishes up his woody fragrance. "You smell nice."

He smiles and opens the door, looking at the karaoke singer and his mother. "Time to go."

Gazing up at the starry night sky above Central Park, from the back seat, she fiddles with her shaking hands as they drive along 5th Avenue, her eyes saying goodbye to Orion's belt as Enrique turns left into the brick red, brightly lit, cobble lane.

"Are we all ready?" asks Elliot.

"Yeas dear," says Barbara, as Pippo approaches the back, looking through to Arabella; his trusting eyes keeping her dark secret, as he grips the handle and opens it.

She accepts his white glove and pulls herself out. "Thanks Pippo," she smilingly whispers.

"You owe me an umbrella," he jokingly whispers, and walks her to the sidewalk; the car doors slamming as her entourage joins her.

Hanging back with Elliot, they watch as Barbara, and Enrique walk the Lyon red carpet. "Why is your mother wearing a leopard print dress?"

He takes her right hand. "I have no idea," he says and starts walking hand in hand, along the red carpet, the fountains soothing bliss caressing their ears, as they ascend the steps. "Are you nervous?" he asks, as she smiles to the doormen.

"A little." She gulps and lets go of his hand, her breathing heavying as the awaiting guests chatter leaks from the ballroom.

This feels all too wrong. She looks left to Chloe, their burning glares exchanging as she walks along the white marble.

Reaching each the ballroom entrance, they turn to each other and look each other up and down. "Ready?" asks Elliot.

Taking a deep breath, she nods and retakes his hand. Together in sync, they enter; the overplaying upbeat playlist drowned out as the room cheers. Making their way along the walnut glossed floor, she smiles, waving to all their friends and family as they reach center of the interchanging blush pink and baby blue lit room. Scaling the room left to right, she blushes; banquets filled with pink blush lilies, eccentric roses, and electric blue orchids, topped with pastel pink and blue hydrangea beautifully placed around the skirting and it's all for her.

She smiles to him. "This is amazing."

He looks around the room. "I know," he says and spots Josh over by the bar. "I'll be right back," he says, and lets go of her hand.

She looks towards the stage, casting her eyes to the crowd in front and squinting, breaking out into laughter as she watches the flaxen blonde goddess attempt to play one awful game of hide and seek. "Clarissa! I can see you," she shouts.

Running out of the crowd like a lunatic quite frankly, she throws her arms around her; their white and pink dresses pressing as they squeeze each other tight.

"Ha-ha, I was just taking the piss." Mmhmmm. Clarissa looks at Beatrice and Tristram walking along and sighs. "I can't believe I'm going to be the last to marry."

"Enjoy it whilst you can," she says and unwraps her arms, as the white coat waiter approaches.

"Champagne ladies?" Smiling their pearlies, they both take a drink, the ringing chime in their ears as they toast.

Arabella wraps her parted glossed lips around the rim and tilts the glass back, swishing the dry fruity flavor around her mouth, as they both look around for Mr. P. "I'll come find you later C. I have to go say hello to the other guests," she says and leans in, pecking her champagne lips against her bronze cheek before turning left to the bar, as Clarissa continues to scale the room for her date.

Grinning at his gorgeous, devilish reflection in the devil red box, Mr. P checks himself out, and unbuttons the top two from his white shirt. The door opens behind him. Show time! Spinning around, he exits into the lobby; patting his security guard on the shoulder as his penny loafers tap along the white marble. He smiles to Chloe. Listening to the sound of chatter flooding from the ballroom, he adjusts his right cuff link and approaches. Turning the corner, with the smirkiest smirk ever seen, he smirks, and smirks some more as he casts his devil's charm back at all the swooning women. Like the bad boy he is, he leaves a trail of his arousing scent, as he spots Clarissa's golden beauty standing alone under the chandelier and sneaks up behind her, lavishing up her flowery scent as he leans into her left ear. "You smell as divine as you look," he seductively whispers.

Hearing that soothing voice, she parts her scarlet red lips and slowly turns around, fluttering her eyelashes as his perfection shoots arousing tingles through her. She runs her crushed, sugar cherry, acrylic index finger down his white shirt. "You decided to show."

He places his right hand on her blushing cheek, sweeping her flaxen locks behind her ear with his left fingertips; his stimulating touch sending shivers down the back of her neck. "I keep my promises," he temptingly says.

Closing her oceanic blue eyes, her heart rapidly beats, as her ears drown out the background noise, puckering her plumped lips as she falls into the princess moment.

He looks left to the bar, met with glaring eyes from Arabella, shaking her head. *Don't you fucking dare!* Tempting fate, he looks back to Clarissa and leans in; his soft lips grazing along her champagne lips. Swiftly moving her hands around the back of his head, she pulls him in, sliding her parted lips between his; their icy, champagne mix colliding as she scratches her acrylics down the back of his head. He places his hands onto her waist, sliding up and down her curvy hourglass.

Opening his left eye, he listens to the sound of angry heels storming towards him, feeling a burning pinch in his waist as Arabella digs her sharp claws into him. He breaks their kiss and looks to her.

She glares at him, switching to a smile as Clarissa opens her eyes. "I just wanted to say thank you for everything," says Arabella, as her blood boils.

"You could have chosen a better time," says Clarissa and rolls her eyes.

He looks to Clarissa. "It's alright. I need a cigar anyway." He looks over to the bartender, as he points down to Clarissa. "There's a bottle of Dom waiting for you behind the bar."

Clarissa's eyes light up. Wrapping her arms around his muscly waist, she rests her right hand against his rippling abs and looks to Arabella. "He's such a gem." She looks up to him. "Don't be too long or I'll have finished it all," she says, and releases him before heading to the bar.

He turns around, catching Arabella's burning glare mid spin. Strolling towards the exit, he turns right, and right again, walking the red carpet towards the garden, unaware that his enraged brunette queen trails closely behind.

Leaning on the glass railing, he flicks open his gold zippo. Slowly rotating the Cuban cigar between his sweet lips, he lowers it onto the deep, blue flame; the cherry ember glowing as the thick, ghost white smoke blocks his exotic botanical view. Listening to the peaceful chirps and buzzing, he closes his eyes, disrupted as the garden door slams open; creating a loud bang as it swings into the wall.

Arabella storms towards him, as he turns around. "Why would you do that!" she screams, as she pushes his chest; the force pushing his waist against the glass.

He starts to laugh, stubbing the cigar out on the ledge and throwing it to the floor. He feels the force, as she pushes him again. "What was I meant to do?"

She pushes him again. "You put your hands on her curves!"

He raises his hands. "Yeah. Suppose I did," he chucklingly says.

She pushes him again; her wrists trapped as he catches them midair. "Why can't you just behave? You purposely put yourself into that position."

"It's just not in my nature…"

She shakes her head as her heart races. "Maybe, just maybe, spare a thought for those around you."

Hit by her words, he feels weird; it's like he doesn't want to be him around her. "Christ. You, Arabella Harper, are something else."

Gazing into his devilish eyes, she listens to the nature in the background as their relentless desire for one another spreads like wildfire across the garden in silence. "Mmhmmm. I am."

He pulls her in closer. "You know, this is where we met," he softly says, letting go of her wrists and curling his fingers between hers.

She looks down beneath their feet, resting the top of her head against his abs. "Actually, it was the second time we met, and you didn't even kiss me."

He gently tilts her head up with his right hand, their green eyes burning their passion as he grazes his smooth fingers above her ears, sweeping her wavy curls behind as her neck tingles. "Let me finish the story then," he beautifully whispers and leans in.

Parting her glossy lips, she catches his warmth between hers; their champagne and cigar flavors mixing, as she throws her arms around his neck, closing her eyes as she stands on her tip toes. She widens the corners of her moist lips, pausing their sliding as she exhales her steamy pleasure around his wet lips; the back of her legs shooting with sensation as his tingling fingertips brush up her smooth skin. He takes grip of her curvy thighs and swoops her off her heels. She wraps them tightly around his waist, as he walks her to the entrance; their passion exploding as he slams her against the door. Tightly gripping his thick hair with her dainty fingers, she swerves her head left and right; tasting every angle of him, as her endorphins explode between the romantic passion. She breaks their locked lips and gasps, pressing her sweaty forehead against his.

With her green gaze locked, as their steamy breath mists between them, she absorbs his sparkling beauty in silence; her breathing heavying as her heart ignites its romantic flame, lightly clawing the back of his hair as she widens her cupid lips. "I love you," she breathlessly whispers.

He gulps, inhaling through his nose as her words ring in his ears, his chest moving up and down as he absorbs her enchanting beauty. "I, I, I—" The door handle moves underneath her, she widens her eyes as her back feels the pushing force. He swiftly spins her around and pops her down. "That was rather funny!" he says, staring out in the garden, as the door swings open behind them.

"There you are," says Clarissa, stepping onto the oak decking with half a bottle of Dom Perignon in her hand, as she looks to him. She casts her tipsy eyes to her. "Elliot was looking for you."

Arabella turns around, smiling her sweaty, flushed face at her and walks past, holding the door as she looks back to them. "I'll see you both inside."

Clarissa walks closer to him, listening to the door swing closed behind her as she examines his face, raising her eyebrow as her chest sinks at the thought. "Why do you have pink lipstick over your face?"

He wipes his sweaty face and looks down to his hand. "Looks red to me."

She squints her eyes, unable to read him as she loses herself in his handsome complexion. "Should we go in?" she ask and accepts his offering hand.

"Your hands are so smooth," he charmingly says.

She giggles. "Moisturizer."

Dancing away to the upbeat track under the chandelier, Mr. P glances through the interchanging lights over to Arabella, by the bar at every opportunity, as he twirls with Clarissa. He looks down to her dripping face, as the track changes. "Do you want a drink?"

She fans her face with her hands. "Yes," she breathlessly says and starts bopping her head to the catchy beat. "This is my tune."

He smiles and heads for the bar, as an older gentleman swoops in and starts dancing with his date. Leaning his left elbow against the blacktop bar, he stands 10 feet away from his queen as he gives her the look. She shakes her head, directing him to look to his right. He casts his eyes right, looking at Elliot chatting away on the red leather couch. Elliot clocks him and waves. He smiles and nods back, casting his eyes back to her, as the new, young blonde barmaid comes over.

"Caribou Lou?" asks the barmaid.

He smiles to Arabella. "Your first day and you already know me too well."

She giggles and turns around, preparing his drink, as they continue to gaze their dreamy romance amongst the chatter and music. "One Caribou Lou," she says and places the glass on the bar top. He turns to the barmaid and reaches into his inner jacket pocket for a white card before handing her it, as Arabella exhales her steam out her nose.

"What does the P stand for?"

He picks up the drink and takes a sip, swishing the refreshing coconut and pineapple mix around his mouth, as he glances out his right eye to his lover. He swallows and looks back to her. "Never you mind," he alluringly says, and places the glass back down. "Thanks." He smirks and turns left, walking amongst the dancing guests as he makes his way towards the exit.

Arabella taps her acrylics along the bar top, watching the barmaid fluster over the white card. She looks left, staring at the back of Elliot's head as he chats away. She exhales out her nose as her heart races. *Screw it!* Making a hasty decision, she decides to follow him. She leans into Elliot's right ear. "I'll be right back," she whispers and takes off.

Clarissa grinds her dancing, with the older gentleman to a halt, sweating profusely as she watches her date exit the room, raising her eyebrow before looking over to the bar. She spots Elliot, but not Arabella. Slowly scaling her scanning eyes left, she spots her blush dress between the guests, heading towards the exit. "Surely not!" Pushing past the older guy, she steps slowly across the walnut floor in her red heels; trying not to fall in her wavy state. Reaching the ballroom entrance, she peeks left around the corner, observing Arabella, who turns her head right at the waiting area and looks at two gentleman in black suits. She casts her eyes at the gentleman, and back to Arabella, watching as she continues down the hall and turns left into the bathroom. Exiting the ballroom, she turns left and down the hall, smiling to the guard in passing. Reaching the bathroom, she rests her hand on the black door; her heart racing as her breathing intensifies, this is too much. Closing her blue eyes, she deeply inhales as her arms rapidly tremble. Here we go! She exhales and gulps, pushing open the black door, the smell of cleaning products hitting her as she steps along the bumpy cream tiles. Making her way to the sinks, she stares through the long-stretched mirror at the line of black door cubicles behind her. All the doors are shut! She looks over her sweaty reflection, cupping her shaking hands under the tap; her nerves numbing the ice cold-water filling inside her palms. Rapidly scaling her eyes back and forth, her blood pressure skyrockets as the sound of an unknown door unlocks. Directing all her attention to the center door, she widens her eyes as it opens and turns around to the brunette queen, the water dropping on the floor as she looks behind her. It's empty.

"What are you doing?" asks Arabella, looking down at her soaking feet with frowning eyes.

"Phew! Don't you worry. I'm just drunk," she says, relieved and flicks her wet fingers at her.

"Stop!"

Clarissa dries her hands under the blow dryer and turns around, giving her bestie a peck on the cheek before walking to the door. "I'll see you in there!" she shouts and exits, as Arabella shakes her head and washes her hand, whilst gazing over her own beauty.

Exiting the bathroom, Arabella turns right, stepping along the white marble as she listens to the leaking music and loud chatter from the ballroom. Reaching the guard, she looks left, her eyes widening as she glances at the empty waiting area. She looks at the guard, their silent exchange sharing the same concern, as he presses the button for her. *Please don't be true.* The doors open. Taking a deep breath, she steps inside, watching the lobbies bright light fade behind her in the reflection. Hit with devil red lights, the elevator starts its ascent. She leans on the metal railing, pressing her oily forehead against the mirror;

her breathing heavying as sweat glides down her sweltering body, feeling woozy as the alcohol hits. She closes her eyes and gulps.

It's time!

The musk yellow dimmed light glows through the gap as the elevator doors slide open. Stepping her rosy gold heels onto the black and white tiles, she slowly walks along.

"—serves us the right to look around," says Agent Sanders, as him and Agent Cody look right, raising their eyebrows at her.

She looks at Mr. P, sitting on the long couch with his arms spread across the top, smiling, with his right penny loafer resting on his left knee. She casts her eyes to the agents and gulps; her chest moving up and down as she gives them the puppy eyes. "What's going on here?" she innocently asks.

Mr. P stands. "Perfect timing. These two fine specimens of society are with the FBI."

Agent Sanders looks to him. "Do you want to tell us why you are running a hotel, full of employees, all linked to the American, and Sicilian mafia?"

"No comment."

Agent Cody looks at him. "Where was you at the time of the city council heist?"

He points to Agent Sanders. "Ask his sister," he smirkingly says.

She shakes her head and rolls her eyes. Talk about immature! "Where are you both going with this?" she asks.

Agent Cody looks to her. "What's your involvement in all of this Arabella? It's quite clear he has a British accent so why lie?"

Mr. P raises his eyebrow at her. Who exactly has she been talking to? She looks to him and gulps. He breaks their contact and looks back at the agents. "Gentleman. You are free to look around, but as you have noted, I am British," he says, and returns to his relaxed position, as they start to look around.

She scurries over to him and sits on his left side. "I should have told you," she whispers.

He leans in. "I will deal with you after," he firmly whispers.

Agent Cody holds up a pair of ruby red thongs with his pen and looks to her. "Are these yours?" She turns to face her lover and hits him in the chest. The agents laugh.

"It's clean," says Agent Sanders. They shake their heads and walk back to the coffee table, looking at him. "Do you have a passport?"

Mr. P rolls his eyes and reaches into his inner jacket pocket, throwing the blue passport on the coffee table. "Now, I preferred the burgundy red one myself. What's your favourite colour?" he chucklingly asks, as Agent Sanders looks it over.

He passes it to Agent Cody, as he shakes his head and looks at Mr. P. "What is your angle?"

He raises his hands. "Angle?"

He shakes his head. "How does a British man find himself in the company of high-ranking members?"

"Now that's a funny story." The room sits in silence, all eyes on him as they stare, eagerly awaiting. He flickers his eyes back and forth between the two agents. "Why are you both staring?" They look at him sternly. He smirks and looks up to the ceiling. "Oh… so it involved two FBI agents and I told them to leave," he aggressively says, as he looks back down.

"It's real," says Agent Cody and chucks the passport back on the table. "Let's go." Turning the corner, they step along the tiles and press the call button. "Trust me, something's up here. We've overlooked something," he whispers. The doors open.

"Arabella said he was a charmer. What if there's a connection?" whispers Agent Sanders, as they step inside and turn around. The doors start to close; met with a smirk from Mr. P through the closing gap.

Standing from the main couch, she walks the Persian rug, turning left, and left again, strutting along the black and white tiles in her rose gold heels. Stepping out onto the violet purple lit terrace, she walking along the black starry floor; the night breeze sweeping across her sweaty, flushed skin, as she looks left, gazing in awe at the pretty, white lit, clear water. She sniffs the air, hit by his strong cigar smoke as she stands beside him to his right, looking up at Orion's belt as her wavy brunette locks blow around her face. "I should have told you," she sighingly says.

He inhales and looks up, blowing the thick white smoke into the wind. "Arabella. Do you know what I value in life?"

She turns to him and rests her right hand on the metal railing as she shakes her head sideways. "You tell me."

He chuckles and exhales. "Loyalty." He chucks the cigar over the edge before turning to her and approaching.

She looks up and flutters her eyelashes to his towering beauty and runs her dainty fingers down his white shirt. "Well, sorry for being disloyal."

He swoops his hands across her glowing cheeks and presses his forehead against hers; her heart racing, as their green flames exchange a whirlwind of explosive passion. "Wrong. You told them nothing. This means everything to me."

She smiles. "You know what means everything to me?" she asks; met with his head shaking sideways, as their noses brush. "Oh, you know exactly what I mean," she passionately whispers.

"You mean the name thing?"

She shakes her head sideways and bites down on her sultry bottom lip. "Three words."

He slides his wet, parted lips between hers and picks her up from her thighs; her legs wrapping around his waist, as her dainty fingers grip his fluffy, black hair, walking her to the glass corner, as their burning passion shoots through them. He breaks their kiss and presses his forehead against hers, losing himself in her eternal beauty; her champagne breath steaming against his upper lip, as his fingertips caress their stimulating touch above her ears. "I love you," he softly whispers.

She deeply exhales, placing her soft palms on his warm cheeks, her eyelashes fluttering away as her heart melts inside. "I love you," she romantically whispers.

He starts to deeply giggle. "Can I tell you something?"

She brushes her nose against his. "Yes."

He passionately glistens his romantic sparkle into her pretty green eyes. "I've never said that before," he says, feeling giggly, as she breaks down; her chest sinking inside as her eyes start to water, sniffling and giggling, as he wipes the streams from her rosy cheeks. "So, England. Ever seen Canterbury Cathedral?" he asks.

She shakes her head. "No."

He smiles. "I think it's time I showed where I'm from."

She brushes her index finger down his lips. "Perhaps you want to tell me what Mr. P stands for first?"

He chuckles and lowers her to the ground. "Soon," he seductively whispers.

THE END

ACKNOWLEDGMENTS

I want my first acknowledgment to be to you, the reader, I appreciate every single one of you. I would like to thank my family, and Louise and hers for always supporting me in everything I do.

Luke – I thank you for being an exceptional hype man. Every step of the way you have made me laugh with your "my word" comments. I can only apologize on your behalf for the amount of fans you have gone through. You will need to be well rested and save money for an industrial one as we have more to do.

Debi – You're an inspiration and you will keep inspiring as our journey continues. We have a special bond which can't be explained. You just keep being you, I will keep being me, and we will keep being a team. Thanks for supporting me.

Billie - Thank you for being my inspiration. I don't need to say much other than my lips are sealed.

Maria – You are exceptional. Always had my best interests at heart. I will never forget it. Thanks for supporting me every step of the way, model.

Gracie – Thanks for supporting me. We have always clicked and supported each other. Good luck with motherhood.

Judo - Thanks for supporting me. You often have a headache. That's ok. So do I.

Elizabeth - Thank you for helping me with the blurb. You will always be special to me. It's not often you meet someone with star signs that align as close as ours. Please keep being the princess and diva you are. I will always be here.

Samantha - Thank you for always supporting me. You have always been a firecracker from the moment we met. Having gotten close over the past year, I've seen you grow, and I want you to know that I am proud.

Keilly - Thank you for reading some of my work and supporting me. You are a lioness, with a soft heart. We have been through many twists and turns with my antics when you didn't have to. You will always be my wifey.

Tanique – Thank you for always supporting me. You are amazing in every way. You would literally take an entire essay to explain, but I can't thank you enough.

Yolanda – You are a mystery, but a good one. You widened my eyes when you revealed your wild side. I was in awe. Thanks for supporting me.

Nathan – We do have our laughs and yes, you will be invited to anything. Thanks for supporting me, not only with the book, but for widening my eyes for the future.

Canette – From one author to another, I have enjoyed speaking to you and I wish you every success on your publishing date. I will be here to support you, as you have been for me.

Holly and Carly – Both amazing, both will go far. You were with me from day one. I miss you both dearly. Thank you for supporting me.

I want to thank everyone else from law. I wish I could write all your names, but you all do mean a lot to me.

I want to thank everyone from the G force. You are all characters; it's what makes the place one of a kind.

Printed in Great Britain
by Amazon